Carefully, with infinite slowness, Annie turned her head to face the beast. It was still moving, heavy on her belly, cool and surprisingly hard; and now feathery light between her breasts.

The head was small, but so close it filled her vision, the tongue shiny and forked and very long.

Then the head disappeared as it pulled back; not until then did Annie close her eyes and turn her face away . . .

THE MOUNTAIN KING
GEORGE ERNSBERGER

THE MOUNTAIN KING

GEORGE ERNSBERGER

A BERKLEY BOOK
published by
BERKLEY PUBLISHING CORPORATION

This Berkley book contains the complete
text of the original hardcover edition.
It has been completely reset in a type face
designed for easy reading, and was printed
from new film.

THE MOUNTAIN KING

A Berkley Book / published by arrangement with
William Morrow and Company, Inc.

PRINTING HISTORY
William Morrow edition published 1978
Berkley edition / December 1979

ISBN: 0-425-04223-5

A BERKLEY BOOK® TM 757,375
Berkley Books are published by Berkley Publishing Corporation,
200 Madison Avenue, New York, New York, 10016.
PRINTED IN THE UNITED STATES OF AMERICA

For Claire

PART

I

The mountain king found himself in motion. He had no sense of having begun to move, nor any memory of having been unconscious. In fact he had been unconscious for many weeks, since he and more than two hundred of his kind gathered in this place, as they always did when cold came, to enter sleep. Now, his body had become mobile before his perceptions awoke, and he found himself crawling over the bodies of his kind toward the light.

He became dimly aware that he had been moving in this way, struggling over shifting bodies, for a considerable space of time. Nothing in his cognitive system was designed to tell him anything of numbers; even the concept "many" was alien to him, and uninteresting. But he was aware, now, of the length and difficulty of his struggle to reach the light.

The mountain king always made his sojourn in the deepest part of the cave. His companions slept wherever they found themselves when sleep overcame them—but

all of them between the king and the cold light of
winter. He had now traveled two of his body lengths,
and it was three more to the sunlight. A brief, effortless
trip over rocky or grassy terrain, but laborious with the
surface shifting under him constantly.

His body felt heavy and stiff; his perceptions were
dim, his complex musculature dull in responding to
signals from his nervous system. The clearest signal he
was receiving was hunger. He knew he must move past
his own kind to find food. Until he left that carpet of
bodies behind he would find none, for many of them
were awake, or half-awake as he was, and would kill
and swallow any food to be found here.

Soon he was on the bare, rocky shelf at the mouth of
the cave, being bathed by sunlight. The warmth was
almost like nourishment to him; as it suffused his body,
his muscles gradually lost their stiffness and became
elastic and responsive. He flexed his body, coiled and
straightened it. As muscle tone returned he began to feel
charged with power. From the rearmost part of his
body, almost as though there were a separate creature
there, came a familiar tingling sensation. Its passage
through the length of his body comforted him, telling
him he was, indeed, alive and powerful.

The mountain king's world was silent; though he was
acutely sensitive to vibrations in the air as well as in the
earth, he did not experience them as sound. Still he
knew the effect the movement in his tail had on other
animals, knew that it had power over them.

He was nearly pure black; he showed some very faint
broken bands of yellow across his back. He was as long
as a tall man is tall, more massive through the middle
than that same big man's arm. It had been more than
twenty years since he had confronted a creature who
was a serious threat to his existence; the deer could
trample him to death, but he had never encountered one
willing to try. The vibration he made with the rattles at
his tail somehow told them that it would be their lives,
too, and perhaps they even knew that death from the

bite of a timber rattlesnake his size was not only certain, but excruciatingly painful. The mountain king was nearly a third longer, and half again heavier, than any other rattler in the region.

As he moved up the face of the cliff alongside the cave, from shelf to sun-warmed shelf, his sensory apparatus brought him complex signals. Nerve clusters in his jaw were exquisitely sensitive to vibration. Messages came from various centers of sensitivity to pressure and warmth. Atmospheric pressure was dropping rapidly—the king was always aware of that, and registered minute changes in it. He knew that a storm was coming. The vast empty space alongside him, the side away from the face of the cliff, grew dimmer as clouds moved in front of the sun.

His vision told him nothing specific about what was more than a few feet from him. He neither knew, nor would he have cared, that some hundreds of feet below him, at the base of a steep forested slope, three houses sat before a large cleared grassy space. But he could see clearly that the sky was becoming darker, and he could feel the air cooling as a result. The still air was taking on a charge of static electricity, and he was dimly aware of that phenomenon, also.

The storm signals made the mountain king uncomfortable. He did not like water, for one thing, though he could swim. On this mountainside the water flowed in fast-moving streams that could pick him up and dash him helplessly, battering his body and possibly drowning him. He knew how that felt; that is, his body had a memory of the rushing water. He sensed that he must return to the deep part of his cave soon.

The mountain king moved through grass when he reached level ground, among the roots of trees and bushes above the cave, flicking his tongue out and withdrawing it to test for scent particles, and paying acute attention to the heat-sensing pits on his head for a signal that living food was near. He would probably find a mouse. They were plentiful. Better if he came across a chipmunk, and still better a rabbit. For the mountain king was massive; a mouse would not satisfy him for long. Though his body had been so quiescent as to seem dead, still it had been many weeks since the king had stretched his jaws. A plump, full-grown rabbit to press his ribs outward for a few days would be welcome.

Soon, though, the storm signals became more urgent than his hunger. He turned and made his way back over his path to the rocky face of the cliff—already discernibly cooler to him—and down it to the mouth of the cave.

Directly below him a few hundred feet, in another universe, the three houses sat impassive.

CHAPTER

1

Annie Axelrod sat in a taxi caught in a traffic jam on Madison Avenue. The weather was freakishly warm for May and the taxi was hot and stuffy. Her day at the office—she worked at a television station—had been typically Monday rotten: all meetings. But Annie's mood was cheerful to the point of giddiness. She was impervious to small discomforts.

Annie was on her way to see her friend Karen Vincenzo, to whom she would bring the news that was making her so cheerful: Annie was pregnant for the first time. Karen had a baby of her own and meant to have another as soon as she and Ted could afford it; meantime, she had announced, she was determined to meddle with the raising of Annie's child, if Annie should have one.

Karen expected the news, so she would probably have champagne on ice. Terrific, Annie thought, and shifted her bottom on the hot, lumpy seat of the taxi—*anything* on ice would be terrific.

But even the muggy heat—first strong taste of the

brutal New York City summer to come—cheered Annie more than it oppressed her. The winter had been long and cold, and the spring chilly and very wet, and she was eager for summer. Annie and her husband Ben, along with Karen and Ted and two old friends of Annie's—Randall Madison and Tim Levine—owned three houses together on the side of an otherwise wild mountain in the northern Catskills. They'd bought the place last fall, enjoyed the houses for four or five weekends, and then closed them for the winter. They were to reopen them this coming Friday, for Memorial Day weekend, and begin their first full season of weekly escapes.

So the hot day in the city, with its glaring light and harsh sounds—car horns were blaring with a sort of sullen stridency—served as a sign to Annie: This is what you will escape from every week. You'll be in a cool, quiet, green place, isolated from everything that's hard and hostile to life, with Ben and your friends. Oh, and with your baby—well, next year.

The three houses had been offered for sale together. They'd once been a private hunting compound for a very old, very rich New York City family named Schuyler. The oldest house was built in 1819. But the Schuylers had not used the place in years—it was Ben's guess that if there were still Schuylers who hunted, they hunted in Alaska or Africa, or maybe the Himalayas.

Ben and Annie had found the place, but couldn't afford it alone, so they'd recruited their friends to form a co-op. They'd split the purchase price evenly—easy for Randall and Tim, who made plenty of money from Tim's travel agency and Randall's acting in television commercials; harder for Ted and Karen—Ted was a designer at the same advertising agency where Ben was a vice-president, and Karen didn't work; and not easy but manageable for Annie and Ben—they made good money between them, but they lived expensively in the city, and now the baby would raise their expenses, and Annie's income would stop.

Annie looked at the briefcase on the seat beside her. I ought to be reading through that stuff as long as we're creeping along here, she thought. Between champagne at Karen's and dinner at Randall and Tim's, I'm not going to get anything done this evening. And then we'll probably take next Friday off. And if I don't keep at it I'll end up having to take work to the country. Baby, she said to her far-off child, I won't be sorry when you come and deliver me from all this. And Ben, for God's sake take that job. We're going to need the money.

Annie and Karen were to meet their husbands at Randall and Tim's; they'd have dinner there when the men arrived from softball practice in Central Park. Ben and Ted, and Randall, who also played on the agency's team—oh, and Alex Klein, she thought with distaste, Well, the hell with him. She wouldn't be disturbed by Alex, not today. What *does* Ben see in him?

Anyway, they'd celebrate the baby some more, and then plan the weekend in the country. Probably, Annie and Ben would go up first and open the houses—connect the pipes, prime the pumps and the like. Ben seemed more interested in mastering those skills than any of the others. Anyway, both he and Annie could take Friday off.

Annie easily resisted the temptation to do some work in the cab. Okay, traffic, she thought, that's about enough, now. I'm pregnant, you know. And the traffic broke; it had been bottled up by a Con Edison excavation, which the taxi now cleared. Well, all *right,* she thought.

Karen Vincenzo's kitchen was spacious, by the standards of Manhattan apartments, sunny and very green. Plants burst from pots sitting on windowsills and butcherblock counters, trailed from pots hanging from ceiling hooks. Karen was feeding Charley, her baby, who was just halfway between his first and second birthdays, when the door buzzer sounded. That would be Annie.

She buzzed Annie into the building and waited at the apartment door until the elevator arrived. Annie stepped out. She looked a little disheveled, and carried a briefcase that hung as though it was heavy, but she was beaming.

"Well?" Karen said, but she knew the news from Annie's expression.

"Yup," Annie said.

"Ohh-hh . . . oh, wow. Sonofagun, wow!" And they embraced in the doorway. Karen, at twenty-five, was ten years younger than Annie, shorter and not so slim; her hair was blonder, and more curly. They separated and went inside to the kitchen. "How do you like the news, Charley?" Karen said to her baby. "You're gonna have a friend."

Karen's grin delighted Charley, who responded with loud nonsense sounds that had all the cadences of a declarative sentence.

"Darn right!" Annie said to him. "You aren't going to be the littlest guy around anymore. There'll be somebody for you to boss around."

"Ho!" Charley yelled. The two women laughed, and Charley looked at them wonderingly for a moment, then added his own noises to the celebration. Baggins, the Vincenzos' big Standard Schnauzer, ambled into the kitchen, cocked his head at Annie, and barked a greeting.

Karen opened a split bottle of champagne that she'd acquired for the occasion, and the women sat at the counter and drank a toast. Karen thought her friend Annie Axelrod was much the wisest of women, and among the kindest, and as valuable a friend as anyone had ever had. But she sometimes thought that Annie was too smart—or anyway too thoughtful—for her own good. She made things complicated, Karen thought. "You know," Karen said, "I just realized a little while ago—I think I was afraid you'd never have a baby. I didn't know I thought that, but now I think I did."

"I thought it," Annie said. "I never said it out loud, even to Ben, but I said it to myself sometimes. I don't know what happened, but finally I just felt like it. And Ben did the moment I did."

Just felt like it? Karen thought. Annie and Ben? Well, terrific. "How does Ben feel now?"

"Well, for one thing, perfectly ridiculous—he's about to burst with *macho*." Annie smiled and shook her head. "No, it isn't ridiculous, it's wonderful. I'm feeling like a lady in a sitcom, or an old *Saturday Evening Post* cartoon, or something—fragile, and giddy and scared of my own shadow. And I think that scares him a little—tough old Annie is turning into a dopey little bride on him. But he loves it, too. He's responding the same way. I mean the opposite way, but the same cliché, you know, he's becoming the other side of it."

Ted and I were like that when I was pregnant, Karen thought. But we were like that even before I was pregnant. Still are.

Annie sipped at her wine and went on, "I began acting that way even before my period was due. It drove Ben nuts at first. Kept screwing up his face at me and saying 'What? *What?*' Once when we were fighting I called him Whatwhat."

Karen laughed. Annie, who had once been an actress, was a gifted mimic. She had shifted easily into a startlingly accurate impression of her husband. Annie's features could have been selected to represent the exact opposite in type from Ben's: the bone structure sculpted cleanly, with an aristocratic jaw, a wide, full mouth, wide-set blue eyes, a narrow, almost pointy nose. But when she was being Ben dismayed and bewildered—"What? *What?*"—she puffed her cheeks and produced wrinkles in her forehead quite unlike the two neat verticals her own frown produced, and you could almost see Ben's curly brown beard on her pale cheeks.

Karen said, "That must have calmed him right down, calling him Whatwhat."

"Well, after a while we began to figure out what was going on, and after that we both calmed down a little—or went easier on each other, anyway."

"So Ben's overjoyed."

Annie nodded. "Yeah . . . but he's scared, too. And it sort of makes a decision for him that he really didn't want to make just yet. He's pretty much got to make a move for the executive vice-presidency at Bradley's."

"For the money, you mean?"

"Yeah. Since I've been a full producer, we've been just fine—we've even been able to sock some away. But now—"

"How long will you keep working?"

"Pretty much up to delivery date, I hope—depends on how I feel. I'm not exactly in my prime for baby-making, you know."

"Oh, you'll be fine." What is Annie, thirty-four? No, thirty-five.

"Anyway," Annie said, "so I want Ben to—well, I don't exactly want him to try for the job if he doesn't want it—it's just too awful working as hard as Ben does if you hate what you're doing—but I guess I want him to want it."

"Ted says the nearer you get to Arthur Bradley, the less fun it is to work at Arthur Bradley Associates."

"Arthur Bradley is a manipulative, exploitive, vulgar, disgusting sonofabitch."

"You always were wishy-washy," Karen said. "Why doesn't Ben go somewhere else?"

"Because the disgusting sonofabitch pays better than anybody else, and we've needed the money until fairly recently. We bought our co-op apartment just as maintenance costs started shooting up. And then buying the country place."

"So you think the executive vice-presidency at Bradley's is his best bet?" Karen said.

Annie nodded. "For now, anyway. It's very good money."

"So you're pushing him, a little."

"I hope not. But I guess he knows how I really feel. . . . You know, what he really wants to do is leave Bradley's and set up as a consultant, and do serious photography on the side."

"Why doesn't he do that?"

"Because it's scary financially. Ben's a very good advertising man; he's very smart and he's creative. But he's not a great self-promoter, and competition is ferocious. I—haven't encouraged him much, I guess, even before now. To tell you the truth, I don't think Ben is—tough enough, I guess."

Karen was beginning to feel restless, She wasn't stupid, or even lazy-minded; yet she didn't like thinking that life could be so complicated—that several decisions might have to be considered at once, each impinging on the others at oblique angles. She wondered again that Ben and Annie had made the central choice, the one that made all the others harder, because Annie "just felt like it." *I* might make a decision that way, she thought, but my life is much simpler. Oh, hell, I don't make decisions at all. Ted does.

Karen shook her head slowly. "You're probably going to have a *complicated* baby."

Annie laughed. "Oh, God, I hope not. Just a nice, dribbly, happy baby, and good grades in school, and a nice happy marriage and make me some grandkids."

Karen smiled and nodded decisively. "You betcha." And that's probably just about how it'll go, she thought. Ben and Annie will worry endlessly, every step of the way, over whether they're doing the right thing. But they will—they'll raise a happy kid. They have good instincts when they don't . . . complicate things so.

"Look," Karen said, "we'll have to be on our way to Randall and Tim's soon. Watch Charley while I walk Baggins, will you, and then we'll start."

Randall Madison and Tim Levine were old friends of Annie's, from the days when she was an actress. Karen envied Annie her history—Annie had been an actual professional actress, and still knew theater people, some very famous. For that matter, Randall himself was famous, in a way—he had even been asked for an autograph in Karen's presence. He was famous now for his commercials, but when Annie first knew him they were struggling young actors together. A very romantic life, it seemed to Karen. And Tim had been a chorus dancer in Broadway musicals—a gypsy, like in *A Chorus Line*.

Karen had grown up in Connecticut, in a small town too far outside New York City to be a suburb, quite. She had come to the city with her parents and seen Broadway shows several times a year, and had seen Tim in musicals more than once—that is, she'd seen shows he was in. She'd never noticed him enough to recognize him when they met. But, boy, did *he* ever know famous people. Tim had pictures on the wall, autographed to him, of Lucille Ball, Zero Mostel, Lauren Bacall, Ethel Merman, Yul Brynner. . . .

Karen walked Baggins nervously, watching for meter maids, who were empowered, or so she understood, to write tickets to people who didn't clean up after their dogs. Karen favored that law, in principle, and she might clean up after Baggins except that nobody else did, and so she'd feel foolish.

Annie and Karen were to go the few blocks to Randall and Tim's apartment on Central Park West for dinner. Randall, whose commercials were produced by Arthur Bradley Associates, played softball on the agency team. When practice was over, the men would come there and they'd all have dinner and plan the coming weekend in the country. And maybe Tim would have champagne, in honor of Annie's baby. Karen hoped so. She was feeling very pleasantly light-headed.

Karen was looking forward to the summer of weekends in the country, though perhaps not so eagerly as Annie. Annie had to go out and battle the city every day during the summer, but Karen didn't; she stayed in her air-conditioned apartment, with just an occasional foray outside to the laundryman for Ted's shirts, or the dry cleaner's or whatever. And anyway, Karen had grown up in a small town, and had played in the woods outside it. It was not so exotic for her. She liked owning a house, though; that seemed very grown-up to her.

Alex Klein would be at dinner, she remembered suddenly; and Ted had said that he'd be their guest for the weekend, too—or somebody's guest; he'd probably stay with Randall and Tim, since their house was the biggest. He and his girl friend, whoever she was. Alex Klein, whom Ted and Ben both seemed to like a lot, gave Karen the creeps. Annie, too.

Karen tugged at Baggins to take him back inside; it suddenly seemed to her that they'd been out longer than necessary. Had he done anything? Oh, the hell with it.

When she arrived back at her apartment, Annie had already installed Charley in his stroller, and so they were off. They walked across Seventy-seventh Street, past the Museum of Natural History, toward Central Park West.

Karen said, "Ted thinks Ben has competition for that job."

Annie nodded. "Alex Klein."

"Scary," Karen said.

"Scares me, all right. Ben says he's pretty sure he can have it—seventy-five percent certain, he said. He's better than Alex, I'm sure of that, but Alex is. . . ."

"Tougher?"

"Yeah," Annie said, "and I think he's treacherous. Ben says no, that Alex might be dangerous, but that he operates under some kind of constraints—some standards he holds up for himself—that keep his meanness—Ben says his hunger—in check."

"Ben understands people very well," Karen said.

"Ben's too busy understanding them to be scared of the ones he should be scared of, or hard on the ones he should be hard on."

"You think?" Karen said.

"Annie sighed and shrugged. They had come to a drugstore at Columbus Avenue. "Wait a minute, will you? I want to buy some Ben-Gay. We're out at home, and this was their first practice of the season."

"Oh, Lord, yes," Karen said. "Have they ever had the sense to stop while they could still move? I better get some too, I don't know if we have any or not."

Tim Levine, a dark, compact man of about forty, wore a denim apron as he fussed over a roast in the oven. He and the two women were celebrating Annie's pregnancy, and gossiping—just like any three married ladies, Tim thought—as they waited for the jocks to show up for dinner.

Tim's joy for Annie was made poignant by a needle-thin stab of regret. He loved Randall, and he loved his life, but he did have just this one regret: that he would never have a child. Even with that, though, his joy was genuine enough. He had known Annie since she was a twenty-two-year-old fledgling actress. He loved her dearly.

She's not, he thought, a fledgling, or an actress, or even young, really, anymore; and I'm not a gypsy, and God knows I was never young. Tim drank at his champagne. The two women were both a bit tipsy; they'd had a head start, and neither of them was a very good drinker.

Tim was jealous of Karen, a little; she and Annie had become very close since they met when their husbands first went to work at the same advertising agency. It had been Karen that Annie had gone to first about the three houses in the country. A married lady did seem to need another married lady—the genuine article, Tim thought wryly—to commiserate with, I guess.

"I'll bet she's another Playboy bunny," Karen was saying. The chief subject of their gossip was Alex Klein and his new girl friend. Tim liked Alex for the same reasons the two women disliked him: Tim liked unpredictable, dangerous people. The girl friend was something of a mystery.

Ben and Ted had reported that Alex seemed to be

seriously involved with a woman for the first time since his divorce, three years past. When they invited him to the country, and he asked if he might bring the lady, Ben and Ted had agreed, of course, but they had not asked who she was—a lapse the three in Tim Levine's kitchen thought criminally obtuse.

Annie shook her head and looked sage. "If Alex is as serious about her as Ben thinks, she wouldn't be *just* a Playboy bunny. Alex is much too ambitious."

"A Playboy bunny working her way through M.I.T.," Karen decided.

Tim said, "Working her way through high school, if I know Alex."

But their speculations were brought to a halt when raucous voices from the living room announced the arrival of the ballplayers: "Fuckin' kid's got to go. Can't cut it." That was Alex. Ted Vincenzo: "Your ass, buddy, he can play as long as he brings his old lady to games. You see her T-shirt?"

The three in the kitchen shared a long-suffering look. The men would be barely fit for civilized company until they'd wound down from their jock mood.

Ben Axelrod's voice: "Madison, you got beer in this joint, or only that French goosepiss you got stuck with?" And Randall: "You love my wine, you fuckin' mooch, you drank a bottle by yourself last time you were here." Ted: "Wait'll it rains." Alex: "What?" Ted: "Wait'll it rains on that T-shirt."

Karen said, "Oh, for God's sake."

Tim said, "The lords of the locker room."

The three kitchen gossips had to wait until dinner was nearly over to learn the identity of the mystery guest for the weekend. There had been much talk of the coming baby, and some about the softball team—the men played in a serious league, played hard and in great earnest—and then Alex had to be filled in on the weekend accommodations and directions to the three-house compound.

Now, Alex was eating his cheesecake in silence, lost in thought. He was, as usual with these people, less than perfectly comfortable. He ate with the peculiar daintiness that was characteristic of him, touching his mouth with his napkin before each sip of coffee. He had showered and changed into soft, tailored jeans and a cashmere sweater; the other ballplayers had washed their hands perfunctorily and splashed their faces, and come to dinner in the khakis and sweatshirts they had played in. It offended Alex, and he envied them the careless ease it seemed to signify.

He remembered as a child hating Gentile kids who wore expensive clothes carelessly. Alex had hated a succession of people—classes of people, rather. People from stable families with successful fathers and warm, comforting mothers; people who lived in clean, roomy apartments with their own johns and telephones.

His sights had risen as he had, and now he hated the rich, mostly. People who own. Like Arthur Bradley, he thought; he owns me. And Ben. Not Ted so much; Ted's just a designer, and he'll probably begin selling his sculptures in a few years, anyway, and be free of the whole world of commerce and industry.

Alex's driving ambition, though, was not to be rich. It was certainly not to be poor ever again, but also not to be . . . the word he gave it was sweaty. His wife had been sweaty: a greedy, scheming social climber—the height of whose imagination, however, was only middle-class respectability, an expensive bar mitzvah for their son. His mother had been sweaty, his father was sweated out.

Sweaty people couldn't help showing you how desperately they *wanted*: by the way their eyes moved, or by constantly plotting, conniving, mistrusting, betraying. Some, he thought with disgust, actually sweat. Alex would do none of that. He would get what he wanted, but he would do it the way decent people did—people who actually believed, and had all their lives, that they deserved what they wanted. He would not connive, or betray. *I am not, by God, Sammy Glick.*

Isn't it the shits? he thought suddenly. I am sweating—straining every nerve and muscle—not to sweat. He let out a breath so big the others noticed it.

Ben looked over at him. "What's that, old fella, aches and pains?"

Alex grinned ruefully and nodded, and gave his attention to the conversation, which was about the country place and had been meant for him anyway—so he suddenly realized.

Annie had been saying, ". . . three houses, and a big lawn in front of them." Her arm was outstretched, palm forward, sweeping slowly. "If you were in an airplane, what you'd see is this flat shelf on the side of a completely wild mountain, all steep and wooded except for this—island, sort of—of flat, cleared land. Four acres."

"Good," Alex said, "that's big enough to practice. I'll bring the bats."

"Glad to know it," Annie said, "I'll take the Ben-Gay. Anyway, we own twenty acres, counting woods, but the lawn is about four. Surrounded by woods on all sides. Wonderfully isolated, about three miles from the country road that runs into town, up our own private road—I mean, we don't own it, but the only reason it's there is to get to our place."

"How high are you?" Alex said.

"About two thousand feet," Annie said. "The mountain's over four thousand."

"Four thousand feet? In the Catskills? That's not the Jewish Alps I used to know."

"No, it's over north and east," Annie said, "north of Woodstock. Anyway, so here we are on our little island in the wilderness—very dramatic setting—and over us, farther up the mountain looking down on us, is The Mountain King."

Annie, Alex thought, is one of those people who

know how to pronounce capital letters. Well, hell, so can Howard Cosell. He raised his eyebrows at her, then shifted his look to Ben.

Ben said, "There's a rocky cliff, like a wall, that runs around the mountain a few hundred feet above us. In the middle of it, right over us, is a face. Annie calls it The Mountain King."

"Well, it all sounds terrific," Alex said. "Now—what's the drill for the weekend?"

Ben began, "Well, Annie and I are going up Friday morning—we're both taking the day off. We'll open up all three houses—I've got everybody's keys. You'll be staying with Randall and Tim, because their house is the biggest."

"Fine," Alex said. "We'll be up Friday night. I gather it's all right to bring a friend?"

Karen recognized her chance. "Oh, that'll be nice," she said casually. "Anybody we know?"

"Well, she knows Randall and Tim, she told me, and both Ben and Ted have met her, I think. She's an actress, used to do commercials for us. Whitney Williams."

The silence that followed was brief, but not so brief that Alex didn't notice it. What the hell? He looked up over his coffee and tried to read responses. Something attracted his attention to Ted. Ted was very studiously attending to his cheesecake, but his ears were pink. Holy shit, Alex thought, Ted's blushing! Karen was looking curiously at Ted.

Then Ben said, just as though the pause hadn't occurred, "Oh, yeah, pretty good actress, I see her in guest parts on TV once in a while. Listen, all, we have to split. My aches and pains are getting really unmerciful. Catchers . . ."

Alex stopped listening. What the hell is *Ben* nervous about? Is he covering up for Ted? No—he hasn't even noticed that Ted's up tight. And now Karen's jaw is all knotted up, and she is definitely flushed. And Annie—*Annie's* stony-faced! What in the hell?

Alex glanced at Randall and then Tim, to see if they were flustered, too. Both seemed quite ostentatiously innocent. *Everybody at this goddamn table knows something I don't.*

Ben said, "Listen, Alex, I'll draw you a map in the office. Remind me in the morning."

The party was breaking up. Before he knew it, Alex was on the street looking for a cab to take him across Central Park and home. He was thinking: Everyone was crazy on his own. Ben didn't notice Ted, Ted didn't notice . . . they were like a flock of chickens all fleeing in different directions. Whitney—for God's sake, I said her name, and . . .

Whitney was in Los Angeles testing for a part in a film, so Alex wouldn't learn why her name should cause such a stir until she got back on Friday. He had a sinking feeling that he wouldn't enjoy the news when he heard it; but that only heightened his curiosity.

Maybe I'll call her, he thought suddenly. Why not? Tell her I miss her. Hell, I do miss her— isn't *that* the shits?

CHAPTER

2

Ben Axelrod waited on the sidewalk in front of an apartment house on West Tenth Street. It was 8:30 Friday morning. He was sitting on a suitcase, surrounded by two briefcases and a totebag with cameras in it, and by cardboard cartons containing pots and pans, towels and sheets, groceries, books, records, a compact stereo system and speakers, candles, rain slickers, and boots. And God knew what else; at least one of the boxes of linens was too heavy to be all linens.

Annie thought of their four-day stay on a mountain in the Catskills—not three hours from their apartment in Greenwich Village, less than seven miles from a busy little town—as a wilderness trek. She felt very adventurous, and Ben thought she might be a little frightened. Here is a woman who's scarcely ever been outside a city overnight. Before last fall, anyway.

Their car approached, a Pontiac convertible of what Ben thought was an excellent year, and pulled up to the curb. Annie got out displaying her businesslike frown. "Did you get everything?"

Ben stared at her and then at the provisions surrounding him. He shrugged and moved to unlock the car's trunk.

She raised her eyebrows. "Cats in their boxes?"

"Yeh, just inside the door."

"Why didn't you bring them out?"

"Because I was tired, for Christ's sake."

Annie stared at him without expression. "Wonderful," she said. "I'm about to spend four days with a red-assed mule." She strode off and into the building.

Ben went to work fitting cartons into the trunk of the car. After three minutes of lifting in, lifting out, turning, tilting, and softly cursing, he scraped his knuckles bloody on the lip of the trunk, forcing a carton down.

Annie had gone inside to make an inspection tour, spray for roaches, change her mind several times about which light should be left on to discourage prowlers, and pick up the cats and the dog. She would leave locking the three locks to Ben, he knew. He looked at his trembling, bloody hand and thought, If she left locking up to me, I'm going to punch her fucking face in. There was no question that she would. She always did. He never knew why.

He went back to packing. He gave up on getting all the carton in the trunk and put the two biggest on the back seat, which left room enough for the rest to fit in the trunk rather easily. The two on the seat would crowd the dog a little and force the cat boxes to the floor, though. Annie would bitch about that—she hated having Albie, the cat, ride on the floor; thought he didn't get enough air. And now there were two, with the brand-new no-name kitten. When she bitched he would certainly punch her fucking face in.

Ben slammed the trunk shut and sat on it. Annie came out carrying the two cat boxes and leading Dinny, their old, stiff-jointed, nearly deaf miniature Schnauzer —who had lost nothing at all in willfulness, Ben noticed. Dinny had dug in his heels, presumably having decided he wouldn't stoop to riding with cardboard cartons. He was a willful, neurotic puppy when I first met Annie, Ben thought, and now he's using the last energy in his decrepit old body on stubbornness.

"Want me to drive?" Annie asked.

Ben shrugged and got down from the trunk and took the cat boxes from her. He stretched into the car to put one on each side of the drive shaft on the floor in back. When Dinny got close enough to the car to recognize it by smell, he jumped in under Ben's chin. He turned around and, with his forepaws on the nearer cat box, stretched out and licked Ben's face.

Ben stood up and set his hands on his hips. Before he could ask whether she'd locked up, Annie saw his knuckles and gasped. There was nothing for it but to go inside and spray them with antiseptic.

She had locked the locks. The spray stung. She used a lot of it.

Annie drove. They traveled in grim silence, except for an occasional tiny wail from the kitten's box, and reassuring coos directed by Annie at the kitten.

The sky was overcast; rain was predicted. Terrific, Ben thought, four days indoors glaring at each other. And I'm going to get soaking wet and cold working outdoors, connecting the pipes. Well, if I do I'll warm up by the fireplace; we left wood in the basement. And meantime, the muted light was very beautiful in its way—the best kind for color photography. As they left the city, across the George Washington Bridge, the world turned green—just about as suddenly as that. Before they'd bought the house, Ben and Annie had rarely left Manhattan, except on great occasions like vacation trips. So Ben was more vividly aware of the greenness in the French countryside than that within a few minutes of their apartment.

The range of greens that met the eye today was less spectacular than in sunlight, but subtler. Not much yellow in any of it, but the middle values were greener in this light, not so washed out.

By the time they were leaving the Palisades for the Thruway Ben was willing to concede, though only to himself, that he *was* red-assed, and to consider why. So, of course, was Annie. And why was that? Annie was crazy a lot these days with being pregnant, so it was hard to tell. In principle, Ben was not merely prepared for Annie to be crazy, he was positively in favor of it. Her feelings were too much buried, Ben thought, and pregnancy seemed to have brought them to the surface, and he was glad. It would be interesting to learn what it felt like, being pregnant. So he approved of her nuttiness, in principle.

In practice, it was frightening and exhausting. He was afraid that it would wear him out, that he simply wouldn't have the emotional stamina to live with all her feelings—or his own—for the stretch. Was that why he was so tense this morning? Wearing thin already? Why was she? Whitney? No, that was settled.

How long had it been? They had decided, when they were fighting last Monday after dinner at Randall and Tim's, that it had been just about five years. Ben had actually left Annie for a few months, five years ago, for Whitney. He remembered it calmly enough now, but it had been almost as wrenching and painful an experience for him as it had been for Annie. And humiliating; he'd been pleased to think of himself as a man in touch with himself, full of understanding, in control of his behavior. His reasons for leaving Annie and living with Whitney had been intricately worked out, sane, constructive, absolutely convincing and utterly, hopelessly delusional. He'd finally felt like a consummate horse's ass.

Enough of that. It *was* five years ago. I was scarcely the first damn fool in the history of the world, and it wasn't the first love affair with a bad ending. If I lied, I didn't know I was doing it, and I didn't use drugs, hypnosis, shackles, threats. . . . We were all three of us adults at the time—well, chronologically—and anyway, it was five years ago.

He hadn't thought of it at all in a long time, and he was pretty sure Annie hadn't, either. Their battle over it on Monday had ended in calm. It might be a little tense at first in the country, but there was no reason for it to be so terrible. They'd probably be off on their own, mostly. Whitney had Alex—not such a bargain, I'd think, but then how would I know? I didn't understand Whitney any better than I understood myself all during that time. Maybe he's just fine for her.

Ben thought the two of them might be serious; Alex, at least, seemed more than ripe to settle down again. He'd been divorced for three years now, and Ben thought he was not really so happy alone and prowling.

He watched the countryside flowing by. Gray-green, green, pale green: tops of trees against the gray sky, leaves and brush and grass under the trees, new grass alongside the road. Near Harriman, they were driving through wooded land, gently rolling but showing rocky outcroppings that foreshadowed the mountains they were approaching.

All right, what then? Annie was being her pain-in-the-ass manager self, for one thing. I *am* going to punch her face in one of these days. He pictures a scene from a western movie: Annie soaring over a balcony, dropping onto a poker table that collapses beneath her; Ben looking down, rubbing his knuckles (his knuckles were still sore from the car trunk); Annie getting to her feet, rubbing her jaw, saying ruefully, well, I had that coming. (But when he carelessly let that fantasy go where it would, she got up and flung a table leg at his face.)

He knew what was making her so tense. It was the damn wilderness. Annie was a city girl. She loved the country place, but she wasn't really at ease there. It was not just out of sight of other people, it was out of ear-shot—my God, you could fire a gun there and it wouldn't be heard. There were animals, of course, but none that were dangerous. Except maybe to Dinny. Albie, at least—the grown cat—would have the sense to run from a skunk or a porcupine, but the dog was stubborn and dumber than hell. Sooner or later we're gonna have to pull quills out of him, or wash skunk off him. Dumbass dog. Ben didn't know how to go about either of those tasks.

It began to dawn on him what it was that was making him so red-assed. He was tense for the same reason Annie was. The idea surprised him, but it was surely true. It was not knowing what to do about Dinny and the quills that triggered the insight. In fact, Ben also was a city person. He'd grown up in a small town, but it was a town, not a wilderness. And wilderness was the word, though that surprised him, too. They weren't many miles from the nearest people; they had the car, they had the telephone, they had solid houses with solid doors, they had lights all over the place, they had those big, square, brilliant flashlights.

Damn it, it *is* a wilderness, nevertheless; I know it is because it scares me. What scares me? To be as concrete as he could, he thought about the house. He was on his own with that damned house, and he only knew how to live in an apartment, with a superintendent on call. He had grown up in a house, but his father, an English teacher, had neither known nor cared to know how to operate one. He called people in.

So Ben hadn't learned. It had only recently dawned on him, in fact, that that was the word for it: operate. He had, he now realized, thought of a house as a big object, when what it was was a big machine. Functioning, wearing out parts, needing repairs and preventive maintenance. It had pipes and wires, it had hinges and latches, an electrical pump, a hot-water heater. It was even in a struggle with the earth—which was also not static. The basement had a leak, caused, so the real estate agent had said, by freezing or settling or something, going on in the earth around it.

It was all those miles to the nearest neighbors, and who could guess what they might be like? If there were a fire, or if a tree fell on the house—no, the trees weren't close enough—well, if there were whatever serious mishap, he'd be helpless. Randall, Tim, Ted—none of them knew any more than he did, and maybe less. It couldn't kill him, this house and this wilderness, but it could humiliate him. The realization settled his mind a little. He was no less scared, now that the fear had a name, and limits—quite narrow limits, really—but he could live with it.

He decided to keep the fear to himself. Annie was already a little afraid, and in her present cranky state, it would do neither of them any good to add to her fear. He didn't trust her to enjoy herself when she was afraid, and he wanted her to enjoy herself. He wanted to enjoy her, too. If she'd stop being such a pain in the ass.

They were past halfway, now, approaching the New Paltz exit from the Thruway—less than an hour left ahead of them. He turned to Annie—she still looked stony-faced—and broke the long silence. "Like me to take over driving?"

Annie turned slowly to him. "Well," she pronounced, "Mr. Redass speaks."

He turned to stare out the windshield and thought: I'm going to punch her fucking face in.

Annie drove in silence, and in a rage. She knew perfectly damn well why Ben was so quiet. That vicious, interfering, destructive—what? *Cunt.* She was a cunt. A taker, a puller-in, a grabber.

Annie's anger was like a fireworks pinwheel: Now that it was lit it spun on its own self-perpetuating energy. Five years ago she had been horribly hurt, frightened, lost and furious with Ben when he'd run off with Whitney Williams; but the full height of rage had seized her only when it was all over, when Ben defended her: "Look, Annie," he had said then, "whatever happened while it was going on, the only one of the three of us to come out of this worse off than before it started is Whitney."

The pompous sonofabitch. And now here she comes

back into our lives, and he says, God *damn* him, he has the crushing insensitivity to say, "What are you *worried* about? I'm sorry it ever happened but it was five years ago. She means nothing to me. I *love* you." Very grand, that. Oh, very. I luuuv you. And I didn't have the presence of mind to tell him what it was that upset me so; and he didn't have even the minimal, tiny ounce of sensitivity that would have been required to know. Not the barest human *minimum* awareness of *me*.

I *love* you, I already love our *baby*. Of course you do, you unfeeling prick. You haven't the remotest idea that *I'm* going to be carrying it for nine months, have you? Eight, now. Seven and a half. Seven and a half months, and how much of that fat and tired and scared and sexless? Unattractive and uninteresting and uninterested and undesirable. Unsexed. How will you feel then, big shot, with Whitney simpering around?

Enjoying the silence, you bastard? Having a good time being mad at me so you can go off into your pornographic fantasy life? Of course I'm unattractive when I ask you to do grubby work. Pack the car. Pick up the cats. Nag, nag. Whitney didn't nag, did she? Oh, hell no. Never any reason to be irritated with Whitney. Just all kissyface. We'll have a picnic in the country, I'll fix the lunch, I'll drive us in my nice MG, all *you* have to do is bring your handsome self and drink my wine and fuck me on a grassy bank. *Cunt!* Not like old Annie the nag. Rather be angry with old Annie, wouldn't you, you sullen little snot?

You love me? You don't even know I exist, you self-centered sonofabitch. You don't know anybody exists but yourself.

Don't even know I exist. . . . The phrase had come to her spontaneously, but when she heard it in her mind, it clanked. Sounded like a line of hackneyed dialogue from, say, a bad movie. The sonofabitch, now he's got me talking to myself like a—like some—like a character in a soap opera. Shit.

But she was beginning to realize that she was enjoying

this inner tirade. Well, it *is* sort of . . . therapeutic. Swearing's very satisfying, for one thing. Fuck. Prick. Self-centered sonofabitch—nice ring to that.

She had learned to swear from Ben, and he found it a useful skill—in her own mind, but also, once in a while, at work. Ben was terrific at it. It sounded natural to him, fit into the rhythms of his speech, adding force and flavor.

He's good at that, isn't that wonderful? What else is he good at? Pouting. He's a terrific sulker. Damn—

Ben's voice interrupted her thought. "Like me to take over driving?" After two hours, he manages to choke out a sentence.

"Well," she said. "Mr. Redass speaks." Like you to drive? Like you to drive your red ass off a cliff, you miserable prick.

She could barely suppress a smile. Miserable prick. . . . The realization was overcoming her that swearing was *not* the only thing Ben was good at, and it wasn't the only thing she'd learned from him, either.

The fact is, I love him, God damn him, beyond all reason. Shit. Annie sighed audibly, and Ben turned to look at her.

Fuck off.

The bedroom was at the back of the house, looking out across the gravel drive at a wall of trees. The room was twilit, the window the only source of light. Rain attacked the windowpane. In the bed, Annie lay with her head cradled on Ben's shoulder, thinking how easy it had been to give up being angry and how glad she was that she had. She could still feel him inside her—though he wasn't.

"Ohh," she said drowsily. "Listen to the rain. You finished up outside just in time. How nice." Ben adjusted the covers over her shoulders with his free hand; his other arm was over her warm, naked back. He shifted the leg next to her and touched her foot with his.

"Mmm," she murmured, "your feet are warm now."

"Oh, yeah," he said softly, "you did a dandy job warming me up."

"Mmm. Warmed up's the word." He'd been as excited as a teenager. She'd forgotten how pleasant it was to have that effect on a man—on Ben.

He nodded, rubbing his chin in her hair. "Funny, I felt at first like you were too fragile, now, or the baby is, or something. I know it's silly . . ."

"Sure is. I want you in me more than ever. If that's possible."

"It was wonderful that you made that so clear. For a little mother, you're a very wicked lady."

She chuckled in her throat. "You're pretty depraved yourself, for an old crock."

"Well, I was so. . . . I knew I was going to be quick."

"You were, too. But by that time, who cared?"

He sighed. "You've been so cranky—"

What? She looked up at him.

"—that I wasn't even thinking about it while I was outside doing the pipes and stuff. When I came out of the shower and you were here—oh, wow, in ambush. . . ." He smiled in her hair.

After a little silence she asked, "Did you ever make love on a grassy bank?"

"Yeah, once."

The quickness of his response stung her. Didn't have to search far back in his memory, did he? Oh, dear, I don't want to know about it.

"In high school. Pretty awful, really. Gritty. Grass wasn't very thick. Chilly, too. Three in the morning, shore of a lake. Beery."

"Oh," she said softly, "that's nice."

He looked at her—that is, she felt him bend his head down and touch her hair with his chin. He said, "Well, it would be, I think, on a proper grassy bank. Nice thick grass, in the shade on a warm day. . . . There are places here. When the weather is nice."

Oh, yes. She smiled against his chest and kissed him.

He asked, "Have you?"

"Mm-hmmm. It was terrific." Why did I say that? She was amused at herself.

"When was that?"

"No, I was lying."

He pinched her.

"*Ow*—I thought you loved my bottom." She moved off him, turned over, sat up against pillows. The bed-clothes fell short of her breasts. She brushed her long, straight hair away from her damp face, leaned back against the pillows and sighed deeply. "You know, I feel like I can do anything when you're inside me." She reached out, under the covers, to touch his thigh, to maintain the warmth of contact. "When you first come in. . . ." She shook her head slowly and fell silent.

"When I first come into you, and you make that sound, I—well, you know, I think I believe in penis envy after all. I mean, not then. Then I just feel like—well, some kind of . . . god. With a great gift." He smiled sheepishly.

"Have we talked about this before?"

He shook his head. "Don't remember. But I have an idea how you feel from the sound, and a sort of—tensing or relaxing, I don't even know which it is—that your body does. It feels like I've just given you something terribly important."

I'm so crazy, she thought. I hate it when I think he doesn't understand me, but when he does I feel—invaded, or something. It's scary. She moved down in the bed and covered her breasts with the sheet.

Her breasts were surprisingly ample—because of her height and broad shoulders, she didn't seem busty when she was dressed—and soft. She had never entirely gotten over regretting that they weren't . . . pneumatic. God damn the movies, she thought. She meant the movies of the 1950s, when she was in her teens. She still—she thought it was silly in the extreme, but with a tiny childish part of herself, she still wanted them to stand out like gun turrets. Bombs. Boobs.

Ben once said they were generous; they had the

generosity that flows from self-approval. They were pleased with themselves. He said the dumbest, loveliest things sometimes. He made them be that way, too—or so it felt to her. A miracle. When he made love to them, it felt as though they grew big and hard. Lovely. Like he did. Big and hard.

She moved the hand on his thigh and found him, warm, still sticky, miraculously growing big again out of his tangled woolly hair. So soon! she thought. She turned to him and rose to kiss him, pulling herself free of the sheets once again. As they kissed, he cupped a breast and her breath caught. She squeezed him gently and he gasped in response. He leaned over to kiss her nipple and—oh, yes, she swelled, she filled and rose to meet his mouth, to fill him as his tongue moved to her and his lips engulfed her; oh, yes, she would fill him, and then he would fill her.

The mountain king had never been below the cave, where the houses were; nor had any of his kind in this cave. It simply didn't occur to them to go lower. Perhaps they were more comfortable where the atmospheric pressure was slightly less. Snakes have no reasons—only habits, driven by instincts. The snakes in this den were the descendants of creatures whose habit it had been to move upward from the cave—those who had ranged below had been destroyed many generations ago. And there were hundreds of square miles of wilderness above the cave, uncomplicated by the incursions of humans.

The king was driven now, as were others that had come out, back into the cave.

There was more motion, more life, inside the cave than there had been earlier. The storm signals were making them restless. He moved over shifting bodies to a shelf that ran along the wall of the cave, moved along this ledge among more restless bodies, until it ended.

There his head and the forward part of his body lifted more than a foot to the beginning of another jutting platform. And so he proceeded through the darkness, shelf to shelf, to the deepest place in the cave.

The cave had been formed, eons in the past, by rushing water, which had carved it into this complicated arrangement of terraces before finding a new channel to run in. All those tens of thousands of years in the past, there had been no deer in these mountains, though there were giant antlered beasts that somewhat resembled deer; there had been no raccoons or opossums, but there had been giant ground sloths. There had been woolly mammoths and a giant cat that humans have since called smilodon.

And there had been snakes exactly like the mountain king: venomous snakes whose shedding skin left dried rings at the tail, each new ring fitted loosely around the last until there were enough brittle rings of hardened skin to rustle together and produce a whirring rattle sound. Thousands of generations of these snakes lived before humans appeared on earth and created the name rattlesnake for them.

The mountain king had reached his spot. His hunger, combined with his unease over the storm threat, made his nervous system alert and sensitive. As his body temperature fell to match the cool of the cave his awareness would dim and his body become quiescent; but for now he coiled and uncoiled restlessly.

He was receiving a strange signal, one his reflexes had no prepared response to—not so much a movement in the rock around him as the promise of movement to come.

An ancestor, thousands of times removed, had experienced such a signal and had left a cave like this one in response to it. That is how that snake had lived to become the mountain king's ancestor. But the mountain king, though his genes contained the same information his ancestor's had, wasn't prepared to act in the same way. It was growing too cold in the cave for his musculature to function smoothly; and then his body was preoccupied with the increasingly urgent storm warnings.

He coiled tightly and vibrated his tail fitfully. Many of his kind were doing the same. But the rattling sound subsided over the next hour as the temperature dropped and torpor overcame them.

CHAPTER

3

Late in her pregnancy, nearly two years ago now, Karen Vincenzo had suspected briefly that Ted was having an affair. Seeing another woman, was how she'd put it to herself. Seeing: she hated the idea of his looking at another woman's—well, no, she had thought, he wouldn't. What she'd meant was, I don't want to think about it; and she hadn't since, until Monday at dinner.

Ted's red ears and silence at the mention of Whitney Williams' name were like thunder and lightning in the room. Not only did she know the truth, she couldn't imagine that everyone there hadn't nearly fainted under its impact, as she had. More: when she thought of the signals she had somehow managed to deny two years ago, signals as undeniable as an avalanche, she nearly burst into tears at the table—tears of humiliation on top of rage.

They had walked home in grim silence, not to disturb Charley's fitful sleep. Ted actually wasn't sure he'd been caught out until Karen pulled the door softly shut between their bedroom and the baby's room.

From that moment her bitter weeping, blaming, pouting, accusing, rage and self-pity, sullen silences and crackling sarcasm had been coming at him like machine-gun fire—for four days now, with breaks only for work and sleep. Which, Ted thought, she's been doing much more of than I have—sleeping.

Ted walked home from work Friday evening, through Central Park. His long-limbed athlete's stride carried him faster than he wished, so he lingered in the park, sitting under a tree to watch some softball. More informal than the league he played in, these teams had girls on them, which was very pleasant to see. They were like picnic or beach games, really, though some of the teams had well-designed T-shirts with companies' names on them—magazines and book publishers. Very nicely set off by the round, soft female bodies, especially.

He was unable to become absorbed in watching the horsing-around style of play, or even the girls' bodies, for very long. He was in no hurry to get home. He was exhausted by the week's recriminations, tired of feeling guilty.

The strength of his remorse had surprised him. He still thought of his fleeting affair with Whitney as a harmless lark, the result of transitory horniness rather than any deep failure of his love for Karen. He had now come to see how much Karen's admiration meant to him. It wasn't what he'd done, but merely that she despised him, that had made him feel ashamed.

But he was becoming weary with all that. He was out of patience—out of guilt. It hadn't stopped for a minute, and it was enough. He pushed himself reluctantly to his feet and resumed the walk home, his irritation growing. His guilt was being replaced, blessedly, by anger.

He found Karen sleeping, as he expected. The baby was sleeping, as well; the door between their bedroom and the baby's room was open, so that when Charley began to stir Karen would wake. I wonder, he thought.

Does she wake up when the baby calls, when she's in this kind of sleep? Is she neglecting—no, that's crazy.

He pulled the door shut between the two rooms and sat on the bed. He looked at her for a while, dreading waking her. She was, of course, angelic asleep and, with her tank top pulled askew revealing a teasing faint edge of nipple, achingly sexy as well.

He touched her shoulder and her eyes came open and blinked. "What?" It was petulant.

He clenched his jaw and said gently, "C'mon, get up. We'll have dinner and decide about the country."

"I decided about the country. I told you. I'm not sharing a mountain with that—your—" Karen frowned her most pettish frown and sat up.

"Now, look." With effort Ted kept his voice soft. "For the ten thousandth time, I don't blame you for being hurt and angry, but—"

"Don't blame me? You told me there was no reason to be upset!"

"That was *days* ago, goddamnit, back in round one, or whatever. Now just shut the fuck up and listen." His voice was still low in volume, but rising in pitch. "I have heard enough snot-nose pissing and moaning for an ax murder, and all I did was get laid a couple of times. I was horny. I shouldn't have done it, but I did it two years ago and haven't thought about it twice since."

"When was the twice?"

Ted clamped his jaw again, rose and walked to the door, wheeled, stood with his hands on his hips, and strode back to where she still sat on the edge of the bed. Looming over her, he said, "If you don't cut that shit out and listen, I'm gonna throw you through the *wall*. No. I'll . . . I *will* tape your stupid mouth shut, I swear I will."

Karen looked up, fury in her eyes, and opened her mouth—and decided, seeing his face, that he might actually do this outrageous thing. She shut up.

By now, the picture of her bound and gagged, her eyes blazing with rage, had formed in Ted's mind and, to his own astonishment, a snort of laughter burst from him. One ridiculous "Hah!" before he caught it.

It was too much for Karen. "You *sonofabitch*. You big goddamn baby, you think all this is a *joke*? Messing over our *lives*? Complicating—" She was crying again.

But the hysteria was on him. He continued to try to contain it, shaking his head, with the result that his abdomen heaved erratically and he produced several widely separated hooting sounds.

She left the room, holding her face in her hands, weeping bitterly. Ted sat on the bed and surrendered to the fit of laughter until, very soon, it subsided, leaving him drained. When she returned, her face was so full of hate he thought he might turn to stone. "Now, look," he began, intimidated a little in spite of himself.

"No, *you* look, you—"

Ted gave in and bellowed, *"No, goddamnit, I'm still talking.* Now, *you* shut up or I *will* by God do what I said."

She shut up, but she turned and stalked out to the kitchen. He nodded to himself, rose and followed. She was watering a plant, her back to him. He said grimly, "If you don't put down that watering can, I'm going to stuff it—" but he stopped that, feeling another fit of helpless hysteria approaching with the picture of the smooth white enamel can disappearing. . . . "Just sit down," he said.

She looked over her shoulder at him, expressionless, cold as marble.

"Do it!" Baggins, their big dog, who had been sleeping on the cool kitchen floor, raised his head and whined. Ted glared at him. Baggins fell silent and put his head back down, but watched warily.

Karen took elaborate pains to finish with the plant, and then she sat on a stool at one end of the butcher-block counter, her hands folded in her lap. Ted sat on the farthest stool from her, facing her, an elbow resting on the counter. "Look, I'm not kidding around. I'm sorry I laughed, I don't think anything's funny, that was, like, hysteria. I'm worn out, I'm exhausted. I don't even feel guilty anymore. It—it's just enough. It's finished, I'm through with it. I'm not gonna apologize anymore. I've felt bad all I'm gonna *feel* bad. It was dumb of me to tell you you shouldn't be upset in the first place, sure you should. But—it's *enough*. . . . If you want to go on sulking and sniveling—" He saw her jaw tighten. "—No, look, I'm sorry, take back the words. . . . But if you want to go on clinging to your hurt, nursing it forever, you're gonna be doing it by yourself. I'm all out—"

"Okay," she said quietly.

"—I'm just out of. . . . What?"

"I said okay," she said flatly. "I'll never mention it again."

He didn't like the response. It was resigned, not far from sullen, and it scarcely promised a return to warmth and intimacy. Still, he was determined to put an end to the weeklong battle, and it was an end, of sorts. Anyway, it cut off his speech, and he didn't know which direction to go next. "Well," he said thoughtfully, "what about the country? If you won't go, you won't, and I won't go without you, but I think you're making a mistake. She'll be with Alex, after all, and they're staying with Randall and Tim."

"Okay."

The tone was still sullen-flat. Ted nodded slowly and said, "It's supposed to be muggy-hot with thunder-showers in the city. It'll be nice to go where it's cool and breezy."

"It's my house. That—she won't keep me from it."

"Good," he said, though he wasn't sure it was.

He heard a thump from the baby's room and looked at her, alarmed, half rising. Karen shook her head. "It's okay. Wait a minute."

In a minute, Charley waddled into the kitchen, wrinkles on his face from the pillow, but bright-eyed and smiling. "Lookit," he said. Of his three or four words, that was his favorite; in this case it might have meant "Look at what I've done" or merely "hello."

"He can get out of his crib?" Ted asked.

Karen, still expressionless, nodded. Charley walked toward her until he bumped into her legs, then hugged them. She picked him up and took a deep breath. "He first did it yesterday. I ran in and there he was, sitting beside the crib looking surprised and pleased with himself." Her voice softened as she spoke to the baby. "You're gonna be a real little terror now, aren't you?"

Charley laughed and looked to Ted, reaching out to be taken. "Lookit," he said.

"That's just fine," Karen said sweetly. "Go to Daddy. He needs changing, Daddy."

Ted hugged the baby and nuzzled his neck and said softly to him, "You rotten little shit. Did Mommy train you to do that?" He carried Charley to the baby's room, the two of them poking at each other and laughing.

Karen picked up the watering can and returned to her end-of-the-week chore. Drained of anger, she felt bleak. Her mind began to fill, all but against her will, with plans for the weekend in the country. Rough clothes they'd need, Ted's Stanford sweatshirt is clean, rain slickers probably. . . .

In Alex Klein's big, airy apartment on a high floor of a new building, three suitcases sat in the living room. One was Alex's, the other two Whitney's. The bags, packed for their weekend together in the country, sat alongside a long white leather couch, under a coldly colorful Vasarely print on the wall.

In the bedroom, on a wall in a corner, hung a poster photograph of Julius Erving in action, soaring, slam-dunking a basketball. It was expensively framed, with glass. It was for Alex's son, who visited him every other weekend. Alex put it up for the visits and removed it when the visits ended, but Whitney had seen the poster in a closet and been touched by its connection with Alex's son. She had asked him to restore it to its place. Alex had grumbled halfheartedly, but he had been pleased.

Alex was pleased by Whitney in many ways. He was pleased by her body. He looked at it now on the bed beside him. It was a dancer's body, lithe and trim, her belly flatter than his, her breasts small and firm, white as ice cream in the midst of her California tan, the nipples engorged now and rising from the mounds, her legs round, smooth and strong. A delicious body, and he wanted to make it his alone.

He lay naked too, his upper torso propped with an elbow, the other hand gently petting her silken belly, moving down into the second strip of white, trailing a finger in fine black hair, teasing. She raised her chin and opened her mouth slightly, clenched her fine little teeth and drew in a hissing breath. She touched, gently, without pressure, that petting hand, and looked at him with her big dark eyes and smiled a tense, small smile.

She was responsive to him, Alex knew that well by now, and he liked that. His mind was already on her coming. She would come easily—early and often—and before she did she would make love to him, enthusiastically, with her hands, her mouth. . . . And Alex loved that. He touched inside her tentatively, with just the tip of a finger, and her gasp was audible. She rose, her body curled, to kiss his chest, tongue around his nipples, and he bent and kissed her shoulder and back. She grasped his balls, her wrist pressing, warm, along his length.

Alex loved it, and yet—and yet he wanted more from her. More than he'd ever wanted from a woman. More than—what? He almost knew. He couldn't think what she might be withholding, there seemed to be nothing she wouldn't do—Oh! her mouth. . . . He lay back to watch her make love to him.

He looked at the curve of her side, the tip of a breast just touching his abdomen, her hair veiling her face. He softly kneaded the back of her neck, felt a tiny seed of anger take root in him. He wanted—though he might never say it to himself—he wanted more than Ben had had, or Ted; wanted more of himself in her than they had had; wanted to touch more of her, lay claim to territory they hadn't reached. He had learned about them only last Monday, on the phone. This was his first time with Whitney since then.

With his hand, he urged her head away from his middle, brought her face to his, kissed her hard, deep, grasped a breast, moved over her and entered her, suddenly and hard. "Oh!" she said, and flinched away with her middle for a split second, but he was in and in a moment that was fine, that was where she was, between her own legs with him, all of her was there.

Alex knew that—that she went there, all of her was there—and it wasn't enough. She looked away, over her head at the wall, she clutched his sides with her hands, moved them down behind his thighs, moved with him—against him—with liquid smoothness, her urgency growing until a tense, tiny trembling joined the long, smooth movements, a kind of undertone. She cried out, a sound that seemed torn from her on the rack, cried again, squeezed him with her hard, strong legs, cried again, the sound becoming a thin, breathy wail, jerked her head, her face against the side of his neck, sucked at his shoulder, hugged him powerfully with her arms, threw her head back again, cried softly, subsided.

It wasn't enough. Alex came out of her, raised up, went to where she was. He went straight between her legs, tongued hard, tasted his own sweat and her hot juices. "Oh!" she said again, that little cry of surprise and discomfort, and then moaned softly, soon began the liquid movements again, against his face, his jaw, testing the strength of the muscle at the base of his tongue, held his head, murmured to him, "Oh, that's . . . ," came again, subsided once more.

It was not enough. He lay back beside her, looked down his front at himself, huge, wet, pink and red, achy with unfulfillment. She saw him and went to him again with her mouth, worked gently with her tongue. "Hard!" he said, and she squeezed with her mouth, hard, and worked her head up and down. He petted her lower back, felt a bit of downy hair there, slid his hand down, touched her at the mouth of her ass, she grunted—with pleasure? he didn't know, or care—but she began to suck, tried to pull him out of himself. Alex loved it, the feeling was intense almost beyond tolerance.

And it wasn't enough. His hand resting, teasing, lightly penetrating her ass—drawing another sound from her throat—told him what was next. He pulled away from her, out of her mouth, pushed her down flat on her belly beside him, moved astride her, pulled her apart, gripped her sides, and thrust. "Oh, *no!*" she cried, and he thrust at a different angle, hard, farther, against her resistance. She was hot and close in there, so tight it hurt him a little. She shook her head violently, clenched her fists beside her head, she was crying now—"*No-oo*"—and he moved down on her, chest against her warm back, grasped her shoulders, pounded deeper, pulled and thrust again, once more—he had never been held so close, so completely—thrust yet again and then suddenly did at last come out of himself, all the way out and into her, with a great racking shudder. She trembled violently, buried her face in a pillow, sighed a long sigh with voice in it, a keening that pierced him to his core.

Looming above her, his weight on his hands, his arms stiff, he nearly laughed aloud in triumph. He had found the rest of her. At once a weakness near to dying came over him. His whole body rubbery, he shrank in her and soon removed himself, sat up and looked at her. She faced away from him, both hands still clenched into fists resting alongside her head, and sobbed out of control. Dismay began to appear in him, replacing the deep, huge satisfaction of having found her. He had gloried in her pain, and now began to wonder at himself. Suddenly she turned and reached around his neck with both arms, pressed her whole warm, wet body to him, legs to legs, middle hard against tender middle, breasts flat against his chest and wept hard against his neck, hugging him.

He held her, petted her clumsily, said, "I'm . . . sorry, I—I'm sorry I hurt you, I didn't . . ." He felt her eyes open against his throat, the lashes brushing him.

Whitney opened her eyes in astonishment. Her weeping stopped. She continued to hold him, listen to his murmurings, hide her face against him. Her feelings were so rich and pungent a stew that she would choke on them if she didn't take time to taste them one by one. She was horrified at herself, ashamed to the center of her heart. She had come with him inside her there, the very humiliation of having him pounding into her against her wish had brought her to a pitch of intense, all-pervading-what? Pleasure? More like pain—and that bone-deep—so beyond her ability to contain, so impossible to *choose* to enjoy or loathe, that she had come not with the middle of her body, as she was used to doing, but with her every cell. Her toes and her scalp had come; all of it had come over her like an army of Huns devastating her carefully nurtured self-control.

She would, she felt, die to have that feeling again, and her horror was compounded. She was horrified to imagine that she might like to be mistreated, humiliated, degraded—she had thought at one moment when he first came out that she could smell her shit—but she was still more horrified that she could want something so much—something she couldn't give herself but must ask for, depend on someone else—a man—to give her. She had felt—filled. Never so filled. Never had a presence made itself felt so intensely inside her. Excruciating, insanely satisfying. Terrifying. Alex could give her that; he could take it away. If she were close to that feeling again, she could imagine herself begging for it. Please—please pound, stab, fill, violate—oh, my God. She shuddered again, and began to sob anew.

He held her firmly, petted her shoulder and head, murmured until her weeping subsided. "I'm so sorry," he whispered. "I didn't—I don't know—I never did—I'll never . . ." he trailed off, kissing her hair.

He was saying he'd never done that before, she realized. That possibility hadn't occurred to her, and now surprised her and started still more tears from her. Now, suddenly, she felt that he'd given her something, as well as taken. She held him hard, knowing they would do it again, despite what he believed.

She had never in her life imagined that it was possible to be so frightened. It was still another terrible feeling she wanted to have again. She loved Alex Klein, and wanted to love him as long as she lived. Oh, what a fear! What a killing terror.

He doesn't know it. He thinks I'm angry. Can I let him know the truth? Another time, she thought; the fear was too much. But he thinks I hate him! Another time. . . .

"It's all right, Alex," was all she could manage.

CHAPTER

4

At nearly ten Friday night, in the basement garage of their apartment house, Randall Madison sat at the wheel of the station wagon, watching over his shoulder as Tim gingerly placed the last suitcase in the rear. "It's just luggage, for God's sake," Randall said, "it's not crystal."

"Then why does it cost as much as crystal? No, I know—because some piss-elegant frog puts his initials on it, that makes it priceless."

Randall sighed as Tim slammed the heavy tailgate and moved around the car to get in. Tim will not give in and really enjoy prosperity, he thought. He directed the car up the steep incline to the street.

Randall was a conventionally handsome blond man who would be recognized by most New Yorkers as the kindly and whimsical loan officer in a series of television commercials for a bank. He and Tim had been together for nearly twenty years now, and for seventeen of them their combined income never got higher than twenty-five thousand dollars—Tim had been understudying a principal in a hit musical for most of that year—and had averaged closer to ten. Now, they were at last reasonably prosperous.

Three years ago, Randall had resigned most of his serious theatrical ambitions and begun doing commercials in earnest. His character for the bank had become famous, and he had just signed a new, exclusive contract at what seemed to him an outrageous annual fee—it embarrassed him to think of the first-rate actors who had never come close to it for doing brilliant work.

They crossed the George Washington Bridge in fog, which became dense on the Palisades. Tim had fallen asleep.

Tim's attitude toward their money had changed from deep mistrust to something like awe to a sort of managerial hard-headedness. For a year after Randall's income had firmly established itself at the new level, Tim had refused to alter their life-style significantly. He was astonished to discover how much had accumulated as a result of his caution—and his stubbornness in the face of Randall's nagging. Then he began to formulate his plan for their future.

Six months later Tim stopped looking for work in the theater and they invested a hefty chunk in his travel agency. In six more months, he had made the agency profitable. Then, finally, they had moved to their new apartment, bought their Buick station wagon—Randall, of course, had wanted a Jaguar—and now they were so secure that Tim had not objected to buying the country house.

Tim's a wonder, Randall thought, he really is. It's ironic—people think Tim's the frivolous one, because of his flitty manner. When really it's Tim's tough—and tiresome, goddamnit—frugality that's kept us off the streets in all the lean years. And he's the one'll see to it we have a comfortable old age. Whereas *I* am as vain and frivolous as any old faggot. I love those ugly suitcases, just because when people see them they know they cost a lot of money.

As they entered the tollbooth onto the Thruway, light flooded into the car, the sound went dead momentarily on the radio and Tim woke up, immediately fully alert. "It's beginning to rain," he said. He had seen the first huge drop smack the windshield as they pulled out of the tollbooth.

"Oh, damn."

"Yeah, it's gonna be no fun for you to drive in." And at once it was thunderously loud on the roof and blinding on the windshield.

"Damn, damn, damn," Randall muttered. "Listen, stay awake and talk to me, will you? This makes me want to go to sleep."

"All right, I'll entertain you. Da-dum tada-dada, your sister *Rose* is dead—"

They laughed at a favorite joke. Like old folks, Randall thought—just the punch line is enough. We could give them numbers.

Tim pondered. "Mmm, da-dum . . . mmwee-ee-*roff* to see d'dum . . . what *are* we off to see, d'you think?"

Randall and Tim were old friends of Whitney Williams'. They had learned only last Monday, along with everyone else, that she was now with Alex Klein, but they had known all along of her history with both Ben and Ted.

Randall smiled. "Off to see a lot of clenched jaws and white knuckles and good manners. Lots of politeness."

Tim said, "I'm ashamed to say it, but it really is delicious, isn't it? I mean, I feel for Whit, but what *possesses* her to come here, with these people of all people on earth? Her whole scarlet past, for God's sake, in one place."

Randall shook his head. "I don't know, except that she and Alex may be really serious."

"You mean, she doesn't want to ask him to drop his friends for her?"

"Something like that," Randall said. "And then, I think she may want to be part of—oh, you know, the *family.* That sort of square, upright world of kids and pets and country houses and all.''

"Like you."

Randall looked over at Tim. "Yeah," he said, "that is what I find attractive about them. They remind me of my real family, a little. Square, solid . . . very different from our other friends. D'you realize that, except for them, *we* are the sanest people we know?''

"What an *appalling* thought," Tim replied.

"It's true, though. Not one of 'em has ever attempted suicide, or—or slapped anybody in public, or—and they don't do drugs. . . . They don't even *drink* too much, for God's sake.''

"Now that you mention it, they're really rather boring, aren't they?" Tim said.

Randall grinned. "Yeah, I guess they are. But—I don't know, it's probably a sign of advancing age, but I'm really sick and tired of *interesting*, neurotic people. It's tiresome watching people fuck themselves up, and it's tiresome to watch them fuck each other up. It's not interesting at all, really, it's the same thing over and over.''

"Well," Tim allowed, perhaps grudgingly, "I think it *is* middle age creeping on, but to tell you the truth I feel the same way sometimes. I'm glad we're not like that anymore. We're not, are we? As much?''

Randall smiled and shook his head, no. He was becoming weary of the tension of this driving. His eyes were tired of the white and red glare from the road. Tim's night vision was terrible, and anyway Tim didn't feel comfortable driving this huge car—that *he* had insisted we buy, damn him. "We're going to have to stop at the Thruway place and get some coffee and rest a couple of minutes," Randall said. "I *am* getting old.''

Feeling better for the rest and the coffee, Randall pulled onto the Thruway once again. The rain had become lighter, but the wind was strong enough to make itself felt pushing against the side of the car. The horizon flickered with an electrical storm ahead of them.

Tim said dubiously, "I hope this trip is worth it."

It was a fiction they maintained between them that Tim's occasional grumping about the country place was a good-natured fraud, that he really loved it there. In fact, he really didn't like it much; and, though he loved Annie, and liked the others well enough, he didn't enjoy whole weekends with them all that much, either. It was Randall's place. Randall had grown up in North Dakota, and felt the need to spend time out of the city. And Randall loved the people—loved them as a group. They were a sort of surrogate family for him; he was totally estranged from his own family.

Tim was glad for Randall that he could have these things, and his good-natured grumping was a way of helping Randall enjoy them. If Tim bitched in earnest, Randall would feel guilty; if he did not bitch at all, Randall would have to feel endlessly grateful. Both of them understood this, and neither of them ever said it.

"It'll be worth it," Randall said. "Sure it will. It'll be like a month of Mary Hartman."

Tim smiled. "I wonder how much they all know about each other? I mean, Annie knows about Ben and Whitney—always did—and Karen knows about Ted—"

"Does now, anyway. Did you see her at dinner Monday?"

Tim nodded. "Thought she was gonna tear his throat out, right there at the table. But does Annie know about Whitney and Ted? Does Karen know about—"

"Oh, Lord," Randall said, "that sounds exactly like—what's the one we used to watch because Robin was on it?"

"*The Young and the Restless*," Tim said.

Randall became thoughtful. "I'll tell you something, I'll bet that, after some tension at first, Whitney fits in just fine. She's like them, you know. She's really amazingly innocent, for a girl who's supposedly been around. Ben and Ted really *are* her entire scarlet past, almost. There was that actor in California—''

"He was going to marry her, too."

"—and what's his face, the choreographer?"

"*That* bitch won't even speak to her now that he's rich and famous and out of the closet."

Randall shook his head. "She does have a gift for picking impossible men, doesn't she?"

Tim said sadly, "Alex is impossible, too, I think. He's a little crazy, you know. Under control, but only just. I'm never sure he isn't going to forget himself and—I don't know, go for someone's throat. Pull a gun. Something."

"Maybe. But Alex wants nothing so much as to be respectable. As . . . *boring* as the others. As stable. And so does Whit."

Tim shook his head. "That's all fine, but what's going to happen when Whitney wants to go live in California all the time? She's going to be good in movies, you know."

Randall sighed. "Yeah, I know she is. Tell you the truth, I felt bad when I heard about her and Alex. I don't think it can come to any good, either. And Whit had begun to seem different to me. Calmer. More —detached about herself. Amused by herself, even."

"Maybe it's the shrink," Tim said.

"Maybe. Anyway, I wanted to think Alex was something different for her, but you're probably right."

Tim nodded. "I wish I weren't."

They were off the Thruway now, circling Schuyler Mountain on the county road, fighting their way through the weather. The rain had grown heavier as they traveled north, and now they were assailed by close, brilliant lightning and battered by claps and rolling waves of thunder.

It was just past one o'clock when Randall turned the car onto the three-mile private road up to the three houses.

"My God," Tim said nervously, "it looks like an alien planet out there." The heavy maples flanking the narrow blacktop formed a canopy overhead in many places, so that their headlights seemed to be penetrating an endless black tunnel.

Coming over a rise, the car headed downward on a gradual slope. The lights fell on a broad expanse of water, beaten to a white froth by the rain. They were almost in it by the time they could see it through the rain-streaked windshield. Randall braked them to a stop. His shoulders slumped. After a deep breath, he said, "well, let's see what we're in for," and put the car in motion again, very slowly, into the flood.

It was deep—more than a foot—and getting deeper, the car still headed downward, when Randall began to feel panicky. He could feel the car—this huge, heavy whale of a machine—being pushed from the side, and he realized that the water was flowing with enormous force from right to left.

Tim could feel it, too. "Darlin', we're being pushed! Stop and back out of here."

"Can't. We'd take water in the exhaust pipe and be fucked for fair." Their forward motion was only just faster than their slow, inexorable sideways slide, the rear end slewing faster than the front, sickeningly uncontrollable, when they felt the road turn up. Just at that moment, the rear end lurched another several inches—"Oo-hh!" Tim screamed—and the headlights turned into the current. The muddy water formed a wave against the front of the car and rose over the lights momentarily, creating a ghostly golden glow on the rainswept surface of the water in front of them.

"*Jesus!*" Tim cried. "We're *under water!*"

"Hang on," Randall said through clenched teeth. He could feel their forward motion becoming upward motion; if the engine didn't drown in the next few seconds, they'd be out of danger.

"My feet are wet," Tim yelled. "It's coming in!"

But they were rising now for sure, and the pressure

against the side of the car was lessening; the car lurched forward as the rear tires gained pavement again, and in another few seconds they were out of it.

Randall stopped the car and gave in to trembling. "Jesus! I thought we were going down the mountain. Under water. Damn! I was—" It was at that moment that the electrical storm discovered them—or so it seemed when the black sky turned so brilliant white in every direction that they could see no source of the light, and thunder at once cracked so loud and close it seemed to be inside their heads.

Randall closed his eyes against it and hunched down. When Tim reflexively grabbed his arm he jumped as though struck by lightning himself, but the contact quickly calmed him.

"What are we doing here?" Tim demanded shrilly.

Randall let out his breath. "Doin' the best we can, hon," he said, and put the car in gear again. Buick, you're all right, he thought. Got some submarine in you, don't you?

CHAPTER

5

At dusk, Annie walked with Dinny through the wet grass along the edge of the woods. Poor creaky old beast, she thought; too bad we didn't get this place when you were young enough to enjoy it. Though, in fact, in his doddering way he did seem to enjoy poking under bushes and around trees, eating grass. You'll just throw it up, you old idiot.

The rain had stopped, but the wind had not relented for a moment. She stuffed her hands in her raincoat pockets. As they walked along the edge of the woods, rainwater blew on them from the trees. The tireless wind created a sound that was part howl, part roar, a keening sound that was more pained than angry, but no less threatening for that.

The others will be here soon, she thought with a pang of regret. She had turned on the outside lights. Set on three widely separated poles, spotlights illuminated most of the big lawn. Though the sky was still twilight gray, the woods that surrounded the lawn were dark as midnight. It would be about sunset if they were on the west side of the mountain, but in fact they faced southeast. She turned and looked up above the houses, past the stone face she called The Mountain King, to the mountaintop. There was scarcely more light in the cloudy sky there, above where the sun would be, than there was across the valley to the east and above the mountain opposite. She moved her gaze downward, over the dense pine and maple forest, over the scattered rocky outcroppings, to the sheer cliff that ran around the mountain to her left and nearly around it to her right before it disappeared into the woods. In the middle of the cliff, above the three houses set widely separated at the rear of the lawn, five hundred feet up a steep, wooded slope, was the face of The Mountain King. It jutted out from the rocky wall with its heavy brow and its underslung jaw, its wide, razor-thin mouth opened just a bit at the very middle. Ben thought that was probably a cave. It looked, Annie thought, like the mouth of a reptile, with its central opening for a searching, forked tongue. She shuddered and looked away from the face, at the waterfalls—one flowing over one side of The Mountain King's forehead, the other far to the opposite side—Annie's right—of the face. They had not been there last fall.

Ben said that it was the water from the heavy rains of this long, wet spring, draining down the mountain. The fall to the right was narrow and fell smoothly. The fall at the face was more turbulent. It fell farther from the wall and more unevenly. Sometimes a tower of spray rose from below it; in the failing light she couldn't see clearly what caused that. The stream from that fall, Annie knew, flowed under a little wooden bridge at the back corner of the property and then alongside the lawn opposite her, through what had been a dry gully last fall. She couldn't see the stream from where she stood. It seemed loud, but its sound was part of the wind's sound. She'd look when they crossed over.

Dinny lifted his leg at a bush and was blown off balance. "That's all right, poor dummy," Annie said, "it really is a terrible wind." She left the shelter of the forest wall to cross the front of the lawn, where the mountain dropped steeply away. She stopped near the foremost point, face into the wind, hair streaming up and behind her. She looked down into the valley, over the forest onto the top of the town of Weaver's Falls, lights alight far below her, and across it to the dark mountainside opposite. To her right, beyond the horizon, was New York City, its location betrayed by a glow on the underside of the clouds. Annie was aware of the curve of the earth between her and the city—the two-and-a-half-hour trip was still fresh in her mind —and she felt like a giant, who could span a hundred miles and more with her gaze.

A hollow opened under her heart. It was a feeling like the feeling in a falling dream, a thrill of freedom and terror. She was too high, and it was all too vast, and the wind was too tireless and powerful and—huge. Annie remembered lying on the earth near this spot last fall. She had parted the grass and found a world of bugs. This earth, her earth, her grass and brushy woods, was alive. It teemed. She was a city girl, and the realization that life—alien life—proliferated in incalculable numbers and varieties all about her, under her very feet, awed her.

Every foot of it had little creatures in it; more little creatures in this twenty acres than people in New York City, maybe. America, even. And this was just twenty acres. Across the valley Annie could see hundreds of acres, thousands, and every foot of it alive. And not just bugs. They'd seen toads and a little salamander. Ben thought there must be garter snakes—whatever they were; he said they were harmless. Last fall on a rainy night they'd heard loud, warbling moans. Ben had searched them down—the foolhardiness of that had appalled her—and discovered a porcupine sitting in a tree just inside the woods. Annie had gone out to see it: a fat, astonishingly golden-colored thing. They'd seen many deer droppings—lovely, like a dozen rabbits had all pooped in one spot—and they'd seen raccoons and opossums. 'Coons and 'possums, Ben said. Raccoons, with their neat little masks, it's like seeing a movie star on the street and thinking, oh, my, he looks just like himself.

Annie had been seized then by a fierce awareness of how much she loved this place. She had never even known such places existed, really, and now she owned one. It was hers; it had been her idea to buy it and, though the others probably didn't think so, she knew it was hers just a little more than it was anyone else's. Maybe Ben's as much as hers. And now it would be her child's, too. She thought she might kill to keep it forever; it was a ferocious sort of love.

It was overwhelming, though. The wind was relentless. Its ceaseless howl in the trees was exhausting. She took a deep breath, trying again to fill the vacuum in her middle. All these creatures allow us here, Ben said, and go on about their business. Ben even liked the damn spiders that were everywhere in the house. Sometimes Annie almost understood that, but the mice—no. She shivered as she remembered Albie, their lovely cat, turned sadistic killer. His playing with his prey horrified her, that was all there was to that, and it was no use telling herself about instincts. Nature's law. Well, it is. It's nature that turns Albie into—she shivered yet again, remembering him eating the disgusting, warm, bloody little thing, head first, skull crackling like . . . oh, God, popcorn. She shook her head to clear the memory away.

Dinny, who was wet nearly all over, was no longer enjoying himself at all. The wind's sound had risen in pitch, or so it seemed. It was so *wearying*. When suddenly the wind stopped pushing on her body, Annie staggered forward a step, toward the edge of the drop. She had been pushing forward against it for so long that she was no longer aware she was doing it. It swirled and placed a giant's palm against her back, shoved her mercilessly toward the vast, empty space between her and the mountain opposite. Panic tore her breath away, almost stole her senses, as she staggered helplessly before the overwhelming force.

She dropped to her knees at the very edge, her hands on the wet earth in front of her. She sank to the ground, pressed herself to it, sobbed. The wind rushed over her; it couldn't get her, as long as she stayed down flat.

Annie raised her head and looked over the edge, down the steep slope. She could scarcely see for tears. But it *isn't* a cliff, she insisted to herself, only a steep slope. It drops a hundred feet or so to thick woods. It wouldn't kill me if I did slide down it, only bang me up. She had a sudden vision of her skin torn and bloody, a jagged end of white bone poking through it just above her ankle. She nearly fainted as the fantasy held her: lying in sickening pain at the bottom of the slope, unbeknownst to Ben. . . . And her baby! What would happen to her baby?

She turned on her hands and knees and moved on all fours a few feet onto the flat lawn. Dinny walked beside her, sniffing curiously at her, whining and licking her cheek as she crawled. She giggled hysterically, hugged the old dog's head and finally got shakily to her feet.

Rain began again, pounding her with big, heavy drops. Annie ran toward the middle house—her house. Vicious lightning flashed brilliant over the mountaintop. Dinny bounced stiffly along beside and behind her. She made herself slow to a walk, so as not to tax his old body. She smelled wood smoke and terror seized her yet again—*what's burning*? Oh, God, it's just the fireplace.

Thunder rolled down, huge and heavy, as she crossed the porch. She could feel it in her feet as the floorboards reverberated with it. She could feel it in her bones. *Get out of me, let me alone.* Dinny howled; he didn't like the feel of that either. "Oh"—she bent down and picked him up, wet and wiggling—"oh, it's okay, old man, it won't hurt us, honest it won't, c'mon in, it can't get us in there." She forced herself to stop trembling, not to make the old dog panicky, and pulled open the big door.

Annie went straight to the bathroom, first to towel Dinny dry, and then to warm herself. She luxuriated in a hot shower, the chill leaving her—driven out as much by the feeling of being enclosed as by the warmth of the water. She knew she would use up the hot water; in the dozen times she'd showered here, it had never once lasted as long as she wanted it, and this time she wanted the warmth to go on forever. She looked at her warm wet belly. Had it grown a little? It pleased her to think so. Certainly her breasts had begun to change.

Suddenly it occurred to Annie that perhaps a shower was a dangerous place to be in an electrical storm. Lightning everywhere. Water conducts—attracts?—electricity. Quickly she turned off the water and stepped out, supposing that she was being silly, but too deeply terrified to care. She toweled hastily and ran from the bathroom, fleeing water and pipes, those magnets for the killer lightning.

She went out to the living room, where Ben was stretched out on a blanket on a rug in front of the fire, his head and shoulders propped up on pillows from the couch. He looked up over his shoulder and said, "Ted and Karen arrived. Karen buzzed on the intercom. They're staying in."

Annie walked up behind him and said, "Well, I didn't use up the hot—" but her voice was thin and strained and her teeth wanted to chatter.

Ben quickly raised his head and turned to look at her. "What—?" She burst into tears and dropped to her knees to throw her arms around him and weep hysterically. He held her, rubbed her shoulders, whispered, "What? What?"

"Oh, Ben!" she said, and sobbed, "I'm *scared*. I'm so scared. I don't—"

"Okay, okay." He held her tighter and nodded, his cheek rubbing against the damp, fragrant towel around her head. "It's okay, we're safe in here, we're really fine. The house is stone, it's been here two hundred years, it's seen lots of storms."

"I'm such a baby, I'm really ashamed."

"No, no, it's a terrible storm, it really is, and we're way the hell up here, I bet even people who live up here are scared."

"It's so—big, Ben. The wind. It's huge. It could just do what it wanted with you."

The windows rattled, as if to confirm her words, and rattled still more alarmingly with a clap of thunder that seemed to have physical shape and substance.

"It doesn't get tired, does it?" Ben said.

"You feel that, too?"

"Oh, yeah. I want it to get tired, to let up for a minute."

"You're scared, too!" Annie was shocked.

"Well, I don't seem to be as scared as you are. I can feel the house better than you can, I guess. It's really some house, you know."

"It's the lightning, too, though," Annie said, "and the water roaring down the mountain—it wasn't even there last fall, like it was in hiding, waiting to get us up here unsuspecting."

"It's staying where it belongs, though, in the gully. And we're in here, and the wind's out there—it's like a science fiction story, like we're in a time machine, or whatever; we're here, but enclosed and separate from it."

They stretched out on the blanket and lay holding each other. After a little time headlights swept the ceiling—that would be Alex and Whitney. The fire danced and jumped, teased by the winds that whipped at the chimney top only fifteen feet above. This sprawling one-story building, the oldest of the three, was low, with a low ceiling. Annie's grip on Ben had eased; each roll of thunder caused her to tense momentarily, but these spasms subsided after a time, too. They both sighed, nearly in unison.

Annie said, "You're as silly as I am. Time machine."

"Yeah, I guess. I am a little tense, I mean I have been all day, about being isolated up here. But it's fun, too. Exhilarating, to be in touch with the world."

"It *is* cozy in here." She turned to lie on her back, her head propped on a pillow from the couch. "My feet are getting hot. Let's turn sideways to the fire."

As they got up, she asked, "Is the door locked?"

"I don't know. I'll see."

Annie took a step toward the front of the house. "I'll—" She stopped.

Ben smiled. "I'll do it." He crossed the room toward the big oaken door. Just as he reached it, a shattering crash sounded stunningly loud all around them and light appeared momentarily in the windows.

Annie's body went rigid as she screamed. Ben turned to come back to her. A second crash tore through the room, different in character—not nearly so loud but of longer duration, with crackling, tearing sounds preceding a heavy thump which they could feel in the floor. He froze in midstep and stared at Annie. He turned and shot the bolt home on the door, turned again and walked to her.

In a fluty voice she said, "Ben, oh God, Ben, what was that?"

He held her. "Lightning struck in the trees just above us. It's okay, take it easy." But his voice was suspiciously high-pitched.

"Ben, you're shaking yourself!"

"Well, but there's a good reason for that. It scared the shit out of me." His laugh was more like a cough. "I think a tree came down."

They held each other in the middle of the room. Annie looked over Ben's shoulder at a window. It glared back at her with a reflection of the room's one lighted lamp in one corner, the nervously jumping fire in another, and impenetrable blackness outside.

"Look," Ben said, "there's trees around to attract the lightning, and they're far enough from the house not to fall on us. And the house is low, and it has lightning rods, anyway. We're okay."

Annie took a deep breath and let it out. She started to speak, but felt the need to breathe deeply again. Her arms dropped to her sides. "Look, I'll settle down here, in a minute. Nothing is going to frighten me as much as that, anyway. I'll be okay."

She put her arms around Ben again, but now she seemed to be reassuring him about herself instead of clinging to him for assurance. "Really, I'll be okay."

They stepped back from one another, hands clasped. After a moment, they dropped hands and walked back toward the fire. Annie stopped and said, "Why not get some cheese and crackers and stuff while I get rid of this towel." She went to the bathroom, removed the turban from her head and brushed out her hair.

"Red wine?" Ben called from the kitchen.

"How about brandy?"

Ben came into the living room carrying a tray. "Yeah, couldn't hurt."

Blindingly bright light suddenly flooded the room, a deafening crack assaulted their ears, and the floor jumped against their feet. Annie's arms went out stiff at an angle to the floor, her fists clenched. Her mouth opened, but no sound came out, only a thin breath of air. Ben's shoulders hunched and his eyes popped wide. They stood frozen, not breathing, for seconds after the light disappeared, until the last rumbling echoes of the crack of thunder had subsided. The wind's howl and the steady roar of the water suddenly seemed almost quiet; that sound was a old friend they much preferred to the raging violence of the sky's electricity.

Annie began to cry softly, Ben to laugh. "Look," he said, "listen here, it's all right, that was lightning out front there." He put the tray on a bookcase and crossed to her as he spoke. "It didn't hit us, and it won't, and it's all right."

Annie's crying stopped and she began to laugh

silently. She grabbed Ben's elbows and put her forehead against his. "It isn't going to hurt us," she said between hiccuping laughs, "but it's going to make me piss my pants before it's through."

PART

II

The mountain king did not become wholly unconscious again through the long, stormy night. He remained in a twilight state, uneasily aware of the terrible threat presented by the violence of the elements. Streams—torrents to the king and his kind—had formed above and beside their cave, and sent the feel of their movement inside through the earth. Lightning and thunder raged outside, and the vibrations from that were painfully intense.

And the ominous new signal was increasingly insistent—that strange, profoundly unsettling indication that the earth was no longer solid. Through the king's long life the rock above and beneath and around him had been impervious, immutable—it was the one utterly neutral factor in his awareness. When he felt motion in it, it was the movement of a stream rushing overhead or alongside the cave.

But now he was getting intermittent, barely perceptible vibrations from the mountain itself, unlike anything he had ever felt. An impulse to leave this place became insistent. His reflexes were dulled by the coolness of the night, and his body was unwilling to crawl out into the storm in any event. Yet something was radically amiss.

He remained in his place, his senses increasingly alert as the temperature rose a degree or two in anticipation of the dawn, his body still almost paralyzed. His body took on a highly charged state of tension, a state which, if it had been contained in a complex brain, would have been called rage.

After hours of storm, after the violent electrical manifestations had ended and the rain had subsided to a steady drizzle, a terrible thing occurred. The earth shifted with a profoundly unnatural lurch. Near a corner of the mouth of the cave the floor fell away. The opening was suddenly wider; more of the sky—a black different, less intense, than the black inside—could be seen. And water now splashed and flowed near the mouth of the cave.

The king and all his kind became terribly agitated; some of them struck at others and even themselves, then settled back into restless turning and coiling. Some of them had disappeared with the falling earth and stone—the snakes nearest the edge of the cave's floor had fallen away from the cliff, onto the forested slope below. The number of snakes seized by the wandering streams of water than newly flowed near the mouth of the cave was growing every minute.

For the first time in many generations of rattlesnakes, there were snakes from this den—perhaps a dozen, perhaps more—below the cave.

CHAPTER

6 .

Whitney woke early, having confounded her body's clock by spending less than a week in California before returning to the east. She had slept uneasily, wakened briefly when Randall and Tim arrived to occupy their half of the house, and again later by a distant rumbling in the earth and a faint, but frightening, vibration in the house.

She woke to uneasiness, too. She was beginning to have second thoughts about having agreed to come here with Alex. Have I just set up a disaster for myself? These men—these women, more to the point—my God, what can they think of me? Annie knew. Now Alex says he thinks—what's her name? Karen—Karen knows, too. Whitney Louise, you're a fool. You want to be pals with straight people. Stability, warmth, security. Okay. Fine idea. But these people?

Oh, damn it, I'm not a monster, I'm a *nice person*. I never meant to hurt anybody. They'll see that, if they get to know me. And I'm no danger to them now, that should be obvious. Well, if they don't see it, the hell with 'em.

Fine words. But in fact she was terrified. She thought of Cary Grant in *Gunga Din*, surrounded by hundreds of ravening, rolling-eyed savages armed with clubs, spears, knives, arrows: "Ye're *run*dah rah-*rest* in the *naeme* of the quaene!"

Good. Luck.

She left Alex snoring softly, his face uncharacteristically relaxed and boyish, and pulled on jeans and a sweater against the morning's chill. She went out the first door she came to, and found herself at the end of the driveway that ran behind all three houses. She stood between Randall and Tim's dewy, window-befogged station wagon—oddly mud-smeared halfway up the side—and Alex's forest-green Mercedes. Away to her left, behind the other two houses, stood two more of these big, cold, sleeping beasts: the Axelrods' black convertible and, thirty yards farther on, the Vincenzos' Volkswagen bus. It was nearly nine o'clock, by her watch. The day was beautiful—sunny and breezy.

Whitney circled the house to the front lawn, looking at all three houses and seeing no sign of life. The lawn was broad and dazzling green in the morning sun. She returned to the back of the house, having decided to climb the steep wooded slope that began just across the driveway. It looked dark and mysterious in the woods, and a vigorous climb would feel good.

She walked along the driveway toward the little wooden bridge where the stream plunged down the mountain, supposing the way would be clearest near the stream. For a few feet up the slope it was clear, but then the underbrush grew right up to the bank of the gully and the going became more difficult. As long as she was alongside the stream, she was in sunlight, which was warm on her back. When she had to change direction, into the woods, the temperature dropped noticeably, and very pleasantly.

Clinging to small trees and bushes to help her climb,

Whitney made her way upward, steadily though not easily, her sneakers slipping on the wet leaves that covered the uneven ground. Soon her jeans were wet nearly to the waist from the thick, rain-wet underbrush. When she emerged from the woods at last at the base of a rocky cliff, she was not sorry to rest. The cliff loomed far above her.

The sound of the rushing water had been steadily growing louder. After standing a moment to catch her breath, she made her way around a bulge in the cliff, moving back toward the stream, and saw the real source of the watery roar. Just beyond a heap of earth and rocks was a magnificent waterfall, brilliant in sunlight, falling from below the top of the cliff, wreathed in a rainbow that shifted, disappeared and reappeared as Whitney watched. Beside the fall was a huge tree, wet from the falling water. Behind the waterfall, which leaped away from the cliff a few feet, the path she stood on continued over a rocky ledge. She could walk to the other side, where the face of the cliff was bathed by the sun. It was a glorious, magical gateway.

She made her way carefully across and sat on the path hugging her knees, warming in the sun. She looked down the slope—ohh-*oh*! Oh, my God, I'm afraid of height! Whitney closed her eyes, took a deep breath, and leaned back against the cliff. The view was still vivid in her mind: the houses below; the vast, deep valley with its little town; the great forested mountain opposite. What a place! Though it scared her—the impulse to fly off into space was powerful—it was very beautiful; and it was delicious to be so alone, at once warmed by the sun and cooled by the breeze. The roar of the fall completed her sense of isolation, enclosing and protecting her with a wall of sound. She just wouldn't look down again.

She stretched out on the path, luxuriating like a cat. She was becoming wet—both from sweat, since the sun was, after all, too warm for the sweater she wore, and from occasional spray blown from the waterfall.

• • •

Ben woke with a mild headache. He didn't much want to get up, but he knew he was awake to stay, at least for a few hours. Never fails, he thought; go to sleep drunk, and when the booze burns out the eyelids snap open.

After the electrical storm had subsided he and Annie had added wood to the fire and sat near it eating cheese and crackers and drinking rather more brandy than was their habit at such late-night snacks. Randall and Tim joined them for a few minutes when they arrived, just as the storm was ending, and told them about the flood in a half-hysterical chatter of jokes, exaggerations and genuinely ominous descriptions. The two men had had some brandy and gone on to their own house to sleep.

Ben and Annie slept deeply, drugged by the brandy and by nervous exhaustion, and were not disturbed by the rumbling in the earth after they had fallen asleep.

Now, Annie slept on. Ben looked at the bedside clock: 7:30. He was surprised it wasn't later, since they hadn't gone to sleep until past two. He looked at his wristwatch for confirmation. Nine o'clock. So—the electricity had been off for an hour and a half. Had to be after we went to bed; the break in the lines must have been over on the other mountain, when the storm got there.

He arose and went to the kitchen to get coffee. But the timer, having been stalled for an hour and a half, had not turned on the coffee maker. He inserted the plug directly into the wall outlet and the pot began to wheeze almost instantly. He went to the bathroom and then back to the bedroom, where he put on dungarees and a sweatshirt. When he'd come back to the kitchen, the coffee was ready. He took a cup with him to the front lawn.

Dinny went out the door with him, and so did the two cats. The cats disappeared at once around the house to the rear, but Dinny trotted over to the edge of the woods in front.

It was breezy, but steamy-warm in the sun. Fat,

brilliant white clouds sailed overhead, moving from behind the mountaintop above him across the valley in front of him, trailing their huge shadows.

The water in the stream to Ben's right—that stream that had been no stream at all last fall—was torrential. It was, as he had assured Annie last night with less than perfect confidence, confined to the gully, and not high enough to menace the little wooden bridge that connected them to the world. Loud, and rushing powerfully, but contained.

Ben felt foolish at not having wondered, last fall, why the gully was so deep, if there was no water to flow through it. The mountain above them was entirely wild; nothing had ever been done to it that would change the flow of water down it. Of course there would be a heavy flow through this gully—else it wouldn't be there. He had, nevertheless, thoughtlessly dismissed it when they looked at the land. It hadn't occurred to him that a stream might run only part of the year.

The feeling that he was in over his head began to come alive in him again. What else was I mindless about? He walked to the front edge of the lawn. Ben had never been at the very edge on a windy day before, and he was startled by the precariousness of it. We're gonna have to put a fence up here, he thought—but right away. This sonofagun's dangerous. Didn't the rich folks ever bring kids here? He knelt for safety's sake and peered over the edge.

Several hundred yards down, the stream, just before it turned to the right into the forest, seemed to widen dramatically to the left. He stared at the place, which was obscured by thick brush. He looked farther to the left, straight down the slope in front of him. He thought he saw something shiny through the trees below. Shading his eyes and squinting he saw it again. Another stream. From the other waterfall over the cliff, he decided; it flows around and joins this one—like a noose around us, Ben thought idly. Where does it go then? Parallel to the road, seems like. Must have something to do with the flood. He was satisfied that the heavier stream, the one that ran alongside the lawn, was well contained down as far as he could see, and posed no threat to them. They weren't going to have to pay for being dumb about the gully last fall.

Ben turned to survey his domain. He saw, on the slope behind the houses, a suspiciously flat-topped pine tree. He thought that might have been a very tall tree before last night, but he didn't trust his memory. The place was not yet intimately familiar to him.

His gaze moved upward to the face and stopped abruptly. The face was different—its expression had changed. The right side of its jaw—Ben's left as he now faced it, the side where the heavy waterfall was—had fallen away. The mouth was now pulled down in a ghastly leer. Jesus, he thought, how many thousands of years has it taken for that to happen? Rain, freezing, the tree roots from above there, and finally. . . .

He decided to climb the slope and have a close look at the cliff. He returned to the house to put down his coffee cup.

The two cats had left the house when Ben did. As Ben and the dog stood on the front lawn, Albie and the kitten explored and hunted in the wooded slope behind the house. On the dark, damp floor of the woods, the kitten bounced and slid, hopped and scrambled uphill, under bushes, over roots. Albie, the big gray tiger, moved gingerly behind, pausing from time to time to shake damp earth off his paws, watching the kitten at times, but also searching the ground for a small live creature to kill and eat. Albie's walk was his stalking stride, belly low to the ground; he placed each forepaw carefully, to avoid noisy twigs and dry leaves, and then lifted each hind paw high and placed it down precisely in a spot vacated by a forepaw as he progressed.

The kitten stopped, having received some mysterious inner signal that it was time to wash. He sat on a thick root, raised a hind leg awkwardly over his head, and began to lick inside his thigh. The root moved, tumbling the kitten off onto the wet earth. He scrambled to his feet and shook his head before cocking it attentively to look up the length of the root. The root moved quickly, liquidly, into an S shape. The kitten raised one forepaw, as though to bat at it. The larger cat watched in fascination, the hairs along his back rising, his tail growing enormous.

The root that was alive had eyes at the end that had risen off the ground, and a tongue that appeared and disappeared, though no mouth ever opened. With a motion too fast for the cat to see clearly, except for a fleeting impression of an open, pink mouth and fangs larger than his own, this root struck the kitten. In reflexive response to the terrible blow, the kitten leaped straight in the air with a little squeaking cry. It fell to earth on its side and was still.

Albie, some four feet away, had by now taken a menacing defensive posture, back arched, legs stiff, his mouth wide open, displaying teeth, hissing. The legless creature ignored him and moved to the stricken kitten, nudging it with its dark, scaly nose. The kitten's whole body twitched, and the awful thing withdrew and became still again. In a few seconds, a second nudge produced no reaction. And then this creature like no other the cat had seen or dreamed of, this legless, dreadful thing opened its pink mouth in a huge yawn, closed it, moved to the body of the kitten, opened up again and began the laborious, lurching process of swallowing the kitten whole. The kitten disappeared in stages, head first. Finally, when only the furry tip of its tail could be seen between the leathery lips, the thing made a convulsive movement and all trace of the kitten was gone.

The cat backed away slowly, showing his fangs to this creature whose larger fangs he had seen. The alien beast, now grotesquely swollen just behind its head, stared dully at the cat and made a whirring, rattling sound that drove Albie into panicky, headlong flight.

The timber rattlesnake was more than five feet long,

dark in color, gray-green, with broken bands of bright yellow across its back. The snake had no memory of the catastrophe that had befallen it in the black of night, nor even that it had been unconscious until just a few minutes ago, when the food creature stepped on its body. The rattlesnake only knew that now it was sated, and comfortable. It crawled slowly to a sheltered spot under a newly fallen tree trunk, green and thick with pine needles, burned black at one end. It would remain there for some days digesting its first food of the new summer season.

Ben moved quietly in the house, so as not to disturb Annie's sleep. The little old dog followed him everywhere, but kept blessedly quiet except for the clatter of his toenails on the hardwood floors. As they walked out the back door together, Ben saw Albie the cat speed across the end of the driveway to his right, out of the woods on the slope and into the trees that bordered the lawn there. Ben supposed he was chasing the kitten. Certainly seemed to be chasing something.

It was cool and dark in the woods as he ascended the slope, mottled with bright sunlight in irregular patches. The underbrush was thick and wet, and footing was uncertain. The earth was covered with wet leaves and pine needles, strewn with branches fallen from the trees, and lumpy with exposed roots.

Entering a small, relatively flat clearing, Ben found the lightning-blasted tree. Firmly rooted in this flat place, it had been the tallest of the pines on the slope until it was sheared off halfway up. Evidence of the violence of the break was vivid: The standing trunk was both broken and torn at the top, showing its white interior in an angled cross section, splintered around the edges, burned black over the top half. Below it, the fallen half of the tree lay not quite flat to the ground, partly supported by its own branches. Its path through the air was blazed by branches hanging from surrounding trees by shreds of bark. It was burned black at the stump end.

Ben made his way between branches to the fallen trunk and sat on it to catch his breath. It settled minutely under his weight. He looked up and down the length of it, wondering at the power that had reached down from the sky, snapped the tree in two and dropped half of it here like a burnt match.

Ben shifted his weight and swung his legs to the up-slope side of the trunk. Planting his feet, he rose, bracing the back of his legs against the trunk. It shifted, noticeably this time, and he had to fight for balance, thrusting his arms in front of himself and bending forward, to keep from tumbling backward onto the ground. Steadying himself, he reentered the thick woods, resuming the climb toward the face.

Dinny, who had gone off on his own, now emerged into the clearing, sniffing the ground and shaking wet leaves off his nose. He approached the spot where Ben had been sitting, but stopped, cocked his head at a peculiar creature moving on the earth, and growled low in his throat. The rattlesnake, swollen now at its middle, moved sluggishly under the trunk and to the other side rather than confront this growling creature. Dinny poked his nose under the log and snuffled. When he got no response he yapped twice, sidled up to the trunk, and lifted his leg.

Satisfied, he trotted around the blasted end and up the slope.

Ben had come to the foot of the cliff, where the sound of the falling water drowned out all other sounds. The cliff rose above his head fifty feet or more. Looking straight up past the irregular wall of the cliff at the sky produced vertigo. The face lost all definition from this angle, below and just to its side. The rock was beautiful, seen close; its rich brown color was really many colors, veined, textured, variegated. Ben made his way along the wall, around the bulge below the face, over the heap of fallen rock, and looked up at the fall and the huge maple tree it fell next to.

The tree grew from a flat area several feet below the level Ben stood on. It was only barely in leaf. Some of its branches touched the cliff below the face; branches near the fall were dripping wet and bent down, some of the smaller ones broken off.

As Ben made his way along the spray-damp ledge behind the fall, he watched his footing carefully. Past the fall, he looked up the path, and lost his breath. Stretched out there, feet toward him, was Whitney Williams, naked in the sun, honey-tan except where she was dizzyingly white and silky black. His legs went rubbery. At less than ten feet from her, he could see beads of moisture on her satiny skin; thought he could see gooseflesh on the neat, small globes of her breasts; knew for certain that he could see that her dark nipples stood taut. As he stood, stunned, not breathing, a fine, barely visible spray of mist blew onto Whitney, creating a shiver that ran her length.

He almost spoke, anticipating her opening her eyes and looking up. At the same time, the trembling in her flesh was paralyzingly beautiful to see—for the brief second that it ran through her he could no more look away than walk away, nor walk away than fly. Oh, my God, he thought, I don't need this.

And so he stood, finally taking a breath, and saw himself and all but felt himself moving over her, lying on that soft body on that hard rock, entering her there, her eyes opening in surprise and delight, there in the sun and the spray, at the edge of a precipice on the lip of empty space. . . . He moved quietly away from her, back under the fall, out of sight.

Ben stood, hands on hips, shaking his head, his mind spinning in an effort to fling out the vision of making love to her again—oh, he knew her body as well as his own—better. He knew inside her, warm and close and sweet to smell—he knew how she felt and how she moved and how she sounded when she—he took a deep breath and sat on the ground, back against the cliff.

Gradually, as he sat, reality struggled to regain the upper hand. He was here with Annie—who'd be awake any minute—and these other people, and Alex. He'd have to just walk calmly back down the mountain as though he'd never seen her. He loved Annie. Annie, for Christ's sake, is going to have my baby! Annie will never know, or suspect.

It occurred to him suddenly that he was going to have to say that he'd been up here. Where else have I been, getting wet? He wanted to take off his chilly, wet dungarees, dry his skin out there in the sun, warm himself. . . . He took another deep breath.

So, I'll have been up here; what if, sometime later, Whitney mentions *she* was up here? The suspicion will *never* go away. Damn. I've got to go get her. I'll just stumble on her, embarrassed, and back off. Right. She'd never tell anybody she was naked, it'll just be that I came up and we met. It'll be our secret. Oh-hh . . . well—in a minute, here, when I've composed myself, I'll go get her.

Later, when he thought back, he would know that at this moment he was deciding to go and make love to Whitney Williams in her preternaturally beautiful mountainside setting. But that wasn't in his awareness now; he was simply going to compose himself, think how to present himself embarrassed, turn his head and back away quickly. That *will* take some doing, he thought. Just turn my head and back away quickly. I will, though. I certainly will.

Whitney had never been so pleased with herself, so comfortable in her body, so relaxed and exhilarated at once. The phobic terror had receded; each returning wave of it was less intense until it stopped coming back. The warmth of the sun, the sense of solitude in a vast space, the overwhelming sound of the fall—it was all nearly too much. The occasional cooling spray startled her flesh and stimulated her. She felt as warm and relaxed as a baby in a womb at one moment, as charged as a lightning bolt the next. It was sensual, and soon it was sexual.

She touched herself momentarily, found herself warm and damp—but she knew that—and took her hand away. She'd keep the feeling for as long as she could bear it, first. She became absolutely still, her hands at the top of her thighs, her legs spread just a little.

After a time, when she could bear this silent excitement no longer, she blinked her eyes open and looked straight up into the vast, dizzying sky. Slowly she moved her hand—and something touched her right there at her center. For a split second, the pleasure held back her terror, then she strangled a scream, jerked her knees up, raised her head and stared down her length at a small gray dog. The dog backed off a step and cocked his head at her. She was about to lie back, to invite the dog's busy tongue to her—what could be more lovely, more natural in this forest stillness? But then it seized her that a person would be with the dog.

Annie Axelrod! It was Annie's dog. She jumped to her feet, picked up her clothes from where she'd been lying on them and, teetering heedlessly on one leg at a time on the narrow ledge, dressed in one long, complicated motion. Oh, God, that's all it'd take for these people to imagine I am some kind of terrible temptress. "Hello?" she called.

Ben was just rising from his spot at the base of the cliff when he thought he heard the sound of a woman's voice over the sound of the water. Oh, shit, who? And then it came again, louder—"Anybody up here?"—and he recognized it. He began to move toward the fall. From that direction, along the base of the cliff, came Dinny, wet from the spray, trotting along looking pleased with himself. He jumped up against Ben's legs. Oh, you sonofa*bitch,* you! Where did you *come from*? He could have killed the old dog. In a moment, he remembered his dilemma and realized that this was a perfect solution to it. But that didn't make him stop hating it.

And following Dinny, fully dressed in damp, wrinkled sweater and jeans, was Whitney Williams, wide-eyed. She quickly smiled when she saw him and said, "Pretty here, isn't it?" her voice moving through two registers.

"Uh—when did you come up?"

"Just a few minutes ago. Nobody else seemed to be awake." Her voice had settled on a neutral, rather flat tone.

"Yeah, it is pretty here. Did you notice the face? No, you'd never seen it before, had you? Look, I want to see the other fall; want to come along?"

And so Ben described the damage to the face, chattering brightly as they made their way along the foot of the cliff. For a little while he felt relieved, delivered from temptation. But a fateful feeling soon came over him. The vision of Whitney glowing golden in the sun would not leave his mind. He found he didn't really want it to. . . .

Dinny had wandered back to the big fall, lured by the vague sense-memory of sweetly pungent human flesh. As he was trotting under the fall, something slapped hard on the edge of the path next to him and fell away before he could turn and look at the spot. He stopped and looked up at the curtain of falling water. Soon he saw, falling behind the water, one of the unsettling ropy creatures he'd seen under the log in the woods. It twisted and coiled as it fell. He barked at it, then fell to whining as he watched for more. Dinny sat crosswise on the path, slid his forepaws out in front of him and rested his chin on them to continue his watch. Two more fell before his eyes, and he jumped to his feet and barked again. Soon, though, when his barking had no effect, and when no more of the creatures appeared, he gave up his vigil and made his way downward through the brush.

Ben and Whitney found the footing sure across the base of the cliff, and soon they had crossed the couple of hundred feet to the other waterfall. It was smaller and quieter, falling steadily, very close to the wall, but dropping several feet farther. The earth dropped away precipitously there and the water fell into a stream bed well below the level they stood on, to run into dense woods and out of sight. No way to climb down there. They turned away and began their careful descent to the houses, grasping brush and tree trunks to let themselves down easily.

Under a thick branch fallen years past from a maple tree, a rattlesnake lay stretched out on the wet earth, half its four-foot length in a puddle of water. It felt vibrations in the earth that it interpreted as the approach of two huge, two-legged creatures, the footfalls ponderous and threatening. The snake pulled itself into a coil, its tail up out of the puddle, and commenced its warning rattle. The characteristic tingling sensation did not make itself felt in the rear part of the snake's body, however, and the giant creatures continued to draw near. The rattlesnake extended its sticky black tongue, then tested the twin tips in the roof of its mouth for scent. The odor was distinctive, but completely new to the snake.

The thunderous footfalls were now barely the snake's own length in distance. The creatures could not be seen because of the fallen branch. The snake had never encountered any animal so huge, except the sharp-hoofed four-legged ones, and they always fled when it made the vibrations in its tail; the peculiar absence of the whirring this time, and the failure of the creatures to be driven away, made the snake still more uneasy. It raised its head from its coil, preparatory to striking, only to find its movement hampered by the tangled branches of a thick bush. Its tail continued its vibration, still without producing the expected sensation.

Ben stopped, leaning against the trunk of a big maple. The going was dense and difficult; they had not picked the easiest way down. "Look over my shoulder," he said. "Can you see what the ground is like on the other side of that fallen branch?"

Whitney braced herself against him, her hand warm and strong on his back, and peered over. Nothing but thick brush; she couldn't see the ground at all. "Nope. Can't tell."

"All right," Ben said huskily, and cleared his throat. "Step back up to that flat place there and move to the right. There's some clear space there."

"Lord, this is hard work," Whitney said. "My legs are tired."

Ben grunted in response. Your legs, he thought, are long and silken, golden sweet. . . . "City folks," he said. "Middle aged."

As they emerged from the woods onto the driveway Whitney, after a pause for breath, said, "*Who's* middle aged?"

Ben sighed and looked thoughtful. "I am," he said. His smile appeared and as quickly disappeared as he turned and walked toward his house.

Whitney watched him go, knowing suddenly that he'd seen her. You dirty peeping bastard, she thought, her mind flooded with unaccountable shame and rage.

Oh, hell, Whitney Louise, she said to herself, if he'd so much as said hello you'd have gone off like a string of firecrackers. That's why you're so furious. She turned toward Randall and Tim's house, toward Alex, who enjoyed being wakened by her hands, her tongue. . . .

But Alex was not in bed. She found him in the kitchen with Randall and Tim. "Good morning," he said brightly. "Randall's making championship omelets."

With an effort, she unclenched her fists, stretched her arms out wide and took a deep breath. She put on a smile for breakfast.

CHAPTER

7

By midday the mists that had lain over the valley floor and in oddly-placed pockets of the mountainside had burned off. The fat clouds overhead were fewer and the sun was brilliant. The tireless wind had abated somewhat, but continued to propel the clouds in a race across the sky, and its sound in the trees had by now gone on so long that it was scarcely heard. If it had ceased suddenly, the silence would have been startling.

Whitney had stretched out on a lawn lounger. Except when one of the great cloud shadows passed over her, the sun was warm and calming. Still May, and she had a tan—the first in New York, it must be. Might as well cultivate it. I'll be three-toned, she thought; this bathing suit isn't as skimpy as the one I wore in California. I'll have to retire my one real dropdead party dress for a while.

Karen and Annie had driven to town to shop for food for the weekend. They had invited Whitney to join them, calling on the intercom system, but with rather forced enthusiasm, it seemed to Whitney. She was careful to be friendly as she begged off, pleading headache and fatigue, with jet-lag the cause. Her excuse was not utterly untrue.

She was grateful for the calming effect of the sun's warmth. She was not accustomed to carrying around the sort of sexual charge that had kept her on edge all this day. She liked sex, expected to enjoy it and usually did; but she expected sex to know its place. The idea of its being in charge, rather than her, was disquieting. And thrilling. And all the more disquieting for being—oh, for pity's sake, she said to herself, stop making yourself crazy. Tell it to Dr. Graebner. He'll enjoy hearing about it. Charley Cheerful, he enjoys hearing anything. And a good thing, too, for a shrink.

It was Dr. Graebner, more than Alex, who had convinced her to come here for this weekend. At least, she thought it was. She had been seeing him off and on for nearly two years—beginning "just after Ted" was the way she placed it—and she was beginning to learn, in replaying conversations with him in her mind, that he didn't always say what she thought he'd said. Maybe I talked myself into it. No. I was scared out of my mind. Oh, hell.

It *is* calming, the sun. I *am* calmer. Calm*er*—not calm. She opened her eyes and looked across the lawn to where Ben, Ted and Alex were playing catch. She had a dancer's eye for movement, both analytical and sympathetic; she could feel the movements of others in her own body.

Once she had tried to become interested in baseball. She watched it on television after seeing photographs of baseball action in a magazine. Whose magazine? Ben's? Whoever. The pictures were interesting and beautiful: a pitcher, stretched out in a long forward step, his arm coming around, the pitching hand trailing the elbow at an alarming angle—the power he was generating in the throw was almost palpable; a first baseman stretched to his limit in a split, maintaining contact with the base with his trailing foot, the glove hand rising at an oblique angle from the line of his body, the bare hand extended toward the ground for balance—she could feel the strain, and the exhilaration of making the catch successfully, which she read in the rising angle of the glove hand.

But baseball was boring to watch. The balletic moments were far too rare, and too quickly done. The pitcher's motions were too repetitive.

It *was* Ben's magazine, damn it. He watched baseball on television, intently. She had found that endearing, at first; later, infuriating. Damn Ben. *Damn* him, I thought he loved me. Her eyes stung suddenly. She looked away from the men, took a deep breath, lay back to welcome the sun's warmth.

The men's movements persisted in her mind's eye. She would have known them anywhere. Alex's play was purposeful, almost grimly proficient; he made it his business to make the catch, to make the throw sharp and accurate. He seemed to be in a contest with the ball, as much as in a game with the men. Ben was more playful. He did a little juggling act with the ball on the back of his hand sometimes, made fancy catches, and sometimes threw with a peculiar jerky motion that made the others laugh. But when they threw high flies he went very certainly to where the ball would come down, with never a change in direction; and the ball never went past him on the ground, either. Ted was careless, effortless, and by far the most powerful of the three. Like a young racehorse. She had the least sympathetic feeling in her own body for his movements; they were so fluid as to be beyond analyzing. His body seemed exuberant, but his mind seemed scarcely present. Like a racehorse, indeed.

She was startled by a sudden insight. They play ball, she thought, the same way they make love. Ted big, beautiful, powerful, exciting—and just slightly removed; Ben intense and playful, involving and satisfying; Alex never far from anger, fiercely maintaining control, making dead certain everything went right. Not yesterday, she thought, he was angry yesterday, but he wasn't in control, he didn't know what was going to happen.

She took still another deep breath. Calm, she thought. The sun makes me sleepy. The sun doesn't make me horny.

The sounds of the men playing—shouts, the slap of the ball into a glove—were joined now by the yapping of Ben and Annie's small dog. Whitney looked around and saw him chasing the Vincenzos' big dog across the lawn. They were beautiful to see together: Baggins a big, rangy, graceful creature, the size of a boxer or a collie, charcoal in color; Dinny a perfect miniature of Baggins, made the same way, square face with flowing whiskers, a smooth body and silky legs, but lighter in color, pewter, and his legs not even half the length, so the chase was scarcely a chase at all. The big young dog waited while the old one stopped for breath, then bolted off again when the little one ran up, yapping mightily.

Baggins managed to stay only just ahead of his small pursuer, keeping him interested in the game. Sometimes he'd start with dazzling suddenness in a new direction. Then Dinny would tumble over in making the same turn, and resume the chase having lost several yards in distance.

When the young dog finally tired of the sport, he trotted to a shady spot under a tree, lay on his back with his legs in the air, flopped and rolled. Old Dinny snarled viciously and leaped on him, bit his whiskers and tugged at them violently, growling in his throat, apparently in a murderous rage. Whitney was alarmed, but the big dog's calm forbearance made her realize that this was all playful and harmless. Soon they both subsided into restful silence, licking each other.

Whitney, all alone on her lounger, felt herself blush as she remembered the small dog's tongue. She was embarrassed that she had enjoyed that so, and knew that she would welcome it again. She wondered at herself, that she was merely embarrassed, not shamed and sickened. Oh, but it was nice . . . natural. Like a natural creature, no emotions, only sensations. No anger, no shame, no fear, no disappointment. . . . She moved her legs just slightly apart. The small dog yapped, and she saw that they were off again. She closed her eyes. Calm, she thought. Sleepy.

Baggins rarely got to run in the city—once a week, in Riverside Park, but the park was crowded with people and other dogs. He stretched, made a soaring leap over nothing—the shadow of a bush—came down running even faster. Dinny had stopped, hopelessly far behind, and sat watching, panting, resigned.

Near the end of his running room, Baggins made one of his magical cuts on the grass at the edge of the rushing stream. But the magic failed him. The grass was still wet, kept damp by spray from the stream, and his feet slipped out from under him. He thumped down and yowled as his momentum carried him, sliding on his side, over the edge into the rushing water.

He was shocked and terrified at first, dashed under the cold, powerful stream, battered on the bottom. He came up yards downstream and began to swim furiously for the opposite bank, which was lower than the one he'd fallen from. Though he was still being carried along by the current, he approached the bank with assurance and the panic left him.

As he made his way toward the solid earth, an object passed in front of his nose on the surface of the water. It was long and slim, rather like his leash, but it seemed to be alive. Gaining dry land, now a quarter of a mile down the mountain, he climbed out, shook himself furiously, and turned to stare at the rushing water. Soon another similar object swirled into view. He plunged into the stream after it, grabbing only a mouthful of water for his trouble. As he turned back to the bank, still another nearly bumped into his upraised muzzle. He grabbed this one in his teeth—gulping along with it considerable water—and carried it with him onto the land. There he shook it, tossing and turning his head violently, growling in his throat all the while.

It was certainly alive. Its writhing movements were erratic, but some of them—the powerful thrashing of its head—were clearly purposeful, and made Baggins angry. With his tongue he could feel the muscles under its tough, leathery skin flex and stretch as it struck repeatedly, each time finding only empty air.

The dog kept shaking it, biting its round, rippling body hard, feeling fine bones splinter satisfyingly between his teeth. He tossed it into the air and it came down with a thump and lay quite still. He picked it up in his teeth again, grabbing at a new point and shaking again. But now it was lifeless. He was standing there holding it in his teeth when the small dog reached him, plunging through the underbrush from upstream, panting heavily.

Baggins dropped the rattlesnake onto the ground. Dinny curled back his upper lip and walked cautiously, stiff-legged, up to the creature—he had seen its like earlier today, but had not managed to get his teeth into one. He snatched this one up and shook it, but soon dropped it. It was dead anyway, and it was a heavy, awkward burden, longer than his own body, indeed considerably longer than Baggins. He yapped at it.

Baggins barked once and turned to make his way back through the woods to the lawn where the people were. He was uneasy in the wild. Dinny wanted to return to the people, too, but he would take this trophy with him. He picked it up again, grabbing it near its head, and dragged it laboriously through the brush.

When the dead rattlesnake became caught on a fallen branch, he tugged at it briefly, but soon abandoned the struggle. Old Dinny had run far more and far harder than he was accustomed to doing, and the snake was heavy. He heard the men's voices not far ahead, and Baggins barking greetings to them. Dinny trotted on, under and around bushes, in the damp green shade, and found all three men in a little clearing with Baggins. He barked at them and ran back toward the snake, trying to get them to come with him to see the thing.

"C'mon, old man," Ben called, smiling. "C'mon, you've had your adventure, let's go home."

Dinny persisted, barking and whining, bouncing his forequarters off the ground, turning back toward the snake and back again toward the people. But they'd gone on into the brush, up the mountain. Ben whistled and yelled back at him. "C'mon, dumbass, this way."

Whitney stood on the small wooden bridge, looking down the stream for the returning men. Beautiful big dog, she thought, I hope he's okay. And wasn't it lovely the way the little one zipped after him? Over the bridge and down the road and into the woods. Dauntless little rescuer.

First to emerge from the thick forest onto the road alongside the stream was Baggins, breasting underbrush, thrashing free. He was wet and bedraggled, and his fringy legs were festooned with greenery, but he trotted cheerily along, head high, unfazed.

Whitney smiled. Dinny came next, looking a good deal the worse for wear, head down, panting, leaves tangled in his bushy facial hair.

To her great pleasure they came straight to her—to be congratulated, so it seemed. To forestall them jumping up against her bare skin, she knelt. She rubbed their heads and picked greenery off them and talked to them and laughed as they licked her face. She returned to her lounger, halfway to the front of the lawn, near the stream, and they came with her, choosing that spot instead of their old place under the tree to flop down and rest. She was pleased to have made new friends.

Ted was the first of the men to emerge from the woods. He paused on the road to catch his breath from the tough climb. He was used to doing hard physical work more easily than others; he was bigger and stronger than anyone he'd known since he played football in college. Still, he was relieved to come to the road. He was wearing cut-off jeans and no shirt, and the underbrush had whipped at his skin, stinging and leaving some small scratches.

Walking up the road, he looked across the stream and saw Whitney on the lawn, nuzzling with the two dogs. He had been dimly aware of her sunbathing as he was playing catch. Lying still, and at a considerable distance, her presence had not been disturbing. But now, kneeling, standing, her legs bending and straightening, body flexing, naked belly wrinkling and going smooth, she might be as much provocation as he would want to handle. He had come to know that body very well in a short time, and had missed it from time to time since—even though sex with Karen was frequent and enjoyable. Or had been, until the middle of her pregnancy, when Karen had lost interest for many weeks. And now, he thought—only she hasn't lost interest, she's just decided I'm not worthy of her precious favors. Ah, well. That'll be over pretty soon. I hope.

He stopped and turned at the sound of thrashing in the brush behind him. The other two men emerged, Ben puffing, his sweatshirt wet with rainwater from the underbrush and probably with sweat, Alex shaking his head and muttering.

The three walked up the road together and crossed the bridge. Ted headed across the lawn to where they had dropped their gloves and the ball, but Ben veered off to the left, toward his house, and Alex to the right, toward Whitney.

Ted stopped, hands on hips, and looked at one man, then the other. "You old farts had it?"

Ben, still puffing, called back over his shoulder, "Yeah, I'm taking a break. Shower. Beer."

Ted said, "All right, I'll come in and get a beer with you." Ben kept trudging as Ted called out to Alex and Whitney, asking if he could bring them anything.

Alex was sitting on the edge of Whitney's lounger, awkwardly petting the dogs' heads. He answered, "Not for me. I'm going in to take a shower, too. I got some paperwork to do." He turned to Whitney and they exchanged words that Ted couldn't hear. Ted strolled toward them.

Alex rose as Ted arrived at the lounger. "Diet soda," he said. "You can get it from Randall's refrigerator."

Ted nodded at Whitney with a tentative, friendly smile. She smiled in return and lay back, closing her eyes. As she stretched her stomach, the horizontal wrinkles that formed when she bent forward disappeared, leaving narrow white stripes that quickly disappeared, finally leaving unbroken golden tan from just under her breasts to the edge of her bathing suit's brief bottom.

Ted quickly turned to Alex and together they walked to Randall and Tim's house. Baggins followed them, and Dinny trotted after Baggins.

Ted was beginning to wonder what Alex knew about him and Whitney when Alex said, "I know about you and Whitney."

Startled, Ted looked sidelong at Alex, trying to think what he might want him to say.

Alex turned to look directly at him, his eyes serious and steady. "I mean, I just thought you might be uptight about it, that's all. No need. Forget it."

Ted nodded and said nothing. He admired Alex's directness, and felt faintly relieved. Alex's knowledge of his past affair with Whitney might serve as a sort of restraint on his own present feelings. His relief was not unmixed, though. He told himself that what had seemed like mind reading on Alex's part was nothing so spooky: Under the circumstances it was natural enough for Alex to raise the subject. And I *was* uptight. And he didn't know it was about those magical white stripes.

Ted hastily fought off a brief fantasy involving his cheek and that warm belly. He wasn't comfortable with such things in his head, walking alongside Alex.

When Ted emerged from the house, he saw that the dogs had returned to Whitney's side. Walking toward her with a cold can in each hand, he saw that she was restless. Twice in a few seconds she shifted her legs just slightly, and she lifted her arms from the lounger, bent her elbows and placed her hands atop her hips.

As Ted reached her side, she looked up at him. Her bathing suit was flowery. Orange in it, and red and little streaks of what might be black, or blue. Warm colors. Warm cloth, but dry and dead. Her belly was damp. A tiny rill of ladylike sweat ran among fine blond hairs, microscopically fine, oddly blond since she was blond nowhere else. The shiny little line of sweat began in the valley just under her ribs, and ended at her navel.

There were, he saw at once, tiny beads of sweat on her upper lip, as well, and even a few of those same infinitesimal blond hairs there. Bleached, he guessed. He suddenly remembered, vividly, kissing those hairs—and the others.

Ted felt himself flush slightly, then realized that he was wearing sunglasses. She probably hadn't noticed his eyes on her navel.

"Tab okay?" he said.

She smiled. "Sure, fine." She drank from the can, lips against cold metal. "How've you been?" she asked.

"Fine. You?"

"Fine, too."

"How's things with Alex?"

She looked at him, expressionless. "Fine," she said flatly.

He stared hard at her. "I didn't mean to—" He took a breath. "Look, you were hurt when we—ended. Weren't you?" This was dangerous ground, intimate, secret territory only the two of them had shared. He liked it there.

She was silent, looking away from him, taking another drink from the can. Ted went on, "I was. I didn't think it'd be hard, but it was. It's good it was short, or it would have been even harder. I'm—"

"It's okay." Her expression had softened. "It *was*

hard. I didn't expect it to be." She smiled with some real warmth. "It helps to know it was hard for you, too. I didn't know . . . I thought it wasn't . . . for men."

She stretched her upper lip over her teeth, brushed above it daintily with a fingertip, removed the little beads of moisture.

Ted looked away from her lips, over her shoulder at the woods, and said, "Alex is okay. I'm glad you're happy with him." He looked back at her with a smile.

Whitney grinned and raised her eyebrows. "I think I might be . . . in love with him." She shrugged. As she did, her bathing-suit straps strained lightly to pull upward at her breasts, each strap slipping an inch across the lightly freckled skin of her shoulders, moved back, caressing, as her shoulders fell again.

Ted took another deep breath and looked away. Lumbering up the road was his car. Karen, driving, turned left to follow the road to the houses. Annie waved from the passenger's side. Karen's gaze was fixed forward.

"Well, I gotta haul groceries," Ted said in a cheerful voice that sounded to him as hollow as it felt.

Whitney smiled and nodded. "Tell them I'll be in after a bit to help with lunch."

She lay back, said to herself yet again: calm. She had not seen his eyes, partly because of the sunglasses, partly because she could not take her own eyes off his chest: broad, deep, sculptured, the curve under the rib cage achingly graceful in its sweep. Skin damp with sweat, flushed pink, lightly textured with whorls of pale goose bumps, warmed and softened by swirls of curly black hair, startlingly violated by a fresh scratch, narrow as a thread, white, passing just under a nipple, turning scarlet, ending in a tiny fold of white skin pulled back by a thorn.

There is no word, she thought, for the feel of a strong man: huge and hard as a granite castle—but no, soft. Soft as velvet. Soft as a bed to lie on. A nervous little breath of a laugh escaped her. She thought if she rose to walk to the house, her legs wouldn't hold her. Walking was not what they wanted.

But the clouds were more numerous again, and she was in sunlight less than half the time now. And she had promised to help make lunch.

But that nipple, that scratch—she knew how it would taste—that soft, hard—stop! Oh, let me alone, she said silently to—she knew not what.

Every man in the place! she thought. And half the dogs.

She sat up, waited until the sudden new heat left her face. Then she arose and went inside.

CHAPTER

8

Annie was tense, a trifle distant. Ben carried groceries in silence and waited for her to provide a clue to what was bothering her. If it went on too long, he'd have to ask her, but he hoped that wouldn't be necessary: If he said anything to her, they'd spend the first ten minutes arguing about whether she *was* tense and distant.

The answer came soon after they had all the grocery bags out of the car. Annie was removing the supplies from the bags, deciding where to store things. Without looking at him, she began casually, "Why didn't. . . ." She fell silent, looked around at him, and started over. "Did you know Whitney had an affair with Ted?"

Ben was shocked. His face went slack, and he thought, oh-h-h damn. "No," he managed. *Damn*—so the level of tension around here goes up another two notches. "No, I didn't know that," he said flatly. Shit, I betcha somehow this is my fault. "When was that?" How the hell could she come here?

"Two years ago, when Karen was pregnant. He seems

to think it's no big deal, just a little horniness that came and went.''

"Oh, c'mon, he never said that.''

"No, no, I'm sure he never said *quite* that. I'm sure he was hangdog contrite, tugged at his forelock, drew circles in the dust with his toe. . . .''

"Oh, Jesus.'' Ben shook his head. "He's going to be a while getting admitted back into the human race, isn't he?''

She glared at him, opened her mouth, closed it again. After a deep breath she said, "You—why don't the two—oh, God damn the lot of you.''

Ben saw that Annie was hurt, more than angry, and though he couldn't think just why that should be, his own anger left him. "Look,'' he said gently, "I know it seems awful, that it should be the same person, and all come together here, but—and I know it's horribly nervy for me to say it, but—well, it *is* in the past. And you know Ted didn't know anything about me and her, we didn't know them then. And she—'' But he stopped. No good would ever come from defending her. I'm nervy, he thought, but I'm not stupid.

Annie nodded. "I told Karen all that. It's in the past, and all. I—''

"You mention Whitney and me?''

"Not very likely.''

"No, I guess you wouldn't. Lord, that *would* upset her—she'd think she was on a mountainside with the foremost seductress on the eastern seaboard.'' He recognized the folly of that line before he got it all out.

Annie's eyes were wide and innocent, but her jaw was as clenched as a fist. "Oh?'' she said.

"Oh, well—''

"Why would anyone think *that*?'' Her voice was like dry ice.

Ben sighed. No, I'm not stupid. Not very.

But for a moment she didn't press it. "I told Karen you had an affair once, left me and all, and we survived it okay. I told her that to comfort her. But I didn't say who. Thought she might leap to some madly unfair conclusion about your old pal. You know, being in a delicate mental state and all, she *might* think—"

"Okay, okay." Ben had sat down at the kitchen table, and was covering his head with his arms.

"I mean, that's *perfectly* silly, of course—" Annie looked around and saw him, abject in surrender, and relented.

He looked up. "Okay, you're right. Look—and I don't know why Whitney's come here, Alex must have pushed her, but—. Aww, shit."

She smiled. "Well, look, I have news. About the mountain and the storm, and all. You know Dart, the tall old man at the gas station?"

"His name is Dart?"

"Dart Klinger. He's the other one's uncle."

"The short one?" Ben asked. "He looks older than the tall one."

Annie replied, "He's his uncle, anyway. Dart told me—"

"You're a wonder. How do you learn all that so quick? That old fart hasn't said seventy words a year his whole life."

"Never mind that, listen to the news, it's important."

"Jesus, you're gonna be the mayor of Schuyler Mountain." Ben never understood how Annie did that. In one more stop for gas she'd have the whole family history.

"*Listen*. . . . That flood, that Randall and Tim came through? It's still there, though it's down to a couple of inches."

"What kind of name is Dart?"

"Ben!" She looked thoughtful. "You don't want to hear this."

He flushed. It made him angry when she interpreted his behavior to him. But she was often right.

Annie went on reassuringly, "Actually, the news is fairly good." And she waited for him to let her know if he wanted her to go on.

"Well, you're right, damn it. I don't want to hear about this—this mountain. I don't understand it, and everything new I learn is something else I can't get under control, or call a cop to straighten out, or take a taxi away from. . . ." He shook his head.

"Lord, I hate it that *you're* scared," Annie said. "I thought you were cool and collected."

"Oh, I'm all right, really," Ben said. "Honestly I am. It's just—I'm really amazed at how disconcerting it is to be in a place like this. How totally citified I've become. But really, it's okay. I'm just a little edgy, that's all."

She nodded thoughtfully. "He doesn't know what kind of a name Dart is, it never occurred to him to wonder. It's just his name."

Ben smiled and shook his head. "I might've known you'd ask."

"Okay, listen," Annie said. "The flood comes and goes quickly in a heavy rain. A few hours. It flows out of the two streams we can see coming over the cliff up by The Mountain King. They meet down below us—"

"I thought I saw the place."

"And farther down, sometimes they spill over into that little low place, there, where—"

"The clear stretch of road? Couple hundred yards with no trees? It dips a little and rises again through there."

Annie nodded. "That's the place. But there's a waterfall still farther down, away from the road—"

"Weaver's Falls?" Ben said. "That the town's named after?"

"Right. And so the water flows very fast, and drains pretty soon. Dart said the flood's very tricky when it's high. It looks flat on the top, and it's very broad when it's at its highest, so you don't realize it's flowing so fast."

"How deep does it get?"

"High as four feet," Annie said. "A Schuyler drowned there once. Car stalled, and he got out to wade through and was swept right away. Found his body in the pool below the falls, a couple of miles down.''

Ben whistled.

Annie said, ''Yes, but it does drain fast—if it's four feet at midnight, it's passable by the next afternoon.''

Ben said, ''Well, but we really are pretty isolated when it's high.''

''Yes, but it only gets that high once every few years, and it's only a few hours, and we're quite cozy up here, after all.''

Ben realized that having Annie reassure him was an interesting reversal of their usual roles. He thought she must be enjoying it. ''What about the electricity?'' he asked.

''Well, it does go sometimes in a heavy wind, and so do the phones, but that never lasts long, either. Dart says he's never had the food spoil in his freezer.''

Ben nodded thoughtfully. ''Actually, that figures. This is a wilderness, but then again it isn't, either. There's some pretty expensive property around here, and some resorts and hotels. I guess the power company and the phone company have to take good care of them.''

She nodded. ''So, you see?''

''It's going to rain again later, though, and the wind never has let up, really.''

''So?'' Annie said. ''Even if we're stuck 'til Tuesday, who cares? It'd be like being snowed in.''

''No school because of the blizzard.''

''Right . . . though, if I was much more pregnant, I don't think I'd be so easy about it. Tell you the truth, all of this made me really panicky when I first heard it, but I calmed down after a bit. Karen was a little nuts at first—actually, I think that helped settle me down.''

''How is she now?'' Ben asked.

''Fine. Same as me. She decided being stranded would be fun, too.''

''Mmm. Even being stranded with—?''

"Miss Twinkletits?"

Ben expelled a snort of laughter. "Miss *what*?"

Annie had sat down from her chores, across the kitchen table from Ben. "That's Karen's name for her." She shook her head. "Everybody's the same person," she said. "It's so silly. Did I ever tell you I grew up wanting bazooms like Kathryn Grayson's?"

Ben nodded slowly, puzzled. "But Karen *has*—" He stopped short, and Annie looked up at him, amused.

"Yes, she has. Had 'em since she was thirteen. But *she* grew up traumatized by Audrey Hepburn."

Ben smiled and shook his head and kept silent. Annie would not be amused if he observed that Whitney's body was scarcely as boyish as Audrey Hepburn's. In fact, he wasn't much amused, himself—Whitney's body was much too fresh in his mind, too achingly real.

It occurred to him that this whole conversation was not a very safe one to pursue. Well, he had a subject in reserve. "Hey, have you seen the kitten?" he asked. After a bit, he would be dispatched to search the woods for the no-name kitten; and that was a thicket he'd rather wade through than this conversation, which seemed to be full of pitfalls. And, in fact, the kitten hadn't been seen since early this morning, though Albie was around. The kitten rarely left Albie's side.

As Ben expected, he was soon off to tramp the woods. Annie was worried, as Ben was himself, a little. He had begun to like the kitten. Tough little guy, Ben thought; brave. Maybe we'll call him Fearless. Furry Fearless. Evel Knievel. That's good. Knievel, we'll call him.

As he left through the kitchen door, he met Whitney, wearing one of Alex's shirts over her bathing suit, carrying a shopping bag with a liquor store logo on it. With one hand she pulled the shirt together in front of her and closed a button. They exchanged nods.

Twinkletits, he thought, with a rush of feeling that was, indeed, nothing like amusement. As he left the

driveway and entered the woods, he drew a deep breath.
Well, they twinkle when they're wet with spray, I'll tell
you that.

Karen's rage was beginning to confuse her. It was
beyond accounting for. It had flared in her fresh and
hot when she'd seen Ted and Whitney—both more
nakcd than clothed—talking on the lawn as she'd driven
up. Talking over old times? Just admiring each other's
bodies?

She looked up at Ted, sitting on a high stoool by the
kitchen counter, watching her unload grocery bags. He
raised his eyebrows and asked, "Can I help?"

Karen said nothing, just shook her head and continued to look at Ted. It was a beautiful body, she
thought. Huge and strong, liquid in movement, capable
of overwhelming her with its power. And mine. It's
mine! As she looked up at him, her anger became
something else, though she couldn't say what for a
moment.

She was walking toward him before she knew why, or
what she intended. He stepped down from the
stool—up, really, he towered over her. She grabbed
him, reached around him, pressed her face to his sweaty
chest, found a fresh scratch, licked it—raw-edged, salty,
warm. The muscle under it twitched, flinching away
from her probing tongue. His arms were around her
shoulders, tentatively touching her head, his big fingers
in her hair.

Karen looked up at him, stretched, slid up his body,
reached with her mouth to his, her tongue to his. He
lifted her off her feet, hands under her arms, and her
hands left his shoulders and reached around to the small
of his back, under the beltless waist of his dungaree
shorts, massaged there, moved around in front, un-
buttoned and unzipped him.

Karen's body was running far ahead of her mind,
grabbing, thrusting, hands now around his broad upper
back, legs around his waist and squeezing. A tiny part

of her was alarmed, but she lacked the will to slow herself down. Her will was in the center of her body, not in her brain. She wanted more of him, all of him, now!

Ted walked clumsily, bearing her full weight, through a door, banging her hip on the jamb, to the stairway to their bedroom. Karen slid down, put her feet unwillingly to the first step, ordered her trembling legs to carry her up. The enclosed stairway was narrow, and after they'd thumped against its walls and each other for two steps, Karen moved ahead. Ted didn't so much follow as attach himself to her, arms about her enfolding her breasts, as she reached back around under her sweater to unhook her bra, climbing, stumbling all the while his strong hands moved under her open clothes, warm on her warm skin. As they passed the half-open door of the baby's room a far corner of Karen's mind noted the silence with gratitude.

That same half-interested tenant of her brain would remember later, with some amusement, Ted's clumsy walk, his shorts tugged down to the top of his thighs. But now she was interested only in what was exposed by the displacement of those rough, denim, brass-studded pants and the snowy-white jockey shorts. In a series of jerky, unwilled movements she had it.

She had Ted—to her own astonishment and, judging from his open-eyed, open-mouthed expression, to his—she had him, on the bed, on his back, deep in her. She was fierce as she came down on him, pulled up, came down again, her hands on his shoulders, her heavy breasts first crushed against his chest, then, as she pushed up, swaying just above him, nipples tickled by the curly black hair until his hands came up to cup them, nipples extending between his fingers. His eyes widened and he began to speak for the first time since she walked to him downstairs—"Oh!"—and she felt a thrilling hot splash inside her, a triumph. And a furious disappointment.

She squeezed him, finding muscles she never knew she had, used him while he was still big, clenched her teeth, threw her head back, held herself rigid, trembling, achieved a sort of deliverance, not a climax, producing a faint shrill sound in her throat, a whimper, and finally collapsed on him.

They breathed in counter cadence, huge breaths that sounded thunderous in the room. As he shrank, Karen pulled herself from him—better empty now than so tantalized—moved off him, lay on her stomach beside him with an arm across his chest, her other arm crossed in front of her, under her breasts. Holding herself as much as him.

Her head spun. Was that me? Oh, I must have scared him out of his wits. Ohh, I . . . I want more. I want to do that again. I *liked* that, being in charge. Feeling he's *mine.* Whenever I want him. She almost laughed aloud, remembering the astonishment on his face. Poor Ted. I want more!

She remembered with a little surprise how pleased she had been, how triumphant, when she felt him come, even though she hadn't been ready for him to be finished. I wanted him, she thought, more than I wanted myself. That didn't make sense to her; she decided to think what she meant by that. Another time.

For now, Karen simply wanted him again. No use, she thought; poor baby, there isn't any more of him to have now. She rose from the bed and dressed quickly, thinking that getting out of this room might calm her, distract her. Anyway, she had promised to help make lunch.

Karen was on the driveway, on her way to Ben and Annie's house, before she realized she had left the bed, the room and the house without a word to Ted. Oh, hell, she thought, he'll survive. Let him be off-balance for a while.

Her anger was returning as she thought that she'd be working with Whitney. *Try him now, why don't you?* she thought. *I just fucked him to death.* It occurred to her that she might actually smell of him. *Good.*

• • •

Ben entered the woods at the end of the driveway where he'd seen Albie dart off the slope, across the gravel, and into the trees that morning. He had imagined then that Albie was chasing the kitten. Anyway, this was the most beautiful part of this whole place; since he didn't really know where to look, it might as well be here.

The ground sloped downward from the houses and cleared land, but only gradually: Walking was walking, and not climbing. There were three or four—maybe more—clear spaces in this three·acres of forest, self-enclosed, transcendentally beautiful and still. Shooting film in one of these spaces last fall, he had sat on the earth, back against a tree, for a few minutes—and had had to leave. He had felt overwhelmed, drowning in the colors: sunlight through scarlet and brown and gold and pale yellow, shards of pellucid pale blue. And the sounds, at first barely audible to his brutalized city hearing, but soon an orchestra: several kinds of birds whistling, burbling, screeching; rustling of leaves falling and occasionally of a small creature's movement on the leaf-carpeted floor of the woods.

It had all been too beautiful to bear. He had thought: *It's breaking my heart.* I'm going to have to leave here, and leave the country, and go back to that fucking city and scuffle for my living; and I won't have the heart for it.

It was different today, not less beautiful, but less spectacular. The colors were all green, and the sounds were all wind. The wind's howl overwhelmed all others except for the very noisiest of the birds' cries. And the leaves that still covered the ground were wet and silent. He regretted not having changed his shoes after playing ball. He still wore low-cut sneakers and no socks; his ankles were exposed to the damp chill of the earth and leaves.

Twice as he made his way through the brush, peering about him at the ground, he caught tantalizing glimpses of movement, each time at the periphery of his vision.

Not the kitten; the movement was silent and very smooth. Stealthy. Snaky? Might be a snake, he thought—there are certainly garter snakes here. Two snakes; the movements were far apart. Mates? Do snakes mate, or hang out in pairs? He had no idea.

He became more alert, and watched his footsteps as well as casting his gaze about him. He had no special phobia for snakes, but the idea of stepping on one was a little creepy. And he was all but barefoot. He felt a little silly; he hadn't actually seen anything at all, except movement. It might have been chipmunks.

There! Near where he'd seen the second one, motion caught his eye again. He stared hard at the spot, between two low, thick bushes, and saw—movement. More than that, he couldn't be certain of. Last year's fall of maple leaves, wet and half-rotted, was nearly black, and mottled by shifting specks of sunlight. But on that confusing pattern of shifting light and dark there was another movement: Some yellow specks were gliding smoothly, in unison, distinct from the shifting pattern of light. It lasted only a moment—perhaps two seconds—and was maddeningly indistinct.

The elusiveness of the sight, the insubstantiality, was profoundly disturbing. But he was more intrigued than frightened. Could it have been as big as he'd thought? It had seemed that the pattern of smoothly moving yellow marks had been a couple of inches tall—certainly bigger than a garter snake.

He moved cautiously toward it, wanting to see more clearly. The ground here, though it looked level enough, was rutted and pitted; the depressions were filled with leaves and pine needles. He put his foot down on apparently solid ground and felt it slip to the side and downward. A stabbing pain as it turned, and then, as the foot buried itself past his shoe top, the shock of the cold, wet leaves.

Ben stepped back, whispered, "Sshhit," stood on his one relatively dry foot to remove the sneaker full of leaves and clean it out. Take it easy, he said to himself;

his momentary loss of control as his foot slipped away from him had scared the hell out of him for just an instant. This is not the Okeefenokee swamp, this is the Catskills.

He was beginning to be half-exasperated, half-amused at himself. Jumping at shadows, scared of thunder and lightning, Jesus, it's silly. Why am I so twitchy?

And where in the hell is that kitten, anyway? There are animals here that could hurt him if he was dumb enough to challenge one—skunks, maybe woodchucks. Could a hawk get him? Probably not; don't they soar around over open fields? An owl? In the daytime? Oh, hell, I just don't know.

Ben's knowledge of such things came mostly from animal shows on television. Annie, he thought, probably knows more about all this stuff than I do. Annie had once done research for a kid's show. Anyway, those shows were usually set in really exotic places—Africa, South America. At least the Southwest Desert, or the Everglades. Real wildernesses, not the Catskills. There isn't that kind of stuff here. Boa constrictors, rattlesnakes, cobras. Jaguars, cheetahs, tigers. Bears. Here we got porcupines, 'possums, 'coons, deer. And a dopey kitten with more courage than sense.

Ben pressed on, feeling foolish for his fearfulness, but watching where he placed each foot.

CHAPTER

9

Annie was shocked by Karen's appearance. Karen had shown up in the kitchen shortly after Whitney's arrival. Annie hadn't seen anyone looking like that since she was a teenager, when people would appear from other rooms at what were called "petting parties" with that telltale flush, tousle-haired, bright-eyed and jumpy.

Whitney noticed it, too. It did nothing to relieve the tension she already felt with these two women. Annie had been a little stiff, but not really hostile, and Whitney had begun to hope the tension might not be unbearable. But Karen's state made her very uneasy.

Karen didn't give a damn. She might have, if she'd been aware of just how glaringly apparent her condition really was—half-laid, Annie might have called it. Or she might still not have cared. Her distraction was nearly total—in truth, a state of controlled hysteria.

"Hi!" Karen said with a sort of bright matter-of-factness. "Sallitches or sam—" She stopped, felt her face flush neon scarlet, started over. "Are we making sandwiches or a big salad?"

Whitney looked away to give attention to her work, cutting and slicing. Annie looked at Karen and swallowed before answering.

"Well, we'd prefer salad, but the men look to be in their good ol' boys phase, hoo-rawing around, playing ball and all, so we figure they're in a mood for sandwiches."

"Good," Karen said. "Let's make salad."

Annie grinned. "That's what we decided. Let 'em stick it on bread if they want."

They decided, Karen thought. Annie and Whitney, a regular partnership already. Karen not needed.

Annie was washing, and Whitney slicing cucumbers, celery, tomatoes. What was needed was cutting the delicatessen meats and cheeses into strips and chunks. Karen moved beside Whitney at the counter.

They worked in silence but for innocuous, chirrupy instructions and thank-yous between Annie and Whitney. "What d'you think? Long strips of cuke, or slices?" "I dunno. What would Julia Child do?" "Sauté 'em with tarragon." "Well, whichever's easier, I guess."

Karen did not become more calm as she worked. Her body refused to let her be, for one thing. Her breasts were warm and felt confined in her clothes; she felt empty at the middle. She had an insistent hunger that popping the odd bit of ham into her mouth did nothing to satisfy. She felt—not angry, exactly, but fierce.

She was oddly surprised and disturbed by Whitney's easy competence with paring knife and peeler. Well, I guess I figured all she did was fuck. The word in her mind surprised her. She didn't talk that way, even with Annie who sometimes did, or even to herself. Well, that's what she does, though. And French cooking is also fucking, when you're doing it for somebody's husband. Makes a dynamite *omelette fines herbes*, I betcha, but let her try frying two up.

Karen was indecisive and clumsy at her own chores. Lifting sliced meat from its wrapper, peeling a salami—she repeatedly dropped things. Her knife narrowly missed embedding itself in Whitney's foot.

Whitney had slim, shapely, lightly-tanned legs, showing the first traces of stubble, invisible only a few inches away. Better do something about that, honey, Karen thought, rising to return to her work. Can't get careless before you have a husband of your own.

She began to be deviled by fantasies of Whitney making love. Her twinkly tits—tits on her shoulders, the bitch—filling Alex's mouth. Ted's. Little button nipples standing up. Her shirt—Alex's, really, from the size of it, a European designer number, gorgeous asymmetrical pattern in a color like mahogany, wish I could get Ted to wear shirts like that—the shirt hung soft from her shoulders, clung to her breasts, fell open above and below the single button that was done up, revealing—well, she looked like a—oh, hell, she looks beautiful. Stunning.

Hard little breasts, flat belly, silky smooth top to bottom, oh, she'd have no trouble reeling them in. Who wouldn't want to. . . . Karen began to feel dizzy. Her fantasy of Whitney's breast in a mouth, belly touched by tongue, slim thighs—it was no longer a fantasy of Alex's mouth, or Ted's. The fantasy now was of flesh, musky-sweet, lips brushing fine hairs. A tiny voice sounded in her mind, calling from a distance: *What is happening to me?* She sucked at her lips, touched them with her tongue, chewed lightly on them.

"Oh!" Karen said. *"Damn!"* Her knife had slipped and cut her—the back of a finger was scarlet from below the middle knuckle to its tip. "Owww." She sucked it.

Whitney looked over at her, alarmed. "Karen?" she said in a small voice.

Annie moved around Whitney to her, gently pulled her hand away from her mouth and looked at the cut.

Karen said quickly, "It's okay, it's not as bad as I thought at first." Blood was seeping again, but not so rapidly.

Annie handed her a kitchen towel. "Here, hold just a second while I get the celery out of the sink." The sink was clear by the time she'd finished the sentence. She pulled Karen to it and turned on the cold water.

"Owwww," Karen said softly as the icy water shocked her finger.

Whitney said, "I'll get a Band-Aid, where are they?"

Karen glared at her. "No."

"But—"

"No. Look, it's okay, I have some Mercurochrome in my house, and anyway I'm about finished here and Charley'll be up soon and Ted'll. . . . It's my turn to change him." And the screen door slapped shut behind her.

Karen's departure left shocked silence behind, but she was far beyond caring about that. *What is happening to me?* I want . . . I don't care. I just *want.*

Tim Levine was no sort of nature lover. As he and Randall explored this Catskills forest, he thought of the jungle that was "outdoors" to him as a child. The outdoors, in his mind, was the teeming, noisy streets of East New York, in Brooklyn—mostly Italian when Tim was growing up, and hostile. Hard, hot, noisy and dangerous. But navigable, once he'd learned a few things. How to amuse the gang kids, how to elude them when they weren't to be amused. Above all, how to get out. By the age of nine he knew the bus that took him to the subway that took him to Manhattan. "To the city," was what they said in Brooklyn.

By fifteen, Tim knew Times Square. It had clearings in it, like these woods, and impassable places. Randall would have been terrified in Times Square, more than Tim was here. God knows what creepy, crawly, toothy, winged or clawed things are behind these bushes, or hidden in the leaves of the trees—but they couldn't be more dangerous than the rough trade in the city.

They were moving toward a clearing, Randall's hand on his shoulder guiding him to the easiest way through the underbrush. Suddenly they were bathed in sunlight, in a glade perhaps twenty feet across. Near the center, a grassy hummock rose, a cushiony platform warmed and dried by the sun. Randall walked to it, sat down, lay back, grinned up at the sky, squinted his eyes against the sun, closed them. He sighed.

Randall was heartbreakingly beautiful. Golden, glowing, strong and graceful. He wore an earth-brown, V-neck sweater, nothing under it, wheat-colored soft denim slacks. After Tim had stood staring in something like awe for a moment, he moved to the hummock, lay beside Randall, looked closely at his face, looked up at the woods. Randall belonged here. Like a deer.

The dry whirring rattle sounded faint under the wind's ceaseless hum. Randall frowned slightly, but didn't open his eyes. Tim thought it was like a sound he sometimes heard in the soundtracks of movies, a tension signal that he always supposed was meant to suggest rattlesnakes.

"What is that?" he asked, but it had stopped.

Randall knew what he meant, though. "Sounds like a rattlesnake, doesn't it?" He smiled. "I'm trying to place it. Tree frog, maybe, I can't remember. I've been in the city too long. It's all right, there's nothing dangerous here."

And Tim knew there wasn't. Randall understood these things. A deer would know if there was danger, wouldn't he? He touched Randall's cheek with his fingertips, and when Randall responded by reaching for his shoulder, Tim curled into him, warm and safe in a clearing in a forest, a strange and wonderful place for Tim Levine of East New York.

Ben's search for the kitten had turned to something else. A sort of test of nerve. He'd become convinced that there were hidden things in dark places on the forest floor. That was the way it occurred to him, that dramatically. For Christ's sake, he thought—things in dark places. Chipmunks. He remembered a late show he and Annie had watched, the most absurd of a long string of nature-out-of-control horror movies: killer rabbits. Giant bunnies running amok, twitching giant noses.

But this inner chatter, twitting himself for his state of nerves, was hard to sustain. The fact was, he had seen something that had looked very like a snake, insofar as he could tell that it looked like anything. And if it was a snake, it was big. At the very least it could have eaten a tiny kitten. Well, at very most, too, he insisted to himself—it is not going to drop from a tree and squeeze me to death and devour me.

And it isn't going to poison me, either. If there were poisonous snakes here, wouldn't we know it? No one in town has ever mentioned copperheads, or anything. Old Dart and his nephew—nephew, for God's sake—have never—well, of course we've never asked them specifically, and I don't guess they'd mention a giant octopus in the creek if they weren't asked.

Having seen two fleeting movements widely separated, he kept searching the ground, thinking he might see another. If he did, he would certainly get close enough to discover exactly what it was. If a snake, what size, what colors? Had they a snake book in the house? Probably not, but they could buy one in town and look it up.

Meanwhile there was no use denying that he was increasingly uneasy. The unending, unchanging, nearly painful sound of the wind was disturbing, for one thing. No other sound could be heard. The little rustles of leaves skittering down through the trees and blowing across the earth, small bird sounds, chittering of squirrels, usually heard in the woods, were not audible. If something moved in the bushes he mightn't hear that, either. He might as well be deaf. And his naked ankles felt terrifyingly vulnerable.

Movement was becoming more difficult. He was in thick undergrowth. He could scarcely see where he was putting his feet, and almost nothing at a distance of more than a couple of yards. It seemed more and more that he had not only become deaf but blind as well, and the helpless feeling was becoming too much to suppress.

By now the conviction had seized him that the floor of the forest was alive with snakes. He didn't believe that to be so—he recognized it as the silliest sort of panic and determined not to be dissuaded from his search—but increasingly it required a huge effort of will to pick up a foot and place it down.

Search for what? he thought. I'm not doing anything here but fighting panic. He froze, utterly immobilized by the distant rattling sound of—what? A locust, or something, of course, but the lunatic snake fear made it a rattlesnake in his mind. Again, he knew that was silly. Rattlesnakes in the Catskills, two and a half hours from West Tenth Street? But he couldn't move.

Ben's throat was constricted, with a feeling like an incipient sob. He felt faint, and reached out to touch a tree. When his hand found it he gripped the rough maple bark until his fingertips hurt. Forcing deep breaths, he worked himself into a state approaching calm. The trembling in his knees subsided.

He had begun to turn back toward the houses when the next sound came—an animal moan, rising to a near-soprano howl, then dying in a sigh that sounded human. It was so appalling, so incomprehensible, the fear was driven from him, replaced by a sort of numb horror. He must learn what dreadful thing had happened.

He moved toward where he thought the sound came cautiously, as silently as he could manage. After only a few steps, Ben found himself just outside one of the clearings. In the midst of the open space, on a grassy rise, were Randall and Tim, nude, holding each other, quiet in the sunlight.

Ben's face flushed scalding hot. Oh, Lord. . . . In his mind he replayed the sound he had heard. It was not a howl of pain, at all. Oh, my, this is my day for peeping.

A sort of silent giggle escaped him, an embarrassed gasp. He turned and moved quietly away. He had never seen such a thing before, or even imagined it very clearly. Two men.

The picture of them remained vivid in his mind. Like a sculpture, but pink with life and glowing in the sun. Intertwined, so . . . intimate. Lovely, really. I guess lovers are lovely, whatever.

He made his way, purposefully now, back to the house.

Ted lay on the bed, head spinning. That had not been the Karen he knew. Sex object, he said to himself. You've just been a sex object. I'll be goddamned. Big fella's been used and discarded. What do you think of that?

He wasn't sure what he thought. It was . . . well, it was exciting, he told himself reassuringly. For her to be so hungry. Usually takes me a while to get her that turned on.

But I had nothing to do with this. Still, it *was* exciting.

All the while he was telling himself what fun it had been, a long, high note of unease was playing over his thoughts. Some shift had occurred. Something new had entered his relationship with Karen, something that would alter the balance in a way he couldn't predict.

What the hell, Ted thought. Karen's horny, all of a sudden. What's wrong with that? He rose to sit on the side of the bed, removed his shorts—finally—and walked to the bathroom. He shook his head as he realized that he was still wearing his sneakers.

He took them off and stepped into the shower. He fixed the water at just warmer than body temperature—less hot made it last longer—and soaped up. Gently, at his middle. He was a little tender: A dull, not unpleasant ache had settled in there. Standing with his face next to the shower head, blinded and deafened by the warm stream on his face, Ted was comforted by the soothing cascade down his body.

His uneasiness wouldn't go away. He sensed that

some . . . awakening had occurred in Karen. That he couldn't give it a name, that when he thought about it hard the whole notion seemed silly to him, only increased his apprehensiveness.

He was surprised, not for the first time this week, to realize how much his sense of himself depended on his awareness of Karen—their relationship, her view of him. If Karen was to be a different person, then the texture of his life would be different. Or its density, or temperature, or . . . speed? He couldn't even find a way of saying to himself what form this change would take. He only knew that, for the first time in years, at least since he married Karen, he didn't know how his life would feel to him in six months, or six days.

He didn't like that. Why be married, if not for stability? He wanted his old wife back.

Ted knew when Karen came in the bathroom. A faint breeze entered the shower, chilling him slightly. Still, he jumped when the shower curtain was shoved suddenly aside and she entered. He turned away from the shower head and looked at her. She wore a small smile. Her eyes still held the burning intensity they'd had when she left.

She touched his ribs with the flat of her hand, urging him gently aside so she could face into the stream of water, but holding him there, both hands moving to his waist. In a moment she was gleaming from head to toe, wearing a shiny second skin of clear warm water.

Ted stood stiffly. He put his hands on her shoulders, but leaned slightly away from her. Karen moved to him, reached around his waist, then leaned back and looked up at his face. She was pressed against his thigh. He looked down through the shower's stream at her gleaming breasts, swaying gently from side to side.

His expression must have been rich, for in a moment Karen smiled and said softly, gently reassuring, "Oh, Ted—it's all right. It's going to be okay. Only more . . . complicated." And she kissed his ribs and lay her head against his chest.

Ted stood, not relaxing, not yet. His hands still rested on her shoulders. He looked down at the top of her head. Complicated, he thought. Is that the word I was looking for?

CHAPTER

10

Annie stood on a step stool to haul down a huge Lucite bowl from the top of a kitchen cabinet. The salad was beginning to take shape.

Conversation between Annie and Whitney had begun to flow reasonably smoothly, after an interval of tentative and brittle politeness. Whitney had seemed edgy, defensive—scared to death, in fact—for a time. And for good reason, Annie thought. Still, her wide-eyed skittishness had been disarming.

Poor thing, she replied to herself. But look · at her—she's just a person like anyone else, doing the best she can. Mm-hmm. Doing it with other people's husbands.

Annie had begun to wonder—later she would think on this, make a theory—whether Whitney had a particular interest in married men, or only in men who were unavailable. Tim had claimed that Whitney was really sweet and decent, more sinned against than sinning. Wonder what he'd say if Randall had been screwing her?

But it was simply not in Annie's nature to judge people, once she came to know them. They always seemed, as she put it to herself, to be doing the best they could—getting through life the best way they could manage. Not such an easy job, after all.

So, after a time, Annie had found herself talking about herself—not intimately, but personally. She had been, she thought, a good actress, and she would never be entirely free of regret for having left acting—so she talked about that.

"Well," she was saying in answer to a question, "I think I quit because it made me crazy. I had other reasons I gave myself at the time, but I think the truth was I just couldn't stand operating with my emotions so near the surface so much of the time. I didn't want to fake it—*indicate*, you know—and I couldn't turn my feelings on and off the way you should, and I just felt—anxious, all the time. And fragmented."

Whitney nodded. "The best work I've ever done was a few months ago in a play in L.A.—you'd be surprised, there are some good theater people out there now, some good things get done. Anyway, I was. . . . I had some moments . . . well—. But I was bonkers. You couldn't talk to me, I'd burst into tears. Pretty soon I was popping Valiums like salted peanuts."

"Pills always scared me," Annie said. "I drank."

"I came out of it a little, toward the end. I scared myself with the pills, so I talked to my shrink a couple of times on the phone."

"And that helped?"

Whitney smiled with transparent pleasure, as if she was still surprised. "Yeah, it did."

Annie nodded. "I went to an analyst for a while, too. It helped a lot . . . Did you get any reviews?"

Whitney grimaced. "No, there was a movie star in the cast and he got all the reviews. Actually, he was good. But the company knew how good I was. He did, too—the movie star."

"So maybe it'll help you, anyway."

"Wouldn't that be nice?" Whitney said wistfully.
" 'Course, it'd be nice if there was an Easter bunny, too."

Annie nodded sympathetically. "I gave a performance like that once, for a week. Downtown, when off-Broadway was still exciting. I was terrible all through rehearsals, but when we opened, it just all came out. Wow . . . people's jaws dropped. And they cried . . . I don't suppose I've ever felt so—full, charged up—since. Well, 'til now—being pregnant makes me feel that way part of the time."

"I've often thought it might."

Annie was remembering. "I was a frightful mess the whole year I was with that company. I was in love with the director. We—" She stopped, felt herself redden.

Whitney looked at her, didn't press her to go on.

"He was married," Annie said. She sighed heavily and looked up at Whitney with a brief, rueful smile.

Whitney said nothing. She felt overwhelmed with warmth, with gratitude to Annie for having given her that gift of complicity. It was forgiveness, or something so close to it as to serve as forgiveness.

The spring on the screen door whined, and Ben entered, shaking his head, limping slightly. He plopped down in a chair. "The woods are full of wonderful things, but no kitten." He shrugged helplessly.

Whitney was sorry the mood had been broken. While Ben and Annie agreed to give up the search for the time being, hoping the kitten would come in at feeding time, Whitney asked herself what it was she felt she needed to be forgiven for. You, you jerk, were the one who got beat up. You didn't seduce anybody. Well-ll. . . . But you weren't alone. Ben, damn him, wasn't exactly Trilby, either. But don't kid yourself, my dear, you did feel forgiven, and grateful for it.

Oh, well, look at them. They obviously belong together, they're so comfortable with each other, know each other so well. . . . And from Annie's point of view, you were the threat.

"It is swollen," Annie was saying, looking at Ben's ankle, "but it isn't turning color. Much."

"Nah, I just turned it a little. It'll be okay."

"You sure?"

"Oh, yeah, I've done worse playing ball. I can walk on it, if I'm a little careful, with hardly any pain."

Annie nodded, satisfied.

Like a mother, Whitney thought, but the mother of a grown-up who could be trusted to take care of himself. I think probably that's how—that's *one* of the ways it's supposed to be.

The screen door made its gentle complaining sound again, and Alex walked in, carrying a holster with a flap on it. Oh, God, Whitney thought, that hateful thing.

"Hello, all," he said cheerfully, then to Whitney, "Hey, hon, want your lesson?"

But Whitney was comfortable, enjoying talking with Annie, and didn't want a lesson in using a pistol. She didn't answer for a moment.

"Is that a gun?" Annie asked. She was staring at the leather holster.

Ben answered for Alex. He was staring at the holster, too, his eyebrows raised. "That's a gun," he said, in a matter-of-fact tone that only Annie recognized as betraying tension. Why do pistols scare the shit out of me? Ben wondered. Because they're small. I don't like a small thing that could kill me. Like a snake. His nervousness from the woods was returning.

"Look," Alex said urgently, "it's a tool. For living in New York—" And as quickly as that he was launched into what was surely a prepared speech. "It's like learning the subway system, or having an umbrella for when it rains, or knowing what streets to stay away from after dark. There are people who'll come into your home and rob you, and kill you. It's crazy to pretend they're not there, and it makes sense to be ready to—uh, cope with them. They'll—well, they're not going to do it to me. Or mine."

His tone had turned defiant, almost sullen, as he

finished. Still, the argument, it seemed to Ben, was not altogether mad. There was violence in the air of New York, more all the time it seemed, and if his understanding of where it came from, and why, was at all correct, it might be another generation before the level would begin to go down again.

"Look, Alex," Annie said. "I don't like that. I wish you'd take it out of here." Her eyes had not left the holster; she was glaring at it angrily, now.

"Look, let me show you something—may I show you something?" Alex looked at Ben when Annie didn't answer.

"Go ahead," Ben said.

Alex unsnapped the flap of the holster and removed the pistol, grasping just the handle with two fingers and thumb. Then he pushed something on the side of the pistol with his thumb, causing the empty cylinder to pop out. With the other hand, he pushed a little rod at the front of the cylinder and looked through the holes where the bullets would go. Holding the weapon with forefinger and middle finger through the empty space where the cylinder would fit, he offered the gun to Ben.

"Now you see," he said, "that's the only way ever to handle it. Not only empty, but with the cylinder out. I knew it was empty, but I still went through the whole ritual. You don't think about it, you just do it, every time, no matter what."

Ben had to steady his hand to reach for the pistol; rather like steeling himself to handle a snake. He put his fingers through the opening the cylinder had vacated. How like Alex, he thought, to know, and practice, all the safety rituals, like a responsible person. But he enjoys the practiced ease he does it with. Flips the cylinder out, peers through; if that doesn't look like Clint Eastwood . . . well, he'll work on it 'til it does.

Changing his grip to the handle of the pistol, Ben found the temptation to flip the cylinder back into place and spin it—like Clint Eastwood—almost overpowering. If he hadn't thought he'd probably toss the damn thing across the room—he'd never had a revolver in his hand before in his life—he actually might have attempted it.

It was not so scary, fully disarmed as it was. And it was an impressive piece of machinery, heavy, solid, obviously extremely well-made, precision fitted, smooth. He'd like to see it work.

Whitney said to Alex, "Look, we still have a lot to do to get lunch ready. I'll have a lesson later."

Alex said, "It's going to rain, later, from the look of things."

"Well, tomorrow then."

Ben interrupted. "I'd like a lesson."

Alex looked at him with a little surprised smile. "Well, okay. Good, terrific. Let's go."

As they left the house, Annie's steady gaze followed them. She was not exactly frowning, but the two little verticals had appeared in the middle of her forehead.

Ben and Alex took a pad of targets from the trunk of Alex's car, then crossed the bridge and started down the mountain road.

Why am I so keyed up? Alex thought. Firing the pistol is fun, but I've done enough of that by now so that I'm used to it. I'm going to teach Ben to fire it; what's so. . . . I'm going to teach Ben, that's what. I don't teach Ben, he teaches me. I'm used to sitting in his office listening to him lecture. Sitting at his feet.

Alex clenched his jaw. Well, all right. I learned things I needed to know from him, and I never would have from Arthur Bradley.

"Just around this curve," Ben said. "There's a clearing right on the road."

Alex was pulled from his thoughts. "Good. We'll need a place that isn't rocky."

Ben nodded. "It doesn't look especially rocky from the road. We'll see."

They looked over the grassy half-acre clearing, searching for a place within ten or fifteen yards of a tree stump or something else they could tack the target to—backed up by several yards of upward-sloping soft ground without rocky outcroppings, to absorb misses. They tramped about, found a dry spot to stand on where the earth sloped upward very satisfactorily, but no tree stump. They decided to look for a fallen log near the edge of the woods.

"A pistol scares me," Ben said, "because it's small. A rifle or a shotgun you handle with two hands, you don't forget what it is, you keep it aimed at the sky. When you aim at something, it's a big deal. But a pistol—just flinging your hand out and firing? I don't see how in the hell you control it. Hit what you're aiming at, or be sure it doesn't go off when you don't want it to."

Having found their log, they began hauling it out into the clearing. Alex spoke in grunts. "Uh-huh. That's why there are all the safety rituals. My friend the cop told me—*unh,* let's rest a minute—says he laughs out loud when he sees cops on television, the way they handle guns." His friend the cop was a semi-celebrity in New York, a young detective who had once been a Rhodes scholar, known by those in the know to be a good bet for major political office sooner or later. Alex hadn't meant to mention his name—though he knew he'd be glad if Ben asked—but suddenly something impelled him to say it. "Randy McNeill, you know the name?"

Ben said, "Oh, yeah—the hotshot who was on television so much around the time of the Knapp hearings? I hear he's gonna be governor some day."

Alex, sitting on the log, nodded. Name dropping—goddamnit, what gets into me? In fact, what had gotten into him was that he had had to ask for a rest before Ben did. He got up now and grabbed his end of the log. "Down there a few yards," Alex said, and nodded toward the spot. Ben nodded and lifted.

Ben was shorter than Alex, and thick set. He looked soft—Alex thought of him as chubby—but he was surprisingly strong. The log was placed on a slope, so that the target would be about waist-high to the men firing from a lower spot.

The lesson began with the litany of safety rules Alex had learned from his friend the celebrity policeman. He popped out the cylinder and cleared the chambers, just as before. "This is a first-class weapon, which makes a difference. See, there's no safety catch. Doesn't need one. There's a built-in safety, inside here"—he pointed to the area of the gun's body just in front of where the hammer strikes down—"a plate in front of the firing pin, that only recedes when the trigger's pulled all the way through two clicks. So you could throw the gun on the ground, or a sidewalk even, as hard as you could and it wouldn't go off. Might break off the hammer, but the gun wouldn't fire. Little cheap Saturday-night specials—which do have safety catches—are ten times as dangerous. Built like cap pistols."

The gun still empty, Ben was finding a stance and grip that would be steady and comfortable. Standing profile to the target first, arm straight out, he peered down his arm and over the sights. "Jesus Christ, I can see the tip waving around. I have no idea where a bullet would go."

"Relax," Alex said. "You'll get the feel of it after a while."

Shifting to face the target, Ben extended both arms and tried a two-handed grip. Though he was awkward and uncomfortable at first, it seemed to Alex that he found steady postures comparatively quickly. Quicker and easier than I did, he thought. Things come easy to this little sonofabitch. Why should that be? Why him and not me?

These days Alex was preoccupied more than occasionally with comparisons of Ben and himself. Alex knew that the two of them would soon be pitted against each other. Arthur Bradley, the man who owned the advertising agency where they both worked—the man who owns *us*, Alex thought—was beginning to feel his periodic thirst for blood. Alex knew the signs very well.

Bradley knows I'm ready to move, and the only move in the shop is over Ben. Alex had made his last move—to vice-president for media—just as Ben was hired to be creative vice-president. Ben had been in more agencies than Alex had, and had come up a different way—from the creative side instead of the sales side. That's why he'd known a great deal that Alex had never managed to learn. That, Alex thought, and the fact that he's just frighteningly goddamn smart.

Ben had "fired" the empty gun a few times, learned to cock it by pulling the hammer back with his thumb before aiming. He was ready to fire live ammunition, so Alex handed him six practice bullets, blunt-tipped, filled with only half a load of powder. Ben inserted the bullets, shoved the cylinder into place, and took a stance profiling the target. *Whamp!* A tuft of grass flew away above and behind the target, a couple of yards to the right.

Ben took a breath and steadied himself again. *Whamp!* "Where the hell did that one go?"

"Dunno, I didn't see it either."

Whamp! A corner of the target paper whipped. Alex added, "Not bad." *Whamp!* Ben looked at Alex helplessly and shrugged. "You're low, now," Alex said. "Look in your line of vision—you center the front sight between the sides of the rear sight, right? And then you lift the front sight up so you see all of it, not just the tip-top."

Whamp! "There, now you're just a little high, did you see it? So adjust for that—see a hair less of the front sight."

Whamp! "Okay," Alex said, "now you're off to the side a little. You'll have it all together soon." *Snap!* Empty. Ben opened the gun, ejected the empty shells, and handed it to Alex, holding it the way he'd been shown, with fingers through the pistol's open body.

"At this rate," Ben said drily, "the target will last us a good long while."

Alex loaded and lined up the target in his sights. *Whamp!* Mud kicked up in front of the target. It was his persistent error—squeezing too hard, he unconsciously pulled the muzzle down. Ben hadn't shown any sign of developing that bad habit, the little shit. He seemed to have the gift of holding firm and relaxing at the same time. How do you do that? Tight is *tight*, goddamnit, and relaxed is loose. I couldn't figure that out when my brother was teaching me to shoot pool, and I couldn't figure it out when McNeill tried to explain it to me, either. *Whamp!* On the paper, low and to the right of the circle. That's better. *Whamp!* On paper again.

Alex had provided Bradley with his bloodletting in the past. He had made most of his career at Bradley's, and every move upward had been the result of a confrontation arranged by Arthur Bradley. For Alex to be right in each case, the other guy had to be dead wrong. Most of those men had left Bradley's soon afterward, whether of their own or Bradley's volition. *Whamp!* Low again.

Alex had stopped enjoying the confrontations when he recognized, after only a couple of them, that he was being used, performing in a game that Arthur Bradley owned. Still, Alex was good at it, and he did want to move upward, and that was how it was done. He had made the kill each time. *Whamp!*

But this time was different. Ben Axelrod, goddamnit, is my friend. And I do not shaft my friends. Bradley, you evil sonofabitch—*Whamp!*—"I think that one was in the eye, was it?" Alex pointed the gun at the sky as Ben went to look. Ben touched the bull's eye with his fingertip and grinned—in your eye, Arthur. He aimed again and—*Snap!*—empty. He opened the pistol.

Ben began to find the target with consistency by his fourth or fifth turn of six shots. *Whamp!* He is capable of settling down to a job, Alex thought. As a matter of fact, he's a tough little prick when he has to be. *Whamp!* His face now was utterly without expression.

No tension, no anger, no squinting and no flinching from the shot—*Whamp!*—just a mechanical blink. He's not a killer, though. I know a killer when I see one, and Ben isn't. I think.

What would Ben do if he found himself in a pit with me—one on one for the executive vice-presidency, loser walks off carrying his head under his arm? *Whamp!* Well, he won't let himself be put in that position if he sees it coming; if Bradley were to do something crude like putting us to work on competitive approaches to the same campaign, Ben'll just come to me and make the work cooperative. But it won't be that crude. It isn't that Bradley's so smart, exactly, but he is devious; he has the instincts of a fucking snake.

No, Ben won't see it. He's not paranoid enough for his own good. So what will he do when he's in it? If he doesn't go for my throat, I'm not going to go for his. Alex Klein does not betray his friends. I've seen the kind of conniving, treacherous, low-class—sweaty, by God—*sweaty* little shits who do that, and *I am not one of them.*

Whamp! Ben had not been off the paper in his last two turns. Twelve rounds from ten yards, first lesson, Alex thought. The little sonofabitch, I wonder if he's telling the truth? That he never shot a pistol before? Oh, cut it the hell out. *Snap!* Empty.

The more Alex thought, the less clear it was just whom he was mad at. *Whamp!* He hated Arthur Bradley, and Ben Axelrod was his friend. *Whamp!* But he wanted the job, and it was going to be Ben between him and the job. And it was Ben, God damn him, who had undermined Alex's killer instinct. *Whamp!* Those goddamn lectures—he knew I wasn't just listening so I could be more helpful on the campaigns we were working on, he knew he was preparing me to do a bigger job. *Whamp!* So I can't take a shot at him unless he takes one at me. *Whamp!* Isn't it the shits? I have put my balls right in Ben Axelrod's fist. *Whamp!*

Alex broke open the pistol and offered it to Ben. Ben

shook his head. "Listen, my arms are tired. We've fired a hell of a lot of rounds here." Indeed there was quite a circle of spent shells on the ground.

Alex grinned. "Kinda hypnotic, isn't it?"

"It is. And I was shooting pretty well toward the end there, when I sat down, did you notice?" In his last turn, Ben had sat on the ground with his knees up, resting his stiff, straight arms on them for steadiness. Firing that way, he had been within the second ring of the target—eight inches in diameter—with all six shots. "Don't know how often you'd get to settle into that position before you had to fire, but I just got determined to put slugs into the target whatever way worked."

As Alex gathered up the spent shells—he would have them repacked for target use—the first drops of rain fell.

"Damn," Ben said. "I do *not* feel like running."

But they ran, once Alex had tucked the gun into its holster and the holster inside his pocket. It was half a mile, mostly uphill, so they eased back to a trot and then to a walk. Soon they were too wet to bother running.

Why, Alex said to himself, why don't you tell Ben all of this about Bradley? No. It's too much to give away. Ben had already taken away Alex's license to fight dirty, and that left him feeling ill-equipped for a confrontation if there should be one. He trusted Ben as much as he trusted anyone, but. . . . And there was something else nagging at him. He couldn't identify it, but there was a strange element in the confrontation this time, a wild card.

Whitney? At first, a little, but no more. She's mine in a way she never was his. It's Arthur Bradley. What does he want this time? And what will he do to set us up? He hated bringing Ben in from—oh Jesus, that's the wild card. He had to bring talent in from outside. And now that he's got what he needed from Ben, he wants him killed off.

That's what's different. Arthur Bradley never wanted me to win, before; this time he does. I'll be goddamned.

Well, I'm not going to let it happen. Bradley, you putrid sonofabitch, I won't kill him for you. But I want the job. . . . No. You don't betray your friends. If Bradley wants Ben dead, he'll have to kill him himself.

They crossed the bridge in a steady drizzle and split up, each to his own house for dry clothes.

CHAPTER

11

Annie and Whitney had set up the lunch on a picnic table on the Axelrods' spacious, roofed porch. It was windy and growing cooler. Rain was threatening again. But they'd be sheltered from the downpour, and they wore sweaters against the wind; they had not come to the country to spend their time indoors. The porch was Ben and Annie's favorite "room" during the day, as the big living room with its stone fireplace was at night.

Annie and Whitney were soon joined by Randall and Tim. The four of them decided not to wait for the others; they began eating the salad, drinking the wine, mostly silent. But it's comfortable silence, Whitney thought, somewhat surprised. I'm actually beginning to feel at ease here. They could hear, dimly, under the hum of the wind in the trees, Ben's and Alex's gunshots.

Whitney tensed a little when Karen appeared with Ted and their baby, but even they looked at ease. And very lovey-dovey. Nice, she thought. Ted sat the baby down on the table and admired the salad. "Terrific idea, chef's salad," he said. "I figured you'd just make sand-wiches. This is much better."

Karen smiled fondly at him. Annie, grinning, said, "We thought you'd like this better."

The baby picked up the big wooden pepper mill, leaving a stack of paper napkins under it to the mercy of the wind, which took them immediately. "Lookit!" he screamed, startled but delighted at their mad, fluttering flight off the porch. "Ho!" he yelled, and banged the heels of his new shoes on the table top. They were walking shoes—his second pair already—and they made a very satisfying thump.

As Ted vaulted the porch rail to chase the napkins, Karen picked up Charley. "Oh, you are going to be a nuisance out here, aren't you? What shall I do with you so you won't get bored and make trouble?"

Annie said, "Put him in the kitchen on the floor, why don't you? Give him all those bottles he likes to move around—I've almost as many here as in the city. He loves that, and you can see him from here."

Karen peered through the window. Shading her eyes against the screen, she could see across the end of the living room, past the dining table and into the brightly lighted kitchen.

Satisfied, she took Charley into the kitchen and sat him on the floor. Because she knew Annie's city kitchen, she was able to go with only momentary hesitation to where the spices were kept here, in a cabinet at eye level. She took down about a dozen small bottles and jars and little square tins, and put them on the floor between Charley's outstretched feet. As she set each one down, Charley knocked it over on its side.

When they were all together in a jumble, he began picking them up and standing them in a row. Soon he was absorbed, talking to himself or to the spice jars in peremptory tones, as if giving orders. He didn't notice when Karen left him.

Charley found it very satisfying to manipulate this assortment of objects, to pick them up and put them down in a more pleasing arrangement. It was always the same arrangement, a straight, or anyway nearly straight, line from his left to his right. But it was *his* arrangement. The line set up, he admired it for a moment before sweeping the bottles into a chaotic heap, in order to begin again.

Pausing, he looked up from his objects across the kitchen floor, his eye drawn there by a movement. It was Albie, the Axelrods' cat, slinking cautiously, low to the floor, to a spot alongside a standing cabinet. Once there he flattened to the floor and stretched his neck, thrusting his nose into the space between the cabinet and the refrigerator.

"Ho," said Charley conversationally. "Kit?" The cat ignored him, his tail sweeping a great arc of floor behind him, the rest of his body frozen in place. Only one of his ears, like a tiny radar screen, swiveled momentarily back toward Charley, but quickly returned urgently to the front.

Charley began placing bottles again. He was startled by Albie's sudden movement. Hopping straight backward, stretching upward on stiff legs, the cat arched his back, his hairs bristling.

From between the cabinet and the refrigerator a small head appeared, just a little off the floor. Emerging behind the head was the oddest creature Charley had ever seen. It had no legs. It seemed to be all neck, in fact, as it moved inexorably forward, its head settling smoothly to the floor, its long body beginning to form an S shape behind it as the cat retreated step by step in front of it. It was dark in color, speckled all along its back, utterly hairless and shiny, though not exactly smooth. Its skin was roughly textured in a scaly pattern.

Charley was fascinated. The creature seemed to have no end—it just kept stretching out from that space, growing fatter as it stretched. Albie seemed to want neither to meet it nor to run from it. When the cat stopped and showed the creature his teeth and hissed, swelling himself by folding his tail—now gigantically fat—up over his back, the strange creature halted its forward motion, though its body continued to flow out from its hiding place until a knobby end appeared.

Charley loved this new creature. What a wonderful shape! And how intriguing that the creature was small enough to pick up and carry around, like Teddy, but yet alive, like Mommy and Da and Baggins. And it had a wonderful trick—it could stick out its funny little tongue, wiggle it, and make it disappear again, all without opening its mouth. Its tongue was black, pointed and divided at the tip. The creature's tiny face was otherwise not so pleasant with its blunt nose, its unchanging, rather angry expression and its pale-yellow, unblinking eyes.

Albie didn't seem to like the creature. Well, Charley didn't like Albie much, either. More than once Charley had tried to pick up Albie and carry him around, and Albie wouldn't put up with it. Once Charley had backed Albie into a corner and Albie had swelled up in this same way and shown him his teeth and hissed, and Charley had been scared and left him alone.

Charley talked to the cat. "Ho!" he said sternly. "Lookit." The cat's concentration was broken; an ear swiveled toward Charley and one of his forepaws, which had been raised as if to swat at the strange creature, dropped uncertainly to the floor. The creature magically changed shape, gathering itself into a sort of heap and drawing its head back.

"Lookit!" Charley insisted, and tossed a spice bottle. It flew almost straight in the air and came down just in front of Charley. Its flight attracted the eye of the long creature, which looked then at Charley and became still once again—except for that darting little tongue.

Charley was charmed. He smiled and stuck out his own tongue at the creature, which looked now from the cat to Charley and back again. It seemed to be uncertain about which of them to go to next. Charley waved at it and spoke again—"Ho, lookit"—trying to get it to come play with him. The creature fixed its gaze stonily on Charley now, and then began to make a dry, rattling sound that somehow seemed unfriendly. Charley began to wonder uneasily if it wanted to play nicely or not.

But the cat had his own ideas. Once the creature's gaze was fixed firmly on Charley, Albie inched closer to its coiled body. When the knobby tail began to vibrate to produce the whirring sound that unsettled Charley, Albie attacked, whipping at the vibrating part with extended claws. His claws caught firmly in that appendage. The sound stopped and the rattles popped off the snake and flew across the kitchen floor. Albie flew after them instantly, and never noticed that the snake struck at his fat tail as he flew by.

Charley was startled by the size of the strange creature's pink mouth, opened momentarily to amazing width, and the length of the curved, needle-sharp teeth as they passed harmlessly through the bristling hair of the cat's tail. The snake slapped down on the tile floor and slid several inches nearer Charley, though still the height of a grown person away from him. It drew itself into a heap again, and made its stub of a tail vibrate again, but now it was silent.

On the porch, Karen heard odd sounds in the kitchen. Both Tim and Randall looked up when the whirring rattle sounded, but it stopped almost instantly. Karen looked inside, hand beside her eyes against the screen, through the door to the kitchen. She could see Charley, ignoring Albie. She looked up and shrugged. "Cat's in there with him, playing with something on the floor."

Annie said, "Oh, good, he must've located one of his toys. He'll bat it under something else in two minutes and it'll be lost again."

In the kitchen, the rattlesnake slid its head down off the coiled heap of its body and moved toward its hiding place. But Albie, who had already lost his new toy by knocking it under the same cabinet the snake had come from in the first place, had now stationed himself there, directly in the snake's path to safety.

The snake reversed itself in a big U on the floor.

Charley watched as it changed directions, away from Albie the cat and straight toward Charley. He supposed the creature wanted to be friends, but when he waved his arms in welcome, it became still for a moment. Then it moved forward once again, so smooth and effortless in its peculiar legless motion that Charley didn't realize that the snake was coming toward him until its mean-looking little blunt nose was almost touching Charley's foot. Charley banged his heel down on the floor.

The creature stopped again, its stony gaze fixed on Charley's foot. Charley became decidedly uneasy. He couldn't take his eyes away from the creature's un-blinking yellow stare. The thing was *not* friendly. It had horrifying long teeth, though they were hidden now, and its wedge-shaped, scaly little head, with the slit mouth and the ridge of bone above the eyes, looked angry. And its shape was beginning to unsettle Charley, too. He was not comfortable, not being sure whether it was even moving or not. Live creatures were supposed to have arms and legs.

Charley banged his heel again, and set off sudden movement on both sides of the floor. As the cat leaped to the top of the cabinet across the room, attracting Charley's attention, the snake bunched its body and drew back its head. Again Charley raised his foot and the creature opened its mouth and extended its fangs and struck, thumping those terrible tiny swords hard against the hard leather sole of Charley's shoe, where they left two tiny indentations, wet with venom.

Thwarted yet again, the rattlesnake drew away from Charley, turned and looked to its original hiding place—now unguarded. The snake moved quickly toward it.

Charley, startled and scared when the creature attacked the bottom of his foot, screamed. "Ho-o!" he yelled, "Maa!" and then began to scream in earnest, bawling his terror, demanding that Mommy come instantly and deliver him from this fear.

Instantly she was there—she always was—swooping

him up in her arms, hugging him, his face against her neck, cooing to him. Charley yelled once or twice more, snuffled, raised his head and looked toward the snake's hiding place. Pointing, he commanded his mother, "Lookit!"

Karen knew that Charley didn't usually mean "lookit" when he said "lookit," but she always looked anyway. There was nothing to see where Charley was pointing except the cat sitting on top of a cabinet switching its fat tail. "Yes, that's Albie—Albee—'s'matter, he doesn't want to play with you? Well, he's a snooty cat and he thinks you're a ruffian. C'mon, we'll go out with the big people."

"Ho?" said Charley.

Annie and Ben were left alone on their porch. Everyone had gone to his own house, having agreed to meet here again for dinner, late. Whitney had wrapped some lunch for Alex and had run through the rain with it so he wouldn't have to come out in such bad weather. The rain was heavy now, with intermittent thunder and lightning, but the wind had subsided.

Annie looked across the table at Ben, who sat with his feet up on the porch railing—they were well under the overhung roof—smoking a cigar, sipping at a glass of beer, reading a book. It was a baseball book by a *New Yorker* writer. One of the stereo speakers was set in the window behind him, and played jazz piano for him.

She couldn't resist interrupting his reading to say, "I've never seen you looking more content."

He looked up, solemnly pensive. After a moment he smiled and shook his head gently.

Annie said, "What?" If that was his third beer, he was probably about to be philosophical. She often liked that, when he wasn't too whimsical to follow.

"You're right, I am content. Very. Your saying it made me think . . . isn't it odd—this is who I grew up to be."

Hmm. He's going to be philosophical, all right. But whimsical, I'm afraid. "I don't understand."

"Well, here's what it takes to make me content. It's not what I would have predicted. Here I sit on my porch on a mountain in the Catskills—not a deck on a beach house at Amagansett, or the balcony of a *pensione* in Portofino, or—and not sipping a unique little *vin du pays* that I have flown in special, but slurping beer—and not even German beer at cellar temperature, but ice-cold Miller's. And smoking a cigar—lovely cigar, by the way, thank you—and listening to Marian McPartland and reading a baseball book. Not listening to Landowska and reading Proust, or Cecil Taylor and *Artforum*, or—well, you see?"

"I still don't. . . . You like those other things, too."

He nodded. "Some of them. But these are the things I picked out, without thinking about it." He smiled again. "It's okay. I'm even content that it's those things that make me *most* content. But I am a little surprised."

She smiled and nodded. "That you're so square."

"Yeah."

"And sitting here with ol' pregnant Annie instead of—who, Jane Fonda? Liv Ullman?"

He sighed a fine, big sigh and puffed at this cigar. "Nah. No way I could have picked anybody better to sit with. Would Jane Fonda remember my cigars? Would Stevie Nicks? Would Jane Curtin? Would—"

"All *right*. Smartass." She got up. "Want another beer? I'm going to get some more wine."

"No, this is my third, already, and it's making me sleepy. Think I'll nap. I'll do my work tomorrow." He closed his book and got up.

"I'll join you," she said.

He came around the table and put an arm around her waist. "Good. I'm not in a red-hot hurry to go to sleep." And his hand moved down her back to her bottom, where he petted her gently. "It's true, you know—there's no way in the world I could do better."

"You're damn right," she said, and held him hard.

Alex lay back, naked, spent, Whitney across him,

spent too. Their breathing had become even and was in perfect complement now. Alex stared at the ceiling, then down at the top of Whitney's head and over her creamy back at her round white bottom and along the length of their intertwined legs, hers tan and smooth, his white, whorled with black hair.

Alex felt as if he was only just coming back to himself, after having been somewhere he couldn't remember. Is it more of her that I'm getting, he wondered—or more of myself? That is scary, how—open I am when—

"Do you know what I think?" Whitney said softly.

"No, what?"

She spoke into his chest, not looking up at him. "I—" He felt her swallow. "I think I love . . . having you—being so close to you and having—I think I love you, Alex. I think I want you to love me."

"I—"

"Or else go away," she said in a tiny voice that seemed to have some bitterness in it, "and let me be."

"Whitney—"

"No. I don't want you to go away, anyway, just—"

"I want you to marry me, Whitney."

Her sob shook them both on the bed. "Oh, Jesus, Alex." Alex petted her head as she wept. He wondered how he was going to like being so confused so much of the time. And scared. Jesus, how did she get me to say that? Oh, Christ, and I think I meant it, too.

Tim looked up from the chessboard. "Y'know, for a second I'd've sworn that sound in Annie's kitchen was the same as the one in the woods, before. That rustling sound."

Randall studied a knight. He had something in mind for that knight, as soon as Tim committed his queen's rook. He would, soon. Never failed. But how soon?

Tim persisted. "It's a creepy sound. I swear it's like a rattlesnake."

"What?" Randall looked up. "Where did you ever hear a rattlesnake?"

"In movies. Westerns."

Randall nodded. Case closed, he thought.

Tim was not satisfied. "Well, did *you* ever hear one?"

Randall nodded, his eyes still on the board.

"Well?"

Randall looked up, irritated. "Well, what?"

"Well, did that sound like one, or not?"

Oh, for Christ's sake. "It might've," Randall said. "It might've been a locust, or a tree frog, too. I don't know. It's been a long time. But there aren't any exotic deadly beasts up here, Tim. I mean, just because there isn't a gay disco in a hundred miles doesn't make it the Mato Grosso, or something."

"The what?"

"Oh, never mind." Randall sighed and moved the knight. Something would develop for it, pretty soon. Tim would deploy that rook.

Tim looked at the board for just a few seconds before he picked up his queen, set her down on Randall's third rank replacing a pawn, and said, "Check. And mate."

It took Randall only a single second to recognize that moving the knight on impulse had exposed him. He looked up at Tim's innocent expression. "You treacherous bitch," he said admiringly.

Ted was sleepy, but so was Karen, and Charley was anything but. The argument about who would drink some coffee and stay awake—each insisting that the other nap—was so loving, so dramatically different from the week-long wrangling that was so recently past, that Ted grinned in wonderment as he sipped his coffee.

Charley had a new toy. He had found a length of clothesline rope that had been around a carton of dishes they'd brought up with them from the city. It had been lying in the empty carton all along, but Charley hadn't been interested before. Now he had decided it was fascinating. It was about twice as long as Charley.

He seemed to have a rather interestingly complex

love-hate relationship with the rope. First he'd drape it over his shoulder and toddle about with it, and then suddenly he'd grab it and fling it. He seemed to mean to slam the rope to the floor, but mostly what he accomplished was simply to toss it away from him. Then he'd yell at it and walk over and stomp on it.

Amazing, Ted thought. Little imagination never stops humming along.

PART

III

The mountain king had attempted to find a way out of the cave during the daylight hours, when the temperature rose high enough that his body became supple. He had found none.

The erratic stream of water that flowed where the floor of the cave had collapsed was still there, and still dangerous, but no snakes had fallen prey to it in some hours. The king had returned to his ledge in the depths of the cave, and had now been there through daylight and several hours of darkness.

This night was warmer than the previous one, and the king and his kind were more alert. The king's persistent sense of uncertainty in the mountain beneath and about him had grown more vivid, then subsided, then returned, only to disappear yet again.

And once again came back, to last only seconds—so brief a time as scarcely to make the king aware he had it again—when the catastrophe occurred. The world of the mountain king lost all solidity and shape. The foremost part of the wide floor of the cave fell away; the remainder tilted radically so that the teeming mass of rattlesnakes slid and tumbled over each other out into empty space.

The ledge on which the king rested fell away, dumping him on the precipitously steep floor of the cave. He slid, writhing desperately, toward the face of the cliff and off it, into the black night air. Flailing helplessly, he flew into a limb of the great maple tree. He slammed off the limb, fell to another, was struck by a powerful rushing wave of water and torn off the second limb, fell again through empty blackness and crashed heavily to earth.

Stunned, he reflexively turned himself so that his stomach ridges could find some purchase on the ground—and in doing so he rolled himself over the lip of still another drop, this time into the torrential stream down the mountain. In attempting to inflate his long, single lung to ensure that he would float, he took in water and nearly drowned as he was swept away, scraped against the bed of the stream, carried still farther down until his body was lifted suddenly where the water rose over a rocky outcropping in the bed of the stream, and flung onto grassy mud.

He was no longer even dimly conscious. His body had absorbed terrible punishment. Ribs were broken and his skin torn, and the multiple shocks to his nervous system had been too much. Even his reflexes were still.

CHAPTER

12

The smell of the earth in the basement of Ben's house was rich and full of texture, a smell so dense he could almost chew on it. The reason the odor was so strong, of course, was that the earth was wet and the basement was far from tight. The rain had been heavy since midafternoon, letting up only minutes ago.

He had come down to see how badly the water was puddling, not because he would know what to do if it was at a worrisome level—hell, he thought, I don't even know how much is a worrisome level. He had come, in fact, in exactly the same spirit that he opened the hood of his car if the engine stopped running—I don't know what to look at in there, either, but I always raise the hood and stare in. I guess I hope that one of those odd-shaped things will look up at me and say, "Me. Give me a little turn to the right and we'll all go back to work for you."

He moved to the wettest of the fieldstone walls, under the stairway down from the kitchen, at the rear of the house. It was dark back there, but he had brought a flashlight with him. The light gleamed off the wet stones. He resisted momentarily the impulse to place the palm of his hand on the wall. After I've stared at the engine for a while, Ben reflected, I think I usually kick a tire.

He had come down here also because he was beginning to get cabin-itis. It was nearly midnight now. The whole bunch had eaten dinner in his house, and all were still upstairs in the living room. It had been very pleasant, really, the talk interesting and funny, the Monopoly game—Ben's first since childhood—wonderfully absorbing and nostalgic. But it was a lot of togetherness for him. Too many people in too little space. Too many emotional currents running, though God knows everybody was on best behavior.

He gave in to the impulse to put his hand against the wet wall. Yes, sir, by God! Feels wet. But, though he mocked himself, he was reassured. The flow was not as fast as it looked in the flashlight gleam. It was, in fact, merely wet—not flowing at all. Well, good. House probably won't wash away down the mountain before morning.

As he was about to pull his hand away he felt a faint vibration in the stone. He held his hand against the wall for a moment, then yanked it away in panic. He thought for a fraction of a second that he was picking up an electrical charge. Then came the sound, faint at first and apparently distant but awesome in depth and growing in volume. An earthquake. He could feel it in his feet.

Oh, God, it's coming apart. This whole enormous goddamn mountain is coming—no, it's not. Something in the quality of the sound and the feel of it had come clearer to him. It wasn't an earthquake, it was a landslide.

The sound was to his left and above him, growing louder—suddenly softer—and then still louder than before, gathering more sounds to itself, sounds of wood splintering mixing with the scraping roar—*the goddamn mountain is coming down on top of us!* "Get down!"

he yelled. Then a single profound thump that he could feel in all his bones, a couple of seconds of after-rumble ending with a small, anticlimactic, almost comically trivial noise of breaking wood and the tinkling of broken glass—perhaps just one window in one of the houses: Ted's house, by the direction of the sound. Then silence, and the light, cheerful plinking of the rain dripping from the eaves.

He could hear voices now. "Ben? *Ben?*" That was Annie. "Charley?" That was Karen. Charley had been asleep on Ben and Annie's bed, walled in by pillows. And both dogs barking madly. Ben breathed at last, and became aware that he'd been holding his breath. He moved out from under the cellar stairs and realized that there were no lights. Well, right. The electricity comes into all three houses through Ted's house. It *was* Ted's house being hit that made the last sound. I wonder if we have phones. Surely not.

With the brilliant flashlight he had no trouble finding the bottom of the stairs, but in leaping up them two at a time he stumbled at the very first leap and banged his shin hard. He discovered that his knees were shaky and weak. Jesus, am I scared? Oh, yeah.

Annie was waiting for him in the darkness at the top. "Ben? Ben?" She was crying softly. Beyond her, in the living room, he could hear voices and nervous laughter, the baby crying and the dogs.

Ben took a deep breath and put an arm around Annie. "We're okay," he said. "We're safe." In fact he was half-sick with fear and self-reproach. How could I—how could any of us—have been so oblivious? Once a little bit of that cliff cracked off last night, we should have known that more of it might be loose. And still is, as far as we know. We're not safe, at all. But he petted Annie's shoulder reassuringly.

Ted, once he had seen that Charley was all right in Karen's arms, moved gingerly through the darkness toward the back door. My house! he was thinking, my thirty-three-thousand-three-hundred-and-thirty-three-dollar house! In the kitchen, at the top of the cellar stairs, he found Ben and Annie, embracing, lit by the flashlight in Ben's right hand. Ben looked up over Annie's shoulder, his eyes tellingly wide and gleaming bizarrely in the flashlight's beam.

Ben said to Annie, "Come on, now, get some candles and the hurricane lamps."

Ted said, "I have to look at my house."

Ben looked at him questioningly, then said, "Wait a minute, 'til we get some candles lit." And Annie moved to the kitchen cabinets.

Damn, Ted thought. My house is buried. My house, which I went into hock to buy. My house, which I may want to live in if I quit working to sculpt, has just disappeared under a thousand tons of rock. *Damn!*

He played back the sound of the slide in his mind. Not such a huge crash at the end, there, maybe it's not so bad. Maybe it's just busted in the wall in the spare bedroom.

As Annie moved out of the kitchen toward the living room, a hurricane lamp in her hand created a wide area of flickering light. Ben handed Ted the flashlight. Ted followed Annie to the front of the house. His rain slicker was on the front porch, hanging from a peg. The living room was full of nervous movements and darting shadows. Alex stood, hands on hips, looking fierce. Lighten up, dummy, Ted said to him silently, you can't punch out a landslide.

He spoke to Karen. "I'm going to have a look at the damage."

"Be careful," she said.

"Yeah, right," Ted said perfunctorily, but he thought, Careful of what?

"I mean—look, are you sure you should go at all? There may be more to come down."

Oh, shit, of course. There might be. "Well, look," Ted said, "uh—if more does come, I'll hear it in plenty of time to get back in here. This house is so solid we're safe in here whatever happens." I hope. In fact, big fella, it really isn't all that smart to go out there. And who knows if it's safe in here?

He was paralyzed for a moment, not so much by fear as by indecision, until Ben said, "Ted, you better go out. See if a car could make it around the front of your house without getting stuck in the mud. I looked out the back door, and it seems like the slide has cut off the driveway behind your house."

So Ben thinks we should get out of here. Oh, Jesus, the car: "How's my car?" Ted asked.

"I couldn't see very clearly, but I think it's okay. We've other cars, anyway. Listen, look at the bridge, too—make sure the slide didn't get it."

Yeah, right, Ted thought. He's in a hurry to get out of here.

As Ted went out the door, accompanied by both dogs, he heard several voices at once. Alex, indignant: "We're not gonna run?" Whitney, her voice bright but thin: "Hey, folks, how strong *is* this house?" Randall, quietly, "Ben, we'll never get through the flood." Annie: "Ben? Ben?"

Annie sounds a little nuts, Ted thought. And, Jesus, Alex's macho's up. Well, Ben will preside over a strategy session. I've seen him do that dozens of times at work. He's good at that; he'll get everybody settled down and thinking calmly pretty soon.

Awkwardly, Ted held the flashlight by its handle as he pulled on his hooded slicker and tugged rubber galoshes over his shoes. The dogs waited for him, still on the porch. Now that they realized it was raining out here, they weren't so eager for the adventure. It had let up quite a lot, though. At least for the moment it was just a steady drizzle. The wind had gone down some time ago.

The porch was faintly lit in spots by lamplight through the windows; all else was utterly, dizzyingly black. The rushing stream that he was walking toward when he left the porch was as noisy as ever, and he used the sound to orient himself. My God, he thought, it's *dark*. But for the ghostly lights in the windows behind him and the flashlight's beam, all was as profoundly, impenetrably black as—nothing. The end of the world. He could scarcely feel which was was up and which down; certainly he could not see where mountain ended and sky began. The very slight slope in the ground under him added to the feeling of vertigo.

Ted shook himself, shaking off the eerie feeling. He directed the flashlight around on the ground. The grass glistened jewelly bright when the flashlight beam struck it just so. The rain was really mist, barely heavier than fog. It glared back at him when he shone the beam of light straight out in front of him. The earth seemed spongy, surprisingly resilient considering the amount of rain. He thought a car might make it.

Swinging the light up toward the mountain above and behind the houses in a hopeless attempt to see the broken cliff, he saw instead, looming shockingly close in front of him, his own porch. He was startled, and froze in midstep. Ted had thought he was much farther out on the lawn, and for a dizzy half-second he thought the house had moved. Ridiculous; it's sitting very comfortably on its foundation, just where it belongs.

Ted directed the beam of light back on Ben and Annie's porch, where it picked out the two dogs, sitting under the roof looking curiously at him out in the rain. He was just admiring their good sense when Baggins, followed immediately by little Dinny, bounded onto the lawn and rushed to join him. Oh, of course, it's past dinner time for Baggins, he thinks I've come over here to feed him. And the little one just follows Baggins. Wet for nothing, stupid dogs.

The front door opened easily, which Ted decided was a good sign. If the landslide had knocked the house out of whack, the door might've stuck. The dogs had caught up with him and followed him inside. He crossed the

living room to the door to what they called the spare
bedroom because they had found a bed in it when they
bought the house—in fact it had never been used and
they hadn't decided what to do with it.

This door opened freely, too, at first. So far, so good.
He pushed it open and the dogs preceded him through it
into the blackness. Partway open, the door seemed to
meet some light obstacle which was pushed along the
floor without giving serious resistance, making a soft
sliding sound as though the door had a leather strip on
its bottom.

What occurred next happened so suddenly, and in so
many parts at once, that Ted was shocked into bewilder-
ment for a few seconds as he sorted it out. First, he
heard the alarming sound of Baggins' deep, seriously
threatening growl—*someone's in here!*—and then a
whirring, rasping noise coming from—where?—all over
the room. Then the small dog yipping. Ted flashed the
light inside the room and saw a broken window and the
wall caved in below and beside it, a sort of mudbank
coming in there and reaching toward the bed, and
movement on the mudbank and on the bed and
—movement everywhere. The room was alive. *What in
God's*—snakes? *Snakes?*

The barking of the dogs was suddenly volcanic. The
bedsprings whined and Ted darted the light beam
toward it. Baggins had leaped up there. He was standing
stiff-legged, shaking his head furiously, growling
savagely, grasping a long snake—five feet, it must
be—in his mouth. Dinny's barking had stopped. Ted
flashed to the floor and saw that Dinny had grabbed up
a snake just as Baggins had, a snake even bigger than
Baggins', which writhed and struck at the little dog,
sinking vicious fangs into his shoulder. Dinny dropped
the snake and howled, but he picked up another and
shook it as his first one flopped, belly up, apparently
broken somewhere.

The flashlight had its own volition, flitting here and

there, to the big dog on the bed, to the floor in front of Ted's feet—a snake was coiled there, seemingly glaring at Ted's booted feet. Ted stood frozen in shock. The whirring sound was an insistent and painful as sandpaper inside his skull, not louder but more penetrating than the now pitiful howling of the dogs. There was a slapping sound as Baggins tossed a small snake out of the mass on the bed, onto the floor, butting it with his nose as he grabbed up another in his teeth to shake and bite and kill.

But Baggins, too, had been bitten, repeatedly—there was even one of the dark, spotted, leathery horrors hanging from his rib cage now, fangs caught in his body. Dinny had fallen over on his side on the floor; the sound that came from his open mouth was a thin, whistling, almost-whine. Baggins had sat down among the snakes on the bare mattress of the bed. He looked bewildered. He sat still, now, a snake dangling from his open jaws for a second before it flopped itself free, to land on the floor with a heavy thud.

"Baggins?" Ted said. But Baggins, who was stiffly maintaining his sitting-up, alert-appearing posture, did not hear. He was trembling violently. More snakes struck him, each with a soft *thump!* His forelegs remained stiff and trembling, but his paws seemed to have lost their grip on the mattress. His legs stretched slowly forward and his wide-eyed, slack-jawed head lowered slowly until his silky chin touched down. There were more thumps, more strikes, but no more need of them.

Baggins had not stopped trembling when Ted felt a powerful blow on his toe. He jerked his foot back and darted the flashlight beam to it and found a snake, two inches in diameter, more than three feet long, fastened to his foot by its gaping mouth. Its fangs had easily penetrated the rubber boot, but were now caught between the rubber and the leather of his shoe.

"Oh, Jesus, oh, God, *get away from me*!" And he

kicked out violently, succeeding only in swinging the snake in a great eccentric arc, its knobby tail snapping past Ted's eyes. Finally, when he stomped the foot down on the floor again the blunt, bony head flopped free and the snake crawled quickly away into the bedroom, over shards of glass, piles of lath and plaster and other snakes.

Finally galvanized into movement, Ted stepped back and yanked the door shut behind him—on the thick body of still another snake, just coming through to the living room. He tugged, crushing bones as the snake darted its head viciously at his retreating ankle, darted again and then darted once more, aimlessly, convulsively—and was still. Ted continued to tug at the door with all his strength, crushing the snake's thick body nearly in two. The door did not latch, but was stuck tight on the tough body.

It required an effort of will to unlock his hand from the doorknob and walk—stagger—away toward the outside door. He wanted to vomit but didn't, he wanted to scream but couldn't get enough breath. He was seized by a fit that was something like sobbing and something like retching, that spent itself quickly.

He stood, shaking and breathing hugely, against the outside door. Jesus, the poor dogs, the poor, stupid dogs. Rattlesnakes? *Rattlesnakes?* But he didn't think he could say it enough times to make himself believe it. Poor Baggins. Jesus, he was brave, though. Killed a lot of them, by God. . . .

But *rattlesnakes*? He couldn't think where they might have come from. Have they been there all the time? Wait—did Baggins kill that many? There were a lot of dead ones on the floor. Crushed, some. Christ, they came down the mountain. They slid down on us.

Ted opened the door and went out into the darkness. As he crossed the porch, just before he stepped off it onto the lawn, it occurred to him that they might be all over everywhere. He was seized by a horrifying vision of a cascade of snakes, a writhing flood descending on the houses from up the mountain.

He shook himself. Nonsense. Some came down with the rocks. They must have lived up there, a family of them. Well, all right. Watch your step.

CHAPTER

13

Annie stood in the doorway between her kitchen and the small end of her living room, where all the others had gathered around the dining table. After an interval of nervous joking and mild hysteria, Ben had moved to an end of the big table and the others had gravitated to it and taken seats. Now they seemed to have settled into a sort of strategy session.

Calmer now, Annie was beginning to be alarmed at how crazy she'd been. At the beginning of the slide, when she'd first felt the vibrations in the floor, she'd thought it was an earthquake; the sensation was that something of awesome size and power had stirred to life within the mountain. She had felt her belly, reflexively touching it with the flat of her hand, feeling for . . . what? She didn't know. Something stirring to life that would be too powerful to contain? Well, yes, my God, a person's growing in there; a whole, complicated being who'll have a personality, a history—a person that I'll have to contain for nine months and then for twenty years, or—a lifetime.

Oh, no, baby, it's all right. Don't be afraid to grow big and strong; you won't hurt me, I'm strong, too, I can hold you and take care of you until you're ready, and then I'll help you be born. And I'll let you be free, too, when it's time. I will.

The first time she found herself talking to her baby—only a couple of days ago—she had laughed at herself. But no more. She supposed she was really talking to herself, but it felt good to think of the baby as already real. It felt right. They were partners.

Annie was standing in the kitchen door listening to the coffee perk. When all the fuss began Ben had told her, rather peremptorily, to make coffee. She had responded automatically—something about the calm authority in his manner, for one thing, and then she'd been glad enough of something practical to focus on at the time. It had required her attention to dig out the old coffeepot, and then she was no longer used to making coffee in a regular pot on the stove.

Ben looked up at her now. "Coffee ready, you think?"

She shook her head and said nothing. As she calmed down she had grown a little resentful at having been summarily assigned the lady's part in an emergency. She wasn't used to that, and it was unlike Ben to expect it, or to give her orders for that matter. Who the hell does he think he is, all of a sudden? Hot cawfeh, ma'am. John Wayne.

She decided it had probably perked enough, so she went into the candle-lit kitchen and poured herself a cup. "It's ready," she said from the doorway. If he thinks I'm going to serve it, he's got another thing coming. But Ben was already up and on his way past her to get it himself; the others followed after a half-second pause. Well, so what was he doing before, giving me orders? Being a big shot, taking charge; taking responsibility.

In fact, she now realized, that was what had happened: Everyone in the place had quickly assumed that

Ben would be in charge of getting them out of here, if getting out was what was wanted. Well, maybe everybody but Alex. Alex looks furious. But then Alex always does.

Though she had scarcely been aware of the conversation around the table, Annie found now that she remembered it clearly enough. Alex seemed somehow to hate the idea of leaving. Not that he likes it here so much, I think. Rather it offends him to have to back down from a mere mountain. Alex would get his big pistol and shoot the next landslide that comes down.

The others were calm enough now. She had thought it ludicrous to call a meeting of the board as a response to a landslide, but it seemed to have worked. Everybody got to vent their fear in their various ways first: Karen fluttering fussily over her baby, saying nothing to the group; Whitney making nervous jokes; Alex snapping; Randall quiet and very grave; Tim joking rather bitingly about the folly of coming to Mutual of Omaha's Wild Kingdom in the first place.

And Ben, she thought, Ben joked with the jokers, bitched with the bitchers, kept everybody talking who wanted to talk. Damn, I believe he knows what he's doing. And gave me something practical to do when I was almost hysterical—and found a constructive use for Ted's nervous impulse to go outside. Sonofagun. But now what? How will the creative vice-president of Arthur Bradley Associates negotiate with a landslide?

A fresh breeze caused her to look at the door. Ted had returned. He was silent, looking around at their faces. He appeared stunned, actually. When Ben came out of the kitchen, Ted spoke. "Ben. Everybody? We have—snakes." He seemed to have barely enough breath to make his voice heard.

Ben asked calmly, "What kind of snakes?"

Ted hesitated another moment before speaking again. "We have rattlesnakes, hundreds of them. They killed the dogs. Both dogs. They tried to get me—" His voice rising in pitch as he spoke faster.

Dinny? Annie thought, My Dinny's dead? My poor little old man? And beautiful Baggins? What kind of a thing would do that to Dinny? Oh, God, *rattlesnakes*?

"They've come down on us with the landslide," Ted said. "They must have lived up there by the face."

"*In* the face," Ben said. "I bet they lived in it. I always thought the face's mouth might be deep. What, uh—what do they look like?"

"Look—? Well, they're dark, black I guess, and spotted across their backs."

Ben nodded. "Sshhit," he said softly. "Yellow spots?"

"I don't know, could be, white or yellow, some lighter or brighter than others. What—?"

But Ben shook his head. "Annie?" he said.

It was a den, she was thinking, for hibernating over the winter. Oh, God, there must've been— "What?" she managed, and then, "Dinny's dead? Oh, Ben, the *kitten*, the poor—do you think—?"

"Could be," Ben said, and went on, his voice smoothly insistent. "Annie, you know about rattlesnakes. Do they live around here? I thought they only lived out West."

"I don't know. I thought so, too. The ones in the film were in the desert. New Mexico." Annie had once edited a film on rattlesnakes from twenty-four minutes down to twelve for a Saturday morning children's program. By the time she was finished she knew the whole twenty-four minutes by heart. But a TV nature film? How is that going to help? This is *real*.

"Tell us what you know," he said firmly.

Annie looked around. There was not a closed mouth in the room. They're stunned and about to panic. Okay, so Ben wants me to make calm noises—a nice reasonable lecture. Right. "Well—there are several species, all pretty much alike, so even though I don't know what kind we have around here, what I know probably applies to these." And she began reciting facts as they came 'to her, as she replayed the film in her mind.

"The rattles are harmless. And, uh . . . you can't tell their age from them because they're brittle, and break off easily. They're rings of dried, dead skin that are left behind when they shed, and they interlock loosely so when they shake their tails they rustle together. . . ."

Alex demanded, "How do you know about rattlesnakes?"

She went right on, "And the tongue's harmless. Looks wicked, but they just smell with it. The teeth are like hypodermics, they're hollow. They inject you —literally—with their poison. The poison is for killing small animals for food, which they swallow whole. So they only look to kill small things, unless they're really seriously threatened. People get bitten-when they step on them or something. Uh—they're immune to their own venom."

Ben said, "Do they live together in—packs, or whatever?"

"Well, no, except, yes, they do in the winter. They come together, to a cave where they won't freeze, to hibernate. They all go their own way during the summer—they don't pair off or anything, either, just mate in season and never see each other again—but there's a transitional stage in the spring when they're dormant, like hibernating, at night when it's cool, but in the warm day they're out and about, active or partly active. In the fall, too."

"How many come together?"

"Two hundred." There was a gasp and some low whistles. "Two hundred is common." Actually, Annie wasn't so sure of the number as she pretended. She thought it might be three hundred. But it was her job now to be as right as she could be, and in any case to sound authoritative—that's how she'd help them stay calm enough to function.

She had become aware that Alex was off somewhere

on his own. He and Whitney had played out a tense and interesting little drama early in her speech. Alex had whispered "sonofabitch," stood up from the table, crossed his arms and hunched his shoulders forward. Getting a grip on himself, Annie had thought—his rage is becoming too much to contain. But she had gone on talking.

Alex had turned and walked away from the table, out of the circle of light from the hurricane lamp. Whitney had stared after him, clearly concerned, then turned her attention back to Ben. Annie thought then, damn right—you know who's gonna keep us safe. But she had kept on talking: "See, they're cold-blooded. That means their body temperature is the same as the outside temperature—they don't have the ability to keep it uniform. And when it gets cold outside, they get cold inside, and become dormant, no matter what time of year it is."

"How cold is that?" Ben asked.

She thought for a moment. No, it's no use faking the answer, I just don't know, and it might be important. She shook her head and shrugged.

She saw Whitney turn away, then rise and leave the table to join Alex in the darkness. They went together into the kitchen. And Annie thought, oh, dear, you're right to do that, but be careful of him—and went on talking.

"They're very primitive creatures. Very simple bodies, extremely simple brains—just a cluster of nerve cells, hardly a brain at all, really. The only thing that's sophisticated about them is their—what would you call it?—their sensitivity. They're very sensitive to vibrations in the air or in the ground. They have no hearing, but some sounds seem to have an effect on them, as vibrations in the air. And they have these pits on their head—the pits are like heat sensors. They pick up the warmth of a live creature, and even tell what direction he's in, so they can hunt in the dark. They can detect a mouse, say, in a dark hole, by the warmth his body gives off.'' She remembered a snake in the film doing that, striking, killing—and she thought of the kitten, horrified.

Whitney had come back from the kitchen, looking uneasy, and Alex hadn't. All right, where is the crazy fool? Annie surreptitiously looked a question at Ben, but Ben just shrugged with his eyebrows and nodded at her to go ahead.

But Randall interrupted. ''Look, folks, none of this matters if we can get out of here. Hadn't we better go down and try the flood?''

Tim said, ''We are not going to make it through the flood. It's rained more today than it did yesterday, and we came within inches of washing down the mountain. I'm not kidding''—he looked around at the others—''we joked about it, but it was no joke. I wouldn't go into it again.''

Randall nodded. ''I think you're right. I don't believe it'll be passable, either. Still, if more of the mountain's going to come down, and now we have—how many, two *hundred*?—*rattlesnakes* to contend with, we can't just sit here and say it's impassable. We've got to go look.''

Tim was insistent. ''We could barricade ourselves against the snakes until the water recedes, and I don't believe there's gonna be another slide—anyway, I'll take my chances before I'll drive into that water again. I'm not kidding, I won't do it, and I don't think anybody else should, either. Please don't.''

''Yeah, all right,'' Ben said. ''And while we're talking, the flood's rising. Let's—'' That was when they heard the first gunshot.

Alex hated the idea that they were going to run away. He knew that's what all the talk was leading to. Ben's going to let everybody blow off some steam, argue until we've gotten confused and exhausted, and then announce that we've got to split. I've seen him do it at work, and he's doing the same thing here. First he says what he thinks maybe we should think about; then he throws the floor open and everybody gets to talk; and we end up doing just what he said in the first place. And everybody agrees, just because they're relieved that someone was willing to take responsibility for a decision.

Well, not me. We are not helpless here. *I'm* not. Alex had opened the trunk of his car and, by its automatic light, was removing the pistol, loading it and emptying a box of shells into one of the pockets of his ski jacket. He reached back in and picked up the flashlight, an old, long five-cell that he hadn't had occasion to use in many months. I'm gonna take the snakes out of the picture, and then we'll see. Clean the sonsabitches out. He moved through the mist toward Ted's house, watching the ground with the feeble beam of the flashlight.

How *does* he take charge, anyway? He didn't say a whole lot, just moved to the table and sat down, and everybody fell into the pattern: Ben's the man. Sonofabitch, for a guy who isn't a killer, he sure gets his own way a lot.

Alex opened the door to Ted's house and shined the flashlight inside. The light went out as he moved it, and he gave it a quick shake to bring it back on. Damn, I forgot it did that. It came back on brighter than before, though. He swept the beam very slowly across the floor. The bottom dropped out of his stomach when he saw two and a half feet of snake protruding from the door on the opposite side of the room. He began shaking, and did not stop when he realized the snake was dead.

He could hear rattling, now, that started and then stopped after just a second or two, then began again and stopped again. . . . He walked across the living room to the door.

Jesus, how many of them *are* there in there? Alex stared at the closed door, took a deep breath, and reached for the knob quickly, without allowing himself to think about it, turned the knob and shoved. The door stuck at the lower corner where the dead snake was jammed in, but as the upper corner gave a little, the rattling became noticeably louder until the door sprang shut again.

Oh, no, Jesus, no. What is in—he shut off the thought and kicked the door, just beside the knob. As it flew open the snake that had been stuck moved its head toward his foot. Reflexively he fired at it—missing. But it was still. It's dead, he realized again, it just scooted across the floor when the door pulled on it. His bullet had missed his foot by only an inch—the dead snake by three or four inches.

Inside the room the light picked out dozens more: on the floor, alongside the body of the small dog; on the bed, on the body of the big dog. For a second he thought there were snakes on the walls and on the ceiling. He had emptied his gun into the room before he ever made a decision to fire. The shots thundered in his ears, reverberating in the small room. It was like being clubbed in the head.

Many of the snakes were still, but many more were in motion, apparently aimless at first. A slapping thump by the bed attracted the flashlight beam. Oh, God, he thought, a big one there and it's come down off the bed for me—his eyes were riveted on it and he stood frozen until something hit him, shockingly hard, in the ankle.

The big snake that had dropped off the bed had not left the spot where it had landed; Alex had been struck, on the boot and not through it, by another, which he'd never seen moving toward him. He leaped back and put the foot down on something that shifted under him. He hopped away from that, teetered on one foot for a moment, waving his arms for balance, darting the beam of the flashlight in a riotous sweeping orbit—it was blinking off and on erratically—and precariously kept his balance. The snake that had struck him moved away, back into the bedroom.

Alex heard the rustle of the snake he had stepped on moving across the floor in the opposite direction, toward the front door. He carefully swept the light to it.

It had taken up its station in front of the door, in a coil, between Alex and escape.

Oh, Christ, he thought, not aggressive, Annie said. Annie's an asshole. This fucker wants me. But seeing himself in a one-on-one showdown had a calming effect on Alex. He took the beam from the snake in front of him and turned to the infested room. There were a couple in the doorway. He could probably step between them to reach the door—they weren't very big. and if they didn't strike above his boots it seemed that they wouldn't be able to hurt him—but in pulling the door shut he'd scoot them out into the living room.

For the moment, they merely held their positions. Confused, maybe. He looked back at the one by the front door—and his light went out. He shook it back on, dimmer this time. The snake there was holding position, too. There seemed to be no move to make—but he had to move. He knew himself well enough to know he couldn't stand being thwarted. The longer he was still, the more terror crept through him. It would paralyze him soon.

He tucked the flashlight under his arm and, as smoothly and unobtrusively as he could manage, he opened the pistol and ejected the spent shells into a jacket pocket. From the other pocket he took bullets, one at a time, and reloaded. He was clumsy at the job; his fingers were shaking. He stopped and directed the light at the snakes in the bedroom: holding still. Now, the last fresh bullet, and he snapped the cylinder into place. With the light, he checked one last time on the snake by the outside door—but it was gone from its position.

It's making a move, the treacherous sonofabitch. He swept the flashlight beam slowly through the blackness and soon found it, coiled beside a big overstuffed chair. He stared at it and decided to try to shoot it from where he stood. It was still, and it was no more than four yards from him.

He raised the gun and pulled back the flashlight to

line it up over the gun and at the snake, so that he could aim. Now . . . I should be able—but the light went out again. It wouldn't come on when he shook it.

He shook it again. The intermittent rattling in the bedroom ceased entirely after a few seconds of darkness, and now the silence reverberated in his ears. He kept shaking the light, producing only an occasional flicker. He shifted it to his right hand, moving the pistol to his left, meaning to open the flashlight and close it up again—sometimes that made the contacts work.

Then he heard a faint rustling from the floor near the front door. *Moving.* The bastard's moving—he listened carefully—toward me! He stomped his foot and the rustling sound stopped. Silence returned for a second, and then the snake began to rattle, seemingly only six feet or so from Alex. The impulse to fling something at it was irresistible. Before he could tell himself that doing so would be futile, he had thrown the useless flashlight, heard it hit the overstuffed chair with a muffled thump, skid and roll across the floor to a stop.

Now he stood, paralyzed, listening. The snake had ceased rattling. He stared fiercely, eyes straining futilely to penetrate the darkness, in the direction he imagined the snake to be. He told himself he couldn't possibly be seeing motion there in this utter blackness. If it moved he would hear the rustling sound on the floor—he had heard it before. Is there a throw rug there? Would it make a sound moving across the rug? The question became moot when the rattling in the bedroom began again. He could hear nothing else over that.

He stood, frozen in place, his ears filled with that evil rasp, his eyes filled with blackness.

CHAPTER

14

The group in Ben's board meeting had sat in stunned silence for seconds after the first gunshot; then, as Ted said, "What in the fuck—" five more came in rapid succession.

"Dumb sonofabitch," Ted went on after a pause, "there's *dozens* . . . ," but he broke off and sat in furious silence.

Randall Madison thought, Who was it said Alex might pull a gun? Poor dumb shit, it really is too much for him.

After a stretch of silence Randall said, "Look, folks, I think I better go have a look for Alex."

Tim said, "I'll go with you."

"In your cute little loafers? No, you stay put." Randall was wearing boots that went over his ankles. "Ben, do you have anything—a hoe or rake, something long—in the basement?"

"There is some gardening stuff in a corner, I don't remember what, exactly, we've never used it. Which do you want? If we have it?"

"Uh . . ." Randall thought back. He had seen his father kill an egg-stealing snake with a hoe when he was a child. He shuddered. "Hoe, I guess. Anything long."

He didn't want to raise the possibility openly—nerves were high enough—but he had begun to suspect that there was something wrong with Alex. The silence had gone on for quite a while. Bitten, maybe, or, hell, maybe he shot himself in the foot. He went through the kitchen to meet Ben at the top of the cellar stairs.

"Look," he said softly, "you better listen for me to yell. If he's hurt, I may need help getting him out of there."

Ben looked thoughtfully at him. "All right. Leave the door open as you go out, so we can hear. Just neglect to close it behind you."

As Randall hauled his hoe through the living room, Whitney said, in a voice shockingly dull and lifeless, "Something's happened to him." Oh, lord, he thought—she looks like she's been shot in the belly. Her eyes were enormous, though she was otherwise expressionless. He slipped into his loan-officer character, a sort of Jack Benny impression: "What could happen? Can the snakes shoot back?" But he looked sharply at Tim, who nodded and moved to put an arm around Whitney.

He left the door ajar. Surprisingly, he could see no light in Ted's windows. As he walked toward the house he wondered, Can Alex possibly have gone in there without a flashlight? In this blackness? No. So—? He stepped up on the porch and across it. Pushing open the door, he shined the beam of light inside and found Alex, standing, gun raised but aimed at nothing, eyes wide. "Alex, are you okay?"

Alex's voice was breathy, almost a whisper. "Yeah. . . . Randall? Listen—"

Randall took a step toward him—Alex seems paralyzed, he thought—and put his foot on something hard and round that rolled out from under him. "Whuh!" he said as his foot flew up, flipping him backward. He dropped the hoe and put down his right hand to break his fall. He slammed to the floor, hand and then elbow before his back hit. "Oh!" he gasped. "Damn!"

He heard Alex say, "Get up, for God's sake," just before he heard the rattle, inches from his ear. He was pushing away from the floor, in a panic to get his face away from that sound, when he was struck in the right forearm. The pain was instant and horrifyingly worse than any pain he'd ever imagined, and immediately grew worse still.

"*Oh-oh!*" he yelled. "Oh, *God*. Oh, god*damn*it, Alex, what—ooOOOH!" he howled. Oh, my God, he thought, that's *bad*. I'm on *fire*.

On his feet, trembling violently now, he directed his flashlight beam at the floor where he'd been. There was nothing to be seen but an overstuffed chair he'd nearly fallen against. Snake under it, probably. Alex had only just now taken a step toward him. "Oh, Alex, you, Jesus, why didn't—" but the pain was now from his fingertips to his shoulder and was so bad he thought he might faint.

Randall was only dimly aware of Alex putting a shoulder into his belly and lifting him. His arm hung loosely behind Alex's back as he was carried out. He would have cut it off willingly if that would have stopped the pain.

Ben was becoming aware that, while his strategy of setting up a board meeting around the dining table had been successful, he'd clung to it too long. They should have tested the flood. It won't be passable, there's really no doubt, but we could have established that by now, and begun to make ourselves as secure as we can be in here.

Ben had a gift for projecting great calm when he was most tense. Even Annie was fooled sometimes—as she seemed to be now. All righf, well, Randall and Alex will be back in a second, and then we'll—

When they came through the door Ben was confused for a second. He took the tangle of legs over shoulder, arms and face to be Randall carrying Alex—which he'd half expected to see—but it was Alex's face he saw, not Randall's.

"Bitten," Alex grunted before anyone could speak. He puffed for breath as he walked through the room to the couch with his burden. "He fell by a snake."

Tim said, "Oh, God damn you, Alex, what have you done to him?" He left Whitney and went to the couch as Alex placed Randall down as gently as he could manage.

Alex looked at Tim, stood up and shook his head unhappily. In a moment, he took off his jacket and folded it under Randall's head, though there were pillows at the other end of the couch.

Ben said, "Annie?"

"Yes," she said, collecting her thoughts. "Yes, look, what you do is what they do in cowboy movies, you must've seen it. You cut across the wounds—can you see them—and suck out the poison. And, uh—and also you put a tourniquet above it."

"All right," Tim said, "give me a razor blade. Do you have a razor blade?" Annie took the hurricane lamp and hurried off toward the bathroom.

"Listen," Annie said when she came back with the blade, "d'you have an open sore in your mouth, a cut or anything? Cold sore on your lip? The poison can hurt you, too, if it can get in your bloodstream that way. Otherwise it's safe, even if you swallow some."

Tim shook his head. Randall's forearm was already twice normal size, and fiery red. At the most grotesquely swollen point, inside the arm just below the elbow, the flesh was white—a horribly sick gray-white—and in the center of that area were the punctures, black-red little pits with torn edges nearly an inch apart.

Ben had tied a scarf of Annie's around Randall's upper arm and now fumbled with the knot and a big serving spoon from the kitchen, trying to remember how to twist the thing to make the tourniquet tight. Where had he seen that done? In the Cub Scouts? In the Navy? You tie the knot around the middle of the stick—the spoon—and you. . . . It was tight, and tighter still as he twisted. Good.

Tim had made the cuts, X-shaped across each puncture, with what Ben thought was astonishing quickness, with no hesitation at all. Ben's stomach clenched as the first gash appeared in the swollen flesh, and when Tim went back into the same cut, deepening it, Ben had to look away. I'm glad it's Tim doing that and not me, he thought; I'd still be gritting my teeth to make the first cut.

Just before he placed his lips over the wound to begin sucking the poison, Tim said, "Bring me some mouthwash."

Annie said, "We have no mouthwash."

"Brandy," Tim said.

And so the work began, and went on, Tim sucking, spitting pink stuff into a bowl from the kitchen, rinsing his mouth with the brandy and spitting that, sucking at the wound, spitting. Randall was conscious now and watching with wide eyes in an ashen face. Ben rose from his side, motioned Karen to kneel on the floor and hold the tourniquet tight. Karen nodded and took the baby, asleep in her arms, to Ted.

Alex stood off to one side, hands on hips, head down. Whitney was standing with him, gripping his upper arm hard, looking no better than before.

Think I should keep both of them in sight, Ben decided. He spoke to Ted. "Hey, is the bridge okay?"

Ted looked startled. "I never got that far," he said. "Sorry. I'll go now."

But Alex snapped, "I'll do it," and was in motion, roughly pulling free of Whitney's fierce grip on his arm.

Oh-oh, Ben thought, no you don't. "No, look, Alex, Whitney needs—"

Alex shot him a murderous glare and Whitney quickly said, "No, it's all right." She looked defiant and terrified, her jaw set, her eyes enormous. Ben thought, it is not, goddamnit, all right. But Alex had flashlight in hand and was at the door, taking Ben's Day-Glo orange rain jacket down from a peg. He nodded at Ben and went out.

The rain had completely stopped. Behind Ted's house, and between the house and the bridge, were scattered boulders and heaps of wet earth. Ted's car was apparently undamaged, but effectively barricaded in place by a mudbank. It looked, though, as if Alex might be able to pick his way through the debris in his Mercedes without circling the front of the house over the rain-soaked lawn.

He liked that idea. He and his Mercedes. They'd get out, and they'd get through the flood, too, by God, and bring help for Randall and get this whole fucking mess straightened out. Alex loved his Mercedes. It was the only fine thing he owned that he loved for itself, even more than he loved owning it.

He walked to the bridge first, to examine it closely. He directed the light under it, then across to the opposite bank and downward at the water. The gully was eighteen, or at most twenty, feet wide at the top, narrowing sharply at the bottom. From the floor of the bridge to the roiling surface of the water was a drop of six feet. Alex had never seen the gully dry, but from the shape of the sides he formed the impression that the water might be another six feet deep at this point—or, he thought a second time, maybe as little as three. In any case, it would be a really nasty fall if the bridge let go, and the way the water leaps and pounds along you wouldn't want to find yourself in it. Not even in a Mercedes.

He thought the bridge might have moved a little; it didn't cross the gap at a perfectly right angle. And oh, yes, it had been hit by something. He saw now that the railing on the right side of the bridge, on the other end, was torn way. He walked out onto the bridge, gingerly—and froze as he felt it move a fraction of an inch, suddenly excruciatingly aware of the empty space between the floor of the bridge and the heaving surface of the water.

He took a deep breath, sucked in his lips, rose to the balls of his feet and bounced gently a few times. Solid. Gathering his nerves along with the muscles in his legs, he jumped a few inches in the air, flexing his legs to land as softly as possible. Solid. He jumped once again, higher, and came down hard. Solid. He breathed once more.

The bridge may have been moved a hair by a falling rock, but it had found a firm new position. Alex was elated. When he first thought he felt the bridge shifting, he had been almost as much afraid of being thwarted in his plan as he was of being dumped into the rushing water. As he moved back off the bridge, the uncertainty of its perch on the banks of the gully made itself felt again, but he ignored that with an effort of will too slight even to notice. He was going to get out of here. He would, by God.

He walked the path that he would drive through the rocky debris on the ground. Here and there a root or tree limb protruded from the mud. When one of these flopped of its own volition he saw that they were not roots or limbs at all. They were partly buried rattlesnakes, some of them obviously not dead. He shuddered and watched his step more closely.

There would be room to drive through. It wouldn't even be all that difficult, if he could get over one heap of stuff that stretched from the back of the house straight across into the woods. Oh, yeah, he and his Mercedes, they'd get across.

Alex walked behind the houses to his car, started it and began his gauntlet run. The O. J. Simpson of cars, he thought happily; it was a little litany he often ran through in his mind. He cut sharply to the left around a boulder. The car responded easily, as it was engineered to do. Not quite the magical moves of a Gale Sayers, but almost, and a lot more power. Back to the right, easy does it—ow! A little scrape at the rear. Okay, no problem. Not as huge and heavy as Jim Brown, but just about as strong, and more agile. Up over the mudbank, front wheels slip a bit to the left, belly scrapes a little but no sweat, rear wheels bite and lift on up. Oh, yeah. Another sharp left and a right.

And onto the bridge—touchdown. But the bridge moved under him, in sickening slow motion to the left, diving straight down; the headlights disappeared into black water and the steering wheel came up into his chest—hard!—as the nose of the car hit the bottom of the rushing stream and he was over, the car somersaulting onto its back and under the water in icy, turbulent blackness.

It wasn't slow motion anymore, now, and it wasn't silent either. He was slammed to the ceiling of the car and the scrape of metal against the floor of the stream was a scream accompanied by the roar of the water—numbingly cold!—through the broken windows. Alex managed to gasp in some air before the car filled—it was almost instantly full. He struggled frantically to free his legs from the steering wheel and pushed himself blindly along the ceiling past the front seat toward the rear of the car, downstream with the flow of the water. The water would pull him right out, if he'd fit through the window—terrible, to be caught up in that torrent, but better than drowning inside the car like a roach in a trap.

His breath was gone; his chest hurt terribly, his limbs grew weak and it was increasingly difficult to keep his throat locked shut. Though he was in utter blackness and his eyes were tight shut, he was beginning to see flashes of bright light. As he reached through the broken rear window with one arm, his jacket—Ben's jacket, Ben's plastic slicker—snagged on a jagged edge of the glass and he was caught.

Sonofabitch! It was silent, but it was a scream. *You*

can't—. He pulled the arm back inside the car, the sleeve remaining caught, and fought to free himself of Ben's jacket, the goddamn killer. He was just free of it when finally an involuntary gasp brought the brutal water inside him. He lost consciousness thinking, *No, goddamnit, I will not.* . . .

CHAPTER

15

Whitney had not expected to hear the car start, any more than the others had. Yet she wasn't surprised. She had a dreadful sense that an inexorable process had begun. The feeling had come awake in her when Alex had gone with his gun to confront the snakes. For a moment when he returned unharmed she thought that she'd been mistaken, but the look in his eyes had told her otherwise: He was going to go and . . . get himself killed. Leave her.

She had first known that, she now realized, when he said he wanted her to marry him. That was when the dread was born. How could she know that? She was beginning to recognize the feeling; she had had it when her father first became ill, when she was a little girl. She had known it with—she cut off the thought. She was about to list the men who had left her, one after another. She had a powerful urge to call Dr. Graebner, right this minute. She thought she might actually do so if the phones were working, but of course they had long

179

since established that they weren't. They'd been taken out along with the electricity, by the landslide.

Now, as the Mercedes moved past Ben and Annie's house, the others were galvanized into action. When the sound of the motor running first came to them, Ted had sworn viciously under his breath. He and Ben had looked at each other for a few seconds—as long as it took for the car to cover the few yards from Randall and Tim's house to Ben and Annie's.

Then they jumped to their feet. Ben ran to the kitchen, where he grabbed a burning candle and went to the basement for another flashlight. Ted handed the baby to Karen and bolted through the door and yelled at Alex just as Whitney heard the rending, horrifying—and sickeningly inevitable—crash into the stream.

She felt as though her insides had been removed. What was left of her body, this hollow, lifeless form of a Whitney Williams, walked through the kitchen and out the back door onto the driveway. She saw Ted holding a candle and Ben a flashlight at the edge of the gully, off to her left, beyond the remains of the landslide. She went to join them, stumbling in the rocks and mud on the driveway, and saw what they saw in the beam of the flashlight.

The bridge lay upside down in the gully, caught on something in the stream. Then it shifted a bit and tumbled a few yards downstream, where it became lodged again, on its side, one rail exposed above the rushing water. She stared at where the bridge had first been. What she saw was boiling white water and, blearily discernible through the surface rapids, the ghostly apparition of Alex's car. It rested on its top, lying at a tilt, its nearer side higher. As the flashlight beam swept the car slowly, she could see little in detail; but when the flashlight beam stopped suddenly she saw clearly, through a rear, side window, the iridescent orange of the jacket Alex wore. She had thought she was beyond being shocked, but learned painfully that she wasn't, quite.

Then Ted put his arm around Whitney's shoulders and urged her back to the house. She walked with him, without will either to resist or to comply, allowing herself to be led toward . . . toward the rest of her empty life.

Not that that feeling was new. Indeed it was an old friend. There was even a dull and sickly loathsome sense of relief connected with it.

Ben and Ted stood isolated by the flashlight's beam on the bank of the stream, Ted tying a rope around Ben's chest. It had not yet occurred to Ben to be afraid; his mind had been too busy. He had gone through a few moments of intolerable sick horror when he first saw the car in the stream—he'd been scared before, and horrified by Randall's snakebite, but, he suddenly realized, he had been rather enjoying the adventure up to that point.

The sight of the car had brought home to him with nauseating impact that this was all in deadly earnest. One of them was not just in danger, but . . . Alex Klein was—well, probably, he thought; we'll see. And beyond that, they were marooned, cut off from help, with a snakebite victim and hundreds of rattlesnakes.

Now Ben was intensely concentrated on the task at hand. Ted would lower him; Annie was holding the flashlight. Karen stood to one side holding Charley. The two women were furious at what they saw as a lunatic attempt to rescue a dead man. But there was no dissuading the men. Ben seemed to feel some responsibility for Alex's suicidal attempt to be a hero, and he would not forgo this slim chance to save him if he could be saved. And Ted seemed to understand and agree; and so the argument had ended.

Now Ben nodded at Ted and dropped to his knees. He backed until his bare feet were out over the stream, then fell to his belly and scooted on back and down over the side. He placed his feet against the slippery wall of the gully, gripped the rope, and began to walk down, lowered hand over hand by Ted.

Since it had not occurred to Ben to be afraid, he was unprepared for the sudden panicky sense of helplessness, of being at the water's mercy, that he suddenly felt when his feet first entered the stream—astonishingly, shockingly cold, slapping powerfully at his feet, tossing them aside and upward. As Ted lowered him another eighteen inches the water tugged at his lower legs, slamming them against the side of the car and pulling them between the car and the wall of the gully, dragging him along, scraping his face and chest—deeper again, now, by another foot and a half, to mid-thigh. Oh, my God, he thought, there's no way I can function.

The part of his body covered by the water was so cold as to have no other feeling at all, and the power of the stream rushing through this little funnel between the car and the stream bank was absolutely overwhelming. And Ted—God damn him, can't he see—just kept lowering.

Ben was in chest deep now, and his chest was losing even the sensation of being rubbed raw by the hard, rough rope. He was being slammed against the car and then the bank, battered back and forth and pulled helplessly almost horizontal. The rope had been pulled up just under his arms and he was afraid to give up his hand grip to wave a signal. He tried to shout, but the water was in his face now, and filled his mouth.

He was about to drown, hanging from this insane rope as helpless as bait on a hook—he thought of bait skipping along the surface of the ocean; he'd seen that once, some kind of small fish, impaled on a hook, smacking along through the breaking waves.

Ben was about to drown, ten feet from Annie —Annie, with my baby, god*damn*—and from Ted holding the rope, in this ludicrous, futile attempt to rescue a dead man. Oh, Christ, why can't they see what's happening?

He was hanging vertical, free of the water, Ted gripping under his arms, before he realized that he'd been pulled up. Stretched out on the wet grass, gasping and choking, he heard Annie shouting at him, "Get up, Ben. Get up." Get up? Jesus Christ! He was still nearly numb through his whole body, both from cold and from the lack of oxygen. He struggled to his feet. Annie was holding the baby, for some reason. What do you *want*—he looked over at Ted, where Annie was directing the flashlight. Ted was walking away, carrying Karen. Oh, Christ, what? he thought; he still hadn't enough breath to voice a question.

"Bitten," Annie shouted. "There are snakes out here, all over."

They staggered together to the house, Annie sweeping the earth in front of them with the flashlight beam. They saw some snakes, but no live ones.

Ted carried Karen quickly through the kitchen door, down the hall and into the living room, where he placed her on a chair. *I want my wife!* he was thinking. I will not have her die, I won't fucking *allow* it!

The bite was in Karen's ankle. Though no one had seen the snake, it had evidently been smaller than the one that bit Randall, judging from the shorter distance between the two punctures. Tim made the cuts—"Bite's not as deep," he said—and Ted began to suck at them.

I want my wife, he thought again. I have a new wife, our life is going to be different. She can't die *now*. The strength and clarity of this feeling surprised him. Since this afternoon Ted's conviction that Karen had undergone some sea change had grown steadily stronger, and his feeling about that had moved from uneasiness to calm acceptance—briefly, in the shower—but then quickly back to uneasiness and then to fear and finally to a kind of sullen resentment. He wasn't sure he wanted Karen at all, under these new terms—whatever they might turn out to be. But now, somehow, he knew: He wanted his wife.

Ted sucked hard, furiously, but very little liquid seemed to come into his mouth. It tasted like blood, nothing else—though perhaps faintly oily. Come out of there, sonofabitch! He wanted to feel great jets of bitter stuff in his mouth, the poison flowing from her into him. But it was like drinking from a warm sponge that he couldn't squeeze. The liquid came slowly and grudgingly, and if the poison had a flavor, then it mustn't be coming at all.

Karen whimpered and Ted turned and snapped, "It's all right!" then softened his tone and said, "You're going to be all right. I'm taking care of it."

Soon he remembered that he was supposed to rinse out his mouth, to avoid infecting the cuts. They had brought him a glass and a bottle of gin; Tim had used up the brandy. Ted disliked gin in any case, and now its perfumy aroma in his nose was especially hateful. It obscured the taste of Karen's blood. If he couldn't have the snake's taste—which he had imagined would be bitter—then he wanted to taste Karen. He wanted her life in him.

She won't die, he thought. It wouldn't be—the bite isn't big enough to kill her, that's all. He went on working, taking her in, taking the snake out of her, sucking hard, spitting, rinsing his mouth.

Ben, sitting near the fireplace wrapped in a blanket, watched Ted thoughtfully. "Annie," he said between fits of shivering, "what happens to people who are bitten by rattlesnakes? Do they really die, or do they just get sick as hell?"

"No, if they don't get treated wth antivenin, they really die," Annie said. "Anyway, they do if they're bitten badly enough. By a big enough snake. And it matters if the bite's near the heart. Or the brain—I forget. No, the heart, because the poison mostly affects the blood system."

"So Randall's in very bad trouble," Ben said.

"Yes, but Karen is too, if we don't get help. It makes a difference how big the person is, too. Randall weighs—what?"

"One seventy, maybe."

"—and Karen's no more than a hundred twenty-five."

Ben looked across the room at Randall, lying on the couch. There was something bizarre and shocking about his face: Randall looked as though he were wearing bright red lipstick. "Tim?" Ben said, "Tim, what's —how is Randall?"

Tim was sitting on the floor at Randall's head. He glared at Ben. "He's unconscious, thank God." Tim reached to Randall's face and, with gentle fingers, pushed the lips open. Randall's mouth looked like a gash made by an ax: Gums and teeth alike were a vivid, shocking scarlet. He let the lips close, and with his handkerchief wiped the blood from Randall's mouth. "His gums are bleeding. Hard. And he has a lot of fever. And the flesh around the bite looks like it's dead and rotting—it's black and blue and yellow and —horrible." His angry tone was accusing: Look what you've done to him.

Ben just nodded.

Annie said, "Ben, what are we going to do? We can't get out, we're ringed in on all sides by water. Can we barricade ourselves in against the snakes? Will they come inside? There are hundreds of them, Ben."

"We have to get out. The flood down the road won't let anybody up here until late tomorrow, and the phone lines are down up here. It could be a *couple* of days, and Randall and Karen . . ."

"Can we cross the stream anywhere? Or the other stream?"

Ben shook his head grimly. "That's what we have to do, all right, get across the water. But I don't see how. The other stream is falling just as hard where it comes off the cliff, and it's much wider down below."

Ted looked up from his work. "I could make it. Up

here—we could lasso something on the other side and I could get across the rope.''

Ben shook his head. "No way. I looked for something like that when we were out before. There's nothing anywhere near close enough over there. The road's too wide.''

Tim put in, "And what time's the next landslide?''

Whitney said, "Oh, *God*!''

Ben looked at Whitney thoughtfully for a moment, then said, "There is a way.''

All looked at Ben blankly. He stared at the ceiling, ignoring the questioning stares. "Yeah, we can get out.'' But he looked grim, rather than triumphant. "Under the waterfall.''

Tim stared at him, incredulous. "You mean climb up the slide? Right through the snakes, right at the *cave*? His voice was rising. "Walk right down their *throats*?''

"Oh, Ben, my God,'' Annie said. "And in the dark?''

"No,'' he said, more confident now, "we'd have to wait for light—but what's that, a couple of hours? It's past three now. And we could get to the county road in—well, only God knows what the terrain's like out there, but with any luck we might get to it in two or three hours, anyway. It runs high over there on that side of the mountain.''

"Wonderful,'' Tim said bitterly. "Just two or three hours through snake-infested woods and sheer cliffs. *If* we get past the cave, and *if* we don't set off another slide, and *if*—''

"No,'' Ben said. "The snakes are down here. If we can get to the fall, and past that, we should be past most of the snakes. It's true it'd be scary that far—''

"Scary!'' Tim muttered. "For God's sake.''

"—dangerous, that far, from the snakes and the loose rocks and earth, but past that we should be okay. At worst, maybe we'd end up stuck somewhere, on some impassable ledge or something—but that's no worse than being stuck here until we're discovered sometime next week.''

Ted was nodding as he rinsed his mouth and spit. "We can do it," he said decisively. "Look, the goddamn snakes aren't supernatural, and they're not invisible. We could take rakes and hoes and stuff to shove them away from us when we see them. Anyway, they rattle to warn you, right?''

Annie said, "The one that bit Karen didn't.''

Ben said, "Who knows what a rattlesnake's like when he's been through a landslide? Maybe their rattles are broken off, or maybe they're a little crazy, or—who knows? But still, we can see them.''

"I just remembered something else from that film,'' Annie said. "Little trivia item, I thought. Their rattles become silent when they're wet. The dried skin becomes soft, I guess, or maybe water just gets inside the rings and makes a cushion.''

"They're not supernatural,'' Tim said, "but they're crazy and they're silent. Charming.''

"Listen, Tim,'' Ben said, "you're not going.''

"What? Look, I didn't say—''

"No, listen, somebody's got to stay with Randall and Karen. They need comforting, and they need—look, I don't see how we can make a house rattlesnake-proof. They're all over the place here, and I don't know why they'd come inside, but if they wanted to, or if they just wandered in, we can't really prevent it. The basement isn't tight, and there are pipes, there's the walls—we find mice, and chipmunk nests and droppings in all these houses, and if they can get in, so can a snake.''

Tim's mouth was open. He closed it and swallowed. "Oh, Christ,'' he said quietly, and looked around the floor.

Annie said thoughtfully, "The mice and chipmunks are a reason for the snakes to come in, as a matter of fact. That's what they eat.''

Ted said, "Look, let's not piss and moan while we

could be sleeping. I'll stay up and watch until daylight—I'm the youngest and the strongest, and anyway, I want to take care of Karen. Now we've all got to be sharp when daylight comes, so the rest of you crap out. A couple of hours is better than nothing.''

Annie stared at Ted, open-mouthed. "Sleep? In a snake house? You must be—''

Ben broke in. "Come on, Annie, we need it. Whitney, that's a lounge chair, you can push it back." Tim took pillows off the couch and curled up on a rug. Ben led Annie into their bedroom, which he examined minutely with the flashlight before they lay down, placing Ted and Karen's baby between them in the blackness.

It was half past five, and half light, when Ted came for them. Annie, to her astonishment, had not only fallen asleep, but had done so immediately. She thought now she might feel worse for it, rather than better, and Ben looked the same—red-eyed and only half-conscious.

But Ted had made more coffee, and after some silent minutes they were all more mobile. Everything from the basement that had a long handle was standing against the wall beside the back door—a leaf rake, a garden rake, a spade and the hoe, which Ted had retrieved from his house where Randall had dropped it.

At Tim's suggestion, they moved Randall and Karen into the bedroom; Ben and Annie's bed was more comfortable than the couch and the chair in which they were sleeping. Moving them produced whimpers from Karen, who remained asleep—or unconscious—and a heart-tearing half moan, half sob from Randall just as they were laying him on the bed. He awoke, his eyes wide and rolling, and he gasped and sobbed, but did not speak.

Tim watched as they set off through the kitchen door, Ted with Charley in a carrier on his back, still sleeping, as he had through all the chaos. They were carrying the garden implements, except for the hoe, which they had left for Tim. There had been a half-hearted sort of argument over whether the women should stay behind, but both were determined to go, for reasons that Tim didn't precisely understand. In Annie's case it seemed to have something to do with wanting to be near Ben. Whitney was even less clear. Tim thought, though it seemed unlikely, that it might have something to do with wanting to be near Annie.

Tim just shook his head. Clearly they were all crazy as bedbugs anyway. "Tim?" Randall was conscious. His voice was as dry as a desert of dust. "Tim, what's going on?"

Tim looked at him and touched his face gently —burning hot. Cowboys and Indians is what's going on, he thought; macho adventures, man against the elements, meeting the challenge of—ah, well. . . . What he said was, "It's going to be all right. They're going to get help for you."

They heard the whine of the screen-door spring then, and saw Ben walk across the living room. In a moment he walked by the bedroom door again, this time wearing Alex's ski jacket and carrying Alex's pistol, broken open to check whether it was loaded. They heard the whine and slap of the screen door again. Whoopee, Tim thought, a real gun. Lawrence of the Catskills leads the charge.

"I'm thirsty, Tim, is there any water?" Randall's voice wavered between a whisper and a falsetto, as though he was resisting sobbing. The pain must be terrible.

"Sure, why not?"

"The pump—the electricity. . . . When the tank runs out, that's it."

"Oh, for God's sake." Tim got up and went to the kitchen. The tap delivered water. Slowly, with little pressure behind it, but the glass filled and he returned to the bedroom.

* * *

The slope near the stream was littered with rocks and earth, crisscrossed with broken trees and brush. It was presumably the most snake-infested part of the mountainside, so they started the climb near the other side of the slope, picking their way slowly, avoiding thick underbrush even though that made the route longer. They constantly peered intently at the ground and beat it with their garden implements, to let snakes know of their presence. They formed a wedge with Ben at the point, Ted and Whitney to his sides and just behind him.

Annie, who had nothing to beat the ground with, stayed close on Ben's heels in the center. Ben had said to her just after they left the house, "What happens to a pregnant woman bitten by a rattlesnake?"

Annie looked him in the eye and said, "What do you think?"

Ben thought of poison in Annie's bloodsteam reaching the tiny, exquisitely delicate embryo. "Oh, Jesus," he said quietly. He placed her in the most protected position. It's probably as safe as the house, Ben thought, and anyway I'd rather have her here where I can see her and see what's around her.

So the climbing proceeded, up a little way, cut left for clear ground, up and back to the right, much of the time single file.

Once Whitney said, "Oh, my God—" and froze. Her rake had flushed a rattlesnake which moved away with what seemed to her sullen slowness, ponderously crawling through a long, long S shape. She never saw its full length, but it was as thick as her wrist. Ted, who was nearest to her at the time, moved to her side. In a thin voice she said, "It's okay, it's gone away."

Ted nodded and grunted. "I've seen a couple already. Don't be too scared, they want nothing to do with us."

They reached the foot of the cliff fifty feet away from the landslide. There was a path, perhaps four feet wide, clear along the cliff. They went along it two by two.

Around the big curve in the cliff before they came to the face, they saw the slide. A heap more than twice

Ted's height stretched down the mountain, mostly precariously piled rocks with some underpinning of earth. At the top of it they would probably be able to look straight into the cave, if there was anything left that could be called a cave. Right down their throats, indeed.

The heap ran down the mountain into the woods to a point where the slope became abruptly too steep to climb across. They would have to cross up here somewhere, or climb a long way down to get around.

"Ted," Ben said, "you know there are snakes in those rocks. Maybe dead, but who knows?"

Ted nodded. "I'm going to ease downslope a few yards there"—he pointed—"where there's more dirt in the heap and less rocks. Stay where you are for a minute." Slamming the underbrush in front of him with his rake, Ted stepped gingerly down toward the smoother part of the slide heap.

At one point he braced himself with the rake against a rock alongside the heap. The rock shifted slightly and a sandpapery sound began to come from it. Ted jumped, then froze, then took a big step past, turned and thrust the rake against the rock, shifting it a few inches this time. Still nothing to be seen, and still the sound continued, to be joined now by more rattles, coming from so many directions at once that they could tell nothing about where the real sources were located.

Whitney whimpered, "Oh-h-h, *Christ*!" She stood, frozen, her face chalky white. Annie took her arm and found her as taut as a drawn bow, and trembling minutely. Or maybe, Annie thought, that's me trembling.

Ted said, "Just take it easy. They can't bite you without showing themselves. We knew they were in here. Just take it easy." He was at a point where the slide heap was seven or eight feet tall and probably not too steep-sided to climb.

Ben said, "Ted—Ted, you can't climb over there with Charley on your back. Come back up and I'll try." Ted looked up and nodded and, after a moment, walked carefully past the rock that rattled to exchange places with Ben.

The rattling sounds rose and fell in intensity. Ben listened to them with acute concentration, trying to determine how many separate ones there were, and to see if he could locate any of them, as he moved to the smooth spot in the slide heap. But registering very carefully when some of them stopped and others began, he formed the impression that there might be as few as five or six. That is, he reminded himself, five or six that are rattling; God knows how many with wet rattles, or just not choosing to make their presence known. Still, all the sound was now above him as he reached the climbable spot in the slide.

The side of the slope was steep, but he found he could climb it partway, at least, without reaching ahead of him with his hands. He used his spade as a staff, and also to dislodge dirt and spill it down the side to make the slope less steep. The top of the heap was formed by one huge, flat rock, eight feet from front to back, ten or twelve feet across, from six inches to a foot and a half thick. He shoved at it with the spade and then with his foot, trying to dislodge it or to discover that it was solidly in place. It hung out over air for almost a foot at the lower end, but that left what must be at least a couple of tons of rock solidly grounded.

Ben stepped on the great slab near the back end, next to the mountain, and it dropped six inches under him. It tipped in exactly the opposite direction from what he'd expected and began to slide, front end high, like a many-ton surfboard, ponderously slow but unstoppable. Ben lost his balance immediately and fell on his side, a horrified passenger on this uncontrollable monstrous sled. He tried to scramble to his hands and knees, looking about frantically for a safe place to jump to. Gazing up, he saw that he was sharing this moving shelf with a rattlesnake that rolled and flailed, striking madly at nothing, rolling nearer to him as the rock slid and the rear edge rose higher. Suddenly the rock stopped short against a tree and the snake, a three-footer, slid quickly at him, off the rock and onto the earth below, striking at him futilely on its way past.

Ben knelt on the rock, his behind against the tree, and shook. His teeth were chattering so that he thought they'd break until he forced a huge yawning breath that settled him some. He looked up the mountain and saw that the rock had slid only eight or ten feet. Farther up, he could see the other three standing, agape, having said nothing and moved not an inch. A thin, breathy wail escaped Annie, but she cut it off quickly. She called, "Are you—"

Ben began to say "I'm fine," but produced instead a brief hoot that might have been taken for a sob or a snort of laughter. With another deep breath, he managed, "I'm okay, I'm fine." And then he did break into a laugh. He stood and shook his head and laughed for several seconds. Ted broke into relieved laughter, too. Annie stared down the slope at Ben.

Her mystified, half-angry stare triggered another burst of laughter from Ben. Oh, Christ, he thought, and remembered what he'd said to himself when the rock started moving under him: I don't like this, were the words that had come to him. Jesus, *I don't like this*, for God's sake. He'd never imagined it was possible to be so terrified.

Ben stepped to the rear edge of the rock and looked over. The slide had revealed a low spot, a sort of saddle in the long heap of the landslide, where they would all be able to cross over easily. He sat down on the edge of the rock and shook his head and laughed again and said, "Oh, hell, yeah, sure it did. Nothing to it. Had that in mind all the time." As the others climbed carefully down to him, the laughter drained out of him and he thought, Oh, God, this is not—I don't live this kind of life. I'm not this sort of person. I'm an advertising man, I work at a desk in New York City. In a glass building. I take taxis. I—

When Annie reached him she violently hugged his head to her. She stood where he sat, her belly to his face, trembling. He wrapped his arms around her bottom and murmured to her, "It's okay now, I really am okay, we're fine. *I'm* fine. . . ." And in a moment, he was.

There was space—a couple of yards—between the slide and the stream. They had only twelve or fifteen feet to go up the slope to regain the path, but the ground was littered with new dirt and small rocks, and they thought it must be snake-infested. So they moved slowly, banging at the rocks with rake and shovel, peering intently at the ground, Ted in the lead.

Ted's eyes were tired; they burned from lack of sleep. He had occasionally to close them for a moment and refocus. He never looked up, or back at the others. He banged with his rake, then braced it next to the spot he had hit and placed a foot there, carefully, testing for solidity. One stride at a time. Soon, chill spray from the waterfall began to rain gently on him. The water now fell through one side of the maple tree below the fall, and produced more spray than it had before the slide.

Charley was awakened by the spray. He cried just once or twice, then twisted around in the carrier to tug at Ted's hair, whimpering. Ted stopped for a moment and pulled a bottle from a jacket pocket and handed it over his shoulder to the baby, who immediately became still.

At the top, they stopped for a breather so that Ted could pull Charley around and hold him face to face and talk to him. Charley was happy now. Ted had put a clean diaper on him before they left the house, so he was comfortable. Drinking mightily from the bottle, he gurgled and pointed over Ted's shoulder. After an effort to talk and drink at the same time, he pulled the bottle from his mouth with one hand and with the other pointed past Ted toward the waterfall. "Lookit!"

"Oh, yeah," Ted said, "water. Can you say water?" Then he saw Ben's face.

Ben was looking where Charley was pointing, at the waterfall and beyond, at the maple tree. His face went slack for a moment, then he said, "Uh—have a look at the tree."

Ted turned. Newly in leaf, barely past the bud stage, the tree's complex, tangled skeleton of branches was clearly visible against the bright sky. It was alive. Festooned. Rattlesnakes—thirty? Ted tried to count quickly. No, more, for God's sake—they're everywhere up there. Like lengths of living tinsel they decorated the tree that the travelers must now pass under.

Most were still, but here and there motion was to be seen, one of the creatures adjusting his precarious position on a branch, another seemingly just restless, writhing nervously. One shifted, curled over a limb and fell into the stream, twisting angrily through the air and smacking off lower branches on its way.

Annie stared up at the dreadful living canopy. She looked at the path under the fall and the tree, and back up to the tree, at the movement. Her lips moved slightly; she was talking to herself and to her baby, silently. Ropes, she was saying, they're like ropes. Only they move a little bit, is the only difference. Move a little bit—writhe, is what they do, coil and slither, and they're not like ropes, they're not like one single god-damn thing on this earth but snakes. Snakes are like nothing else but snakes and they're the worst thing on the face of the earth and *I don't want any more of them*—

"Annie," Ben said. "Go ahead. Just walk along next to the cliff and I'll walk right behind you with the shovel over your head like an umbrella, okay?"

"Wait," Ted said. "Annie, take Charley. I don't want him on my back where I can't see him or see if anything's falling—"

Annie nodded and went behind Ted and lifted Charley from the carrier. She held him against her breasts and leaned a little forward and, without saying anything further, walked straight out onto the ledge,

under the tree and the fall. Ben had to move quickly to
fall in behind her. As he walked, staring up into the tree,
he carried his shovel at the ready, at port arms. They
crossed without incident.

My God, Ben thought, will you look at her with a
child? She looked like a snake would break his teeth on
her back. But now he looked at her face. She stood erect
again, holding the child tight to her, looking at Ben. Her
lower lip trembled visibly and tears rolled down her
cheeks.

Ben smiled at her. "Y'done splendid," he said.
"Really, you were wonderful. We're past them
now—all of 'em, probably." He put his arm around her
shoulders.

They looked back and watched Whitney and Ted
making the crossing. Whitney walked huddled over, as
though to ward off a blow to her back, and stared
fixedly at the ground just in front of her and to her
right, where the cliff met the ledge they were walking
on. Ted came behind her, looking up, handling his rake
with thoughtless ease, as though it were an oversized,
just slightly clumsy baton.

As they were under the densest part of the tree, a
snake fell from a branch near the trunk, well away from
them. Whitney heard it falling through the tree and
froze in place, her hands over her head. Ted, looking up
into the tree, bumped her just slightly on the shoulder
with the handle of the rake and Whitney shrieked and
fell to her knees. Ted then bumped her with his shin and
teetered forward, making a huge hurdler's stride over
her in an attempt to regain a solid footing.

For a second, then, they were caught in that awkward
tableau, Ted straddling Whitney, trembling as he fought
for balance—unsuccessfully. As he dropped the rake
and teetered over the edge Whitney uncovered her face
and looked up at him and reflexively grabbed him with
both arms around his thigh, anchoring him solidly to
the spot.

After another second, Ted said, "Okay. Okay, you

can let go now." And she did. Ted leaned against the cliff with one hand and with the other reached down to touch Whitney's shoulder. Whitney crawled forward, out from under Ted's legs and on off the ledge, crawling all the way. Ted followed.

When they reached the gently sloped grassy mound where Ben and Annie waited with the baby, Ted looked solemnly at Whitney, swallowed and said, "Um—I was gone, y'know. I was—over the side, if you hadn't grabbed me. That was—uh, well, that was quick thinking. I mean—well, look, you saved my life, is what I'm saying."

Whitney looked bewildered. "I almost killed you."

Ted laughed. "Well, yeah, but what the hell—scared as you were, to grab me like that—well, that was really good."

Ben said, "C'mon, troops. Snaky part's over, but we got some pretty nasty terrain to cover."

"All *right*," Ted said. "Look *out*, mountain, here we come to *git* your ass."

The mountain king came back to consciousness hours later, in daylight. He was still in a state of shock; the violence done to his body in the fall had taken a terrible toll.

He was stretched his full great length in plain view of any creature who might happen along. Painfully he flexed his body, drew into an S and began to move, gripping the earth with the tough ridges along his belly, away from the stream, horizontally along the face of the mountain, to seek cover.

He found it soon enough, eight or ten of his body lengths from the stream, under a log on a flat space. The log was not thick, but it was long enough to conceal his full length if he moved under it stretched out nearly straight, and he had no strength to search farther.

CHAPTER

16

Tim stood on the front porch of Ben and Annie's house. His face was wet with sweat and some tears, and he was trembling slightly. He was filled with pity and rage. He had come out through the living room to the front of the house to get away from the bedroom. He carried a sheet and a blanket and a bucket full of vomit and vomit-soaked rags and paper towels.

Randall had gulped the glass of water eagerly and had lain back on the pillow. In a moment his eyes came open and his teeth began to chatter. He looked questioningly at Tim, and then suddenly erupted, spewing stuff onto himself and the bed. Horrible! And still more horrible for Randall, who was near phobic about vomiting—it made him panicky; he seemed to feel out of control in a way he couldn't tolerate.

And then his excruciating, futile dry heaves, finally producing pink and yellow stuff and causing pain like the tortures of hell in his whole body.

He was unconscious again now—mercifully, Tim

thought. The only thing for him to wake up to was some new agony.

Tim had removed the fouled bedclothes—the top sheet and blanket—and replaced them from a closet. He had pulled Randall's T-shirt off and had washed his chest and face. The water was still holding out—though it was flowing so weakly now he didn't expect it to last much longer.

Karen, blessedly, had not come to consciousness during that ordeal. She was in a sort of quiet delirium, stirring restlessly in her sleep, muttering and whimpering; and she was soaked in sweat. She was passing through the same stages as Randall, though with less severity, and her gums had not bled.

Randall is not going to come to consciousness again. Ever. The thought took Tim by surprise. He felt as though he had been punched hard in the stomach. Oh, my God, it's true. Randall is going to . . . die? Randall? No, by God! I won't let him.

Tim turned and hurried through the living room, into the bedroom—to find Randall and Karen both conscious, looking at each other with shaky little smiles. Neither seemed strong enough to utter a word, and both—Randall, especially—looked blank, confused. Then Randall's eyes closed again.

Tim took a clean towel from a dwindling stack beside the bed and gently patted Karen's face and neck dry. She nodded and smiled gratefully and whispered, "Water, please, Tim?"

He almost said, No, it'll make you throw up. But then he thought, well, her body must need the liquid, she's soaking wet with sweat. So he decided to get her just a tiny bit to sip at, to wet her lips and throat at least.

He walked quickly to the kitchen, which was much brighter than the bedroom, with more windows and the shades up—and, as his eyes adjusted to the brightness, froze in midstep. In the middle of the tile floor, stretched out in a long, sinuous curve, was a brightly speckled black rattlesnake more than four feet in length.

Oh, you evil sonofabitch. Oh, you killer, you loathsome—I'm gonna kill you. Tim backed slowly through the door, turned, shaking uncontrollably, and walked to the bedroom. He stepped inside and smiled calmly at Karen—or so he meant it. In fact, he grinned hugely, like a skull—and picked up the hoe, which leaned against the wall next to the door.

He walked carefully. The light was dim until he turned the corner toward the kitchen, where sunlight came in through the back door. With the hoe low in front of him like a mine detector, he approached the kitchen door, turned, and—the snake was gone. He surveyed the whole floor in long sweeps of his gaze. Nowhere to be seen.

Come out. You vicious, sneaking coward, you *bastard*! *Come out here*. . . . All right. All right, you fucking snake, but I'll be back. I'll hunt you down. But he scarcely believed himself.

He reached for the cabinet door, face high, to get a glass for Karen—and could not bring himself to open it. He could not even touch the handle.

He backed away and raised the hoe. Awkwardly, he managed to hook its corner in one of the door handles—and still could not raise the courage to pull on it. He was only about three feet from the cabinet. He couldn't handle the hoe over a greater distance than that.

Swallowing hard, he tugged on the hoe. As the door swung lazily open, there tumbled out from the cabinet a cascade of dish towels. He heard, and felt in his throat, a faint, breathy scream. Ohhohh, oh, my God. . . . Oh, God, I even knew those damn things were in there, I saw them before. I even knew they were poorly stacked. How could there be snakes five feet off the floor?

Still, he backed off another step before he caught the hoe in the other door and pulled it open. There was no snake in the cabinet.

Tim took down a glass and put it under the tap, not to waste a drop of the dwindling water supply. When he turned the water on, it came in a trickle, accompanied by banging and shaking in the pipe and a dry, rasping sound under the sink. Quickly he turned off the water, with just a sip in the bottom of the glass. The banging stopped, but the rasping sound continued.

Oh, *Christ*! He leaped back from the sink and stared at the cabinet under it. The sound stopped. All right, I'm gonna kill you. I'm gonna make two snakes out of you, you—. But first, he would take the water to Karen. He would need a moment to gather courage to open that cabinet and stir around with the hoe among the Ajax and Drano cans and pull him out and chop—. He shuddered.

When he got back to the bedroom, Karen was once again unconscious. Tim sat on the side of the king-sized bed, his shoulders slumped.

Alex Klein came to consciousness reluctantly. He was bone-cold, except for his head, which was burning hot, and he was in considerable pain. He began to taste stale vomit. Oh, let me sleep some more, then I'll be all right later.

Alex remembered then that he had not passed out after drinking some insupportable quantity of martinis—no, he had drowned. The idea that he was dead didn't bother him so much, if only he were allowed to feel a little better. A moment of profound horror washed through him as he realized what was meant by *dead*. But that feeling was quickly replaced, as he became more fully conscious, with the realization that he was being absurd.

He forced his eyes open—though that hurt, too; he was in bright sunlight. Why was he so cold?

Alex was lying on the bank of the stream that tumbled down the mountain past the lawn. His legs were in the water. His face hurt. His cheek, which had been scraped raw, rested on gravelly mud. He lifted his face and looked about. He did not recognize the place. He could tell, though, from the flow of the stream, that he'd been cast up on the opposite side of it from the houses—so he could get out and send help, if he could walk.

Alex dragged himself painfully up out of the water and turned to lie on his back. His legs were without feeling, which terrified him. He surveyed his position more thoroughly. A slab of rock jutted up from the stream bed just above where he was; he supposed he had been hurled against it and then up and to the side, and had been saved thereby.

Yes, he could almost feel that happening. It was as if he was remembering it. He'd hit the rock face first. But he couldn't remember pulling free of Ben's jacket in the car . . . or could he? The current through the car had certainly been strong enough to pull him free, if he got loose from the jacket. . . . Well, the hell with it. Here I am. Isn't it the shits?

Jesus Christ, what a taste. I must've coughed it up and puked it up and—hah, by God. Here I am.

There was a sickening sort of numbness in the lower part of his face. Alex tried to move his jaw and felt as much as heard, near one ear, a crumbly sound, like pebbles grating together in a little bag. He stopped instantly and took a deep breath, bracing himself for a killing pain from the place in his jaw where the crackling came from—but nothing came. There was only the numbness.

There was a long gash on his forearm—the car window, probably—partly scabbed over. It hurt when he turned his wrist and the muscles under it moved, and it seeped blood a little, but it didn't seem to be too deep. That arm had been out of the water while he'd been unconscious. His legs were beginning to pain him terribly, with an overall prickly feeling as though he were being jabbed by hundreds of needles. He was very grateful for that feeling.

After a time that sensation became less intense. Alex tried to stand, pushing himself up with his good arm, and found that he could—though he was at once so faint he nearly fell back down. When that faintness cleared, though, he took a step, and then another, up the mountain. His arm began to bleed more freely, so he carefully removed his shirt and used it to wrap the arm tightly.

I'm going to get out of here after all, by God. They're still stuck up there, but I'll get out. He decided to make his way up the mountain to the road. He could walk out easily, at least as far as the flood—but the flood might be down by now, anyway. He looked at his watch —okay, Rolex, what do you say? It was working. Damn right it's working. Ten after eight.

Well, if everybody's right about that flood—which is doubtful, considering the hysterical state they're in—it won't be down yet. But still—that flood can be gotten around, down there. Somewhere, I'd have to come to a road.

Is that right? Alex stopped for a moment. His legs still hurt, and he needed to relax to plot his course. For one thing, he realized that he was not far below the private road. This stream joins another one only a few hundred yards down the mountain, and I'm not down that far. Let's see. . . .

But his mind was still fuzzy. Hell with it. I'll solve the problem when I get to it. He started upward, and discovered after only a couple of strides through the underbrush a rattlesnake, clearly dead, apparently broken in more than one place, punctured and bloody, tangled in a fallen tree limb. Oh, yeah. Watch your step, fella, the next one might not be feeling as bad as this one.

When the four travelers had stood on the grassy mound just past the waterfall and the maple tree with its deadly fruit, they had felt proud of themselves and each other and eager for the next step in their journey. Now they half sat, half stood against a steep bank, in the shade, puffing, trembling from exhaustion, bitter with disappointment.

An hour after they began they'd heard truck traffic on the county road that was their objective. They had been that close. They couldn't see the road because of the trees, or the mountain's shape. But they were near enough to hear the traffic sounds, and they supposed their ordeal, and that of the people they'd left back at the house, was about to end.

But the mountain turned dead sheer in front of them just there, and they'd had to double back. It was more than an hour later, now—past eight o'clock. They had climbed nearly as much up as down, and far more sidewise. They were lower, though they couldn't be certain by how much, and they had been forced back in the direction they had come from so far that now they could hear, clearly, only a few yards in front of them, the falling stream they had left behind two hours ago.

Whitney had several times been in such terror looking over the edge of a path they were inching along that she had nearly fainted. She had kept her fear to herself, though; none of the others knew. Like everyone else, she had torn flesh from her hands gripping bushes, and from her legs sliding downward from one flat spot to the next. But she had not fainted, and had not fallen, and had broken no bones, nor even sprained an ankle. Nor had any of the others.

"Listen, what the hell," Ted was saying. "We *are* getting back toward the stream, but that's not so terrible, either. We'll come down to the private road pretty soon, now, and we can walk out on it, easily."

"Gotta start watching our step, though," Ben said. "Close enough, there's gonna be snakes again." They had only one implement left with them, the spade. They'd discarded the rest as too awkward to climb with, and passed the spade from one to the other, freeing hands in turn.

"Oh, damn, damn, *damn*!" Annie said.

Whitney didn't care about the snakes. The thought of achieving that broad, flat road made her weak with anticipation. She nearly wept with relief at the thought. Her exhaustion was as much emotional as physical. It wasn't only the now-and-again scalding terror of looking over a cliff. There was the constant, profoundly disturbing, disorienting sense of being . . . up. High. On ground that was never level enough to relax on. Having the infinitely vast sky not above her but at her side or in front of her or—worst of all, sometimes behind her. Always tugging at her.

Oh, that road. Flat. Under trees. Oh, yes. But not so quick, Whitney Louise. Look at what's right in front of us. I think Ben stopped to rest here because he saw it. I don't see how we're going to get around that cliff. Climb up? There's no way down. Are we stuck finally?

She craned her neck and peered at the cliff's face. Her eyes picked out a way across it, though it made her stomach lurch. A little shelf, perhaps a foot wide, ran out ten or twelve feet, then ended. There you could step up, across a gap of a couple of feet, to a wider ledge, maybe a foot higher. Then—but she tore her eyes from it. Obviously they weren't going to try that. She was just making herself crazy, clambering across it in fantasy.

Hello darkness, my old friend. . . . Randall Madison was vaguely irritated that his mind should be haunted so persistently by pop music. The phrase had come to him more than once. Sometimes he thought it had been twenty times, or fifty—but it might have been only two or three times.

The darkness was his friend, though, that was true; consciousness was unending pain and dread. *Hello darkness, my old friennn*—Stop it! He thought he might be dying. He didn't believe he was, but he recognized that the idea was not absurd. He didn't believe it because the pain had not subsided; so long as he was conscious some part of his body burned. It was in his chest now. He felt as though some relentlessly destructive acid had been injected into each of his cells.

And he couldn't believe that you could die in such pain; the notion simply offended his sense of order, of justice. You might have the pain—though in fact he'd never known that pain like this existed—or you might have death, but both—the idea was intolerable. *Hello dark . . .*

. . . old friend. Oh, Jesus, how much time did I lose in there? Oh, goddamnit, please, let the pain just . . . just let it please go away for a minute. Ten seconds. I could gather strength. . . .

I cannot be dying with Simon and Barfle in my mind. My body knows if it's dying, my cells know, and if I were dying, it would play Bach. I'm a trivial-minded man, but not if I were dying. Beethoven. *Missa Solemnis.* Am I a trivial person? Will I die a trivial person? I haven't done—I never—*Hello darkness—friennnd.*

Ah, Tim, you're a love. Why is Karen in bed with me? Keeping me company, lovely loving sister . . . *my old friennnnd.* Stop it! Oh, pain, *stop it*! Please? *Hello dark—*

Randall's eyes had been open, though blank and unfocused; now the lids fluttered and closed. In a moment tears welled out of them. Karen was conscious, now, suffering fever and chills and some stomach pain. She had taken the water, feeling deprived that Tim would allow her so little, and retched afterward, but had thrown nothing up. Her mind was clear enough at the moment, though too tired to follow a thought very far.

She had been in terror earlier, as she had seen some of Randall's suffering and supposed the same thing lay before her. She no longer believed that would happen. She believed that Randall would die no matter when help arrived, and that she would not if they came soon. But please, soon. How long had they been gone? It seemed forever. She was very tired of being in pain, and of not knowing what would become of her.

Tim sat on the edge of the bed, patting Randall's face gently with a towel, though Randall was not perspiring very much now. Tim knows Randall's dying, she thought. Poor Tim.

Her gaze shifted around the room. It had seemed to her earlier—delirium, she now realized—that there were snakes all about. On the walls, even. She had been terribly afraid, then, and insanely angry with Ted for having left her.

She was still angry with Ted. He's been gone so long! She supposed it was right for him to go; they had explained it to her carefully before they left, but she'd been barely able to comprehend words then. Big and strong and agile. Very difficult terrain. Terrain. They might come to a place only Ted could climb, or leap across. But he can't leap with Charley. He mustn't.

Karen was beginning to become fuzzy again. She guessed she'd sleep for a while. Oh, yes, my mind is becoming feverish—I see a big devil of a snake coming through the door. I'll go to sleep. . . .

I'll tell Tim, anyway. I'm going to sleep, Tim dear, because of the snake. She pointed, and he looked. His face went slack and then his eyes bulged.

Oh, God, it's real! She came awake again, and very alert. The snake, the first she'd seen, was bigger than she expected. Ten feet? She didn't know how to estimate its size. No, ten feet is the height of the basket, and Ted had to leap hard to dunk the ball. Half that? Five feet? It made a long S, then stretched forward with its head and brought its tail up to form the S again.

Its motion seemed aimless at first, but it came toward the bed and out of her line of vision. She looked at Tim, who pulled his legs up onto the bed and sat, hugging his knees. They were like survivors on a raft.

We can't just stay here like this. He'll find a way up here. Onto our terrain.

If he's real. . . . I'll go to sleep 'till Ted comes. Maybe he's outside right now, right this minute. . . .

The cliff was not so much a cliff, really, as a very steep slope, both above the ledge and below. Much too steep to climb on, or slide down safely, but still. . . . Ben thought it might be possible to lean against the rough stone, sort of lie down on it, and walk sidewise across the narrow, broken ledge to the other side. It was twenty feet, maybe thirty, to where the slope became more manageable. As near as could be seen, it would be clear sailing from there on down—and just a little more sidewise, around a sheer drop—to the road.

They were all equally certain that they could see the private road below them—or anyway, that a certain gap in the treetops indicated the road. The stream was no more than twenty yards from the other side of the cliff, from the sound of it, and that did mean snake danger—but they probably wouldn't have to get any closer than that.

"It's the worst yet," Annie said. "I don't know . . . maybe you and Ted should go ahead."

"Don't think you can make it?" Ben asked.

"I can make it, but I'm not so sure about Whitney."

Whitney said, "I can make it if you all can. I'll watch how you do it." *She looks terrified,* Ben thought, *but she's done okay up until now.*

Ted said, "I don't think it's even going to be all that hard. The angle of the slope is just about perfect to lean on."

Ben nodded. "All right, I'll go first, just to see how it goes, then I'll come back." And he stepped out, right foot first, face and chest against the rocky slope. In fact, he felt pretty secure. Much of his weight was supported by his hands.

The wind, a pleasant little breeze in the shelter of the trees, did not grow stronger once you stepped onto the ledge, but did become a factor in maintaining balance. It could be constantly felt, pushing gently, and the others should be warned. As he pushed away from the mountainside a few inches to make his next step, the wind swirled between his body and the rock and shoved him away, backward toward the emptiness, but he collapsed his arms and easily fell forward.

Another step, pushing away with his left hand and reaching and grabbing the rough rock with his right, then dragging the left foot up to the right. *Could Annie do this? Could Whitney? Annie can, I can talk her* across. And if worse comes to worst, Whitney can stay back there on the grassy place until we can get somebody here with climbing gear who would know how to rescue her. Or maybe Annie would want to stay with her.

"Hold it!" Ted called. "Your right foot is just short of the break now."

Ben looked down at his foot and over the edge, down the mountainside. The slope dropped thirty or forty feet at maximum steepness, then there was a ledge three feet or so wide, covered with grass and moss, that ran downward at an angle until it disappeared after another ten or fifteen yards in brush and trees. It would be an extremely nasty fall, even if you stuck on that ledge and didn't bounce on over—though it probably wouldn't kill you. Past the grassy ledge the cliff dropped, more sheer than up here apparently, another—well, he couldn't see. There were what looked like maple leaves growing up out of the space beyond it, and out past that the tops of trees that seemed to be pretty tall. So that drop was a mystery, but probably huge—a killer.

Well—the drop under the George Washington Bridge is huge, too, but there's no good reason to fall off it. Let's just see about this step, here. The step across the break in the path was only a couple of feet, and the other side—wider than the path he stood on, almost a comfortable width—was only a few inches higher. An easy enough step for me. Annie? Yeah. Even Whitney.

And Ben took it, telling himself to forget that there was nothing between his feet. He reached with his right hand to get a new grip, then flexed his left leg and pushed off with some vigor, the better to take all his weight on his leading right foot. Right. Not difficult.

He stood on the second ledge now. It was, in fact, comfortably wide. Ben looked ahead of him to be very sure that he saw every step they'd all have to take. It would be easy, he saw, from here on; all straight-ahead walking, and then just a little comparatively easy climbing down. His sense of relief was overwhelming.

His muscles ached with fatigue, from the incessant climbing and from insufficient sleep. He was covered with bruises, scratches, and cuts. And there had been a space of an hour or more when he'd half believed that they would not find their way out at all, but would end up marooned. While Randall and Karen slowly and painfully died. Now the end was in sight.

Ben turned and grinned at the others across the face of the cliff. "It's easy," he called. "Wait a minute, I'll come back." He turned and stepped back across the gap, forcefully reminding himself again to concentrate intensely on each step and handgrip. He didn't want to overlook any difficult spot, and especially he didn't want to fool himself that it was easier than it really was. *Did* he really want Annie to attempt it?

When he reached the others again, he said, "Yeah, we can do it. A lot of your weight rests on your hands, against the cliff. It actually isn't as dangerous as the place back there where we crossed that mossy rock. The fall would be worse here, but the footing's much better. The gap out there is only a couple of feet, an easy step even for Whitney, who's the smallest, and the ledge after that is wide enough to walk straight ahead on—"

"How's the wind?" Ted said.

"The wind will scare you a little—it tugs at you. But it really isn't strong at all. If you keep close to the cliff it can't get you."

"Can I make it with Charley on my back?" Ted asked. "He overbalances me a little."

"No problem," Ben told him. "You really are almost lying down out there with your body against the slope."

Annie said, "All right—who goes first?" She thought that she should go before Whitney, so Whitney could see her do it.

"I do," Ben said, "and you with me, and Ted behind you. Then Ted and I'll go back for Whitney." Ted nodded and handed Charley to Whitney.

Annie was suddenly aware of just how tired she was, how weak her legs felt. For the first time, she felt a moment's resentment toward her baby. You are taking too much from me! Oh, no, it's all right, baby, Annie said silently, Ben'll take care of us. Ben took her hand and sidled out onto the ledge. He said, "Now I'm going to let go of your hand—" Oh, no, don't do that!—but he had. "You'll need it to hang on with, and I'll keep touching your arm, see, so you'll know I have you." He moved a step farther out to make room for her.

Annie leaned against the cliff and stepped out. Though she could feel her weight being supported quite securely by the cliffside as well as by the ledge beneath her feet, it was impossible not to be aware of the drop-off inches from her foot. The sound of the wind, and of the stream falling nearby, swirled in her ears, and somehow accentuated the vastness of the sky behind her and the earth stretching away impossibly steeply below her. But she kept her eyes on Ben.

He smiled. "Fine, you're doing fine. Reach just as far as you'll be comfortable with your hand and find a new grip, then step, then pull your back foot up to your front—that's fine, fine."

The wind was pushing at her now; it was gentle, but insistent, and she felt that if she were the least bit careless, or if it grew only slightly stronger, it would grab her and fling her, flying, soaring, slowly spinning. . . . Annie closed her eyes and flattened herself to the rock for a moment. No, listen, baby, I made that up, it didn't happen, we're all right.

She opened her eyes and smiled at Ben, who looked relieved. He was standing facing her straightaway, not face to the hillside, and he was a long step away from her now. "You're at the gap," he said. "Hold your right foot still and slide your left foot up to it—good. Now reach out again, then just take a big step, up just a little bit, toward me, and I'll grab you. You'll make it without me, you don't need me to grab you, but I will, anyway."

Just as the picture of the drop was beginning to form again, before it could get a grip on her, Annie reached and stepped. As she leaned out a little from the cliff, the wind took her hair, swirled it up and away, out into space, tugged at her head. She missed her grip with her reaching hand and felt, before she was expecting it, firm, solid, immovable rock under her striding foot, and Ben took hold of her outstretched arm. He pulled her to him, into his arms. She was fine. She'd made it.

Ben murmured into her hair, "You were wonderful, wonderful, I'm proud of you, that was fine."

He left her on the broad shelf then and returned, following Ted, back to the other side. It looked terrifying, this trip that she'd just made. Step, reach—step. . . . If he miscalculated the tiniest bit in putting his foot down, he'd go—. My God, did I do that?

Whitney seemed stiff as a puppet, and scarcely more in command of what she was doing. Oh, Christ—leave her, she won't make it. But she was making it, one jerky step at a time, until Ben, moving ahead of her, made the stride across the gap to stand beside Annie. "All right," he said, "you're at the gap. Hold your—" but Whitney had looked down, through the gap. Her mouth slowly opened, and her eyes grew impossibly wide. She gripped the rock fiercely and pressed her body to it as though she would never move.

Oh, God, Annie thought, this is bad—she isn't going to move. Ted, unable to urge her on, looked over her at Ben.

Ben said, "Whitney. Look at me." But Whitney's eyes did not move up. Her face was now soaked with sweat—it had flooded out of her as suddenly as that. She was rock still, except that her ribs heaved with huge, yawn-like breaths. Her jeans whipped around her ankles, flapping in the wind.

Ben said softly, with infinite calm that Annie knew was a signal that he was seriously frightened, "Whitney, don't do anything, just hold still and I'll get you." And he gripped the rocky cliff with his right hand and stretched out with his left to take hold of her wrist. But when she felt his hand she yanked hers away. Wet with perspiration, it slipped through his fingers, and Whitney was thrown off balance, teetering out from the cliff for a split second before she restored her contact with it.

Ted had a firm grip on her upper arm, but he could accomplish nothing with it, because his footing was too precarious, and he had the baby in the carrier on his back again now.

Annie was beginning to know what Whitney felt. Annie had been stuck on the roof of a tool shed once, when she was a little girl. She had been in the same state of frozen panic that Whitney was in now. Annie had not been willing to jump into her mother's arms, but she did it for her daddy. Jumped right to him. But Whitney. . . . Why won't Whitney. . . . "Ben," she said. "Let me get there." For some reason, Whitney doesn't trust Daddy. She wants Mommy. How do I know that? I don't know that, I don't know anything. I don't know aything. Oh, hell, it's worth a try.

But Ben wasn't about to move to let Annie stand on the edge of that drop. "Ben, it's all right, I'll kneel down, and you can reach over me. She needs to see me, that's all." He moved aside, very carefully, and Annie knelt on the ledge.

"Whitney," she said. And Whitney's gaze shifted, from straight down the mountainside to Annie. Nothing about her expression changed, though, and when Annie's hair billowed out in the wind again, Whitney's saucer-like eyes grew larger still. Oh, goddamnit, hold still! Annie reached up and grabbed her hair and pulled it down alongside her face. Then she reached out again—she could almost touch Whitney's waist. If she leaned just a little—but Ben grabbed her shoulder to prevent her from doing that. All right, all right.

"Whitney, dear, come to me, it's all right." Tears tumbled out of Whitney's eyes and spread through the perspiration on her cheeks, running down to drip off her chin and be pulled away by the wind. Her nose was running, too. I'm right, Annie thought, she's a tiny little

girl. All right. . . . "Come here, darlin', I'll get you."
Darlin'. Is that the right thing to call her? Can I say
come to Mommy? Mama? How else could I—What was
it she called herself? Oh, yes. . . . "Whitney Louise,
come—"

And Whitney came, simply collapsing toward Annie,
falling almost straight down through the gap. Ben
grabbed for her and missed, and Annie grabbed for her
and caught hold of her arm and was pulled. Suddenly
her secure perch was gone and Annie was tumbling forward, after Whitney, past the gap and the little ledge
and into that dreadful, sickening empty space.

CHAPTER

17

Alex had reached the road. It was lined with trees where he emerged from the bushes, and he could see neither up the mountain nor down, but he could still hear the stream clearly. So—they said this road was three miles. Well, then, he had three miles to walk.

He sat on the ground, knees up, head between them, catching his breath and settling his mind. All right, now think about that flood. There's no bridge where the flood is, just a low stretch in the road—Alex had, in fact, driven through it Friday evening, though it had been too shallow to pay much attention to, then—so the stream doesn't go through, it just floods out to the side. So I should be able to walk—or climb—around it, and be on my way out to the county road. Yeah.

All right, nothing complicated about it. I'll walk out of here and get help. I'll—but he heard strange, confusing sounds above him on the mountainside. Sounded like people shouting: one man's voice, maybe two, and a woman—Whitney?—screaming. From the house?

Alex got to his feet and was attacked again by dizziness. After he stood for a moment, the feeling lifted from him and he cocked his head to hear more. No more sound came. He tried to call out, but his jaw was slack and exploded with pain—ohh, God . . . decided to hurt, did you? Oh-hh—so that he produced only a sort of feral howl.

Jesus! Well, I know what I heard, and it was not back at the house, it was straight above me. He plunged into the underbrush on the uphill side of the road and began climbing, grabbing at trees and bushes, falling forward and sliding back, struggling furiously upward.

After a few minutes, Alex was confirmed in his judgment that the sound had come from above him. He heard a gunshot.

Ted and Ben had watched the two women fall, slide really, to the first ledge, thump hard on it, almost on top of each other, and bounce on over it into the chasm beyond it, all in what seemed like the tiniest part of a second. Now it played over in Ben's mind in slow motion, in precise detail.

They had fallen differently, Annie sliding, tearing her hands trying to grip the mountainside, battling the mountain for her life. Whitney had been like a rag doll. Whitney had half bounced, half slid along the grassy ledge a little way before she slid on over. Annie had bounced straight on into the abyss. There had been a scream—Whitney—but that had stopped short when she hit the ledge. Silence since.

"Jesus," Ted said solemnly. He still stood on the precarious narrow ledge, Charley on his back. He looked at Ben, who had just seen his pregnant wife fall, probably to her death. He looked at him guardedly, as if expecting to see him fling himself over after her. But Ben was calmer than he'd been in all this time, since the landslide last night.

"Ted, go on for help," he said. "I'm going to climb down there and see how they are. But you can be out of here and have help on the way in half an hour. So, besides a 'copter to the house with the snakebite stuff, tell 'em to send—whoever, a rescue squad of mountain climbers, they must have mountain rescue people around here—whatever, send help here, too."

"I—"

"Go on."

"Right." Ted wasn't really inclined to argue. Karen had a limited amount of time, no one knew how much. Randall, too.

Ted stepped over the gap to the wider ledge and followed Ben a few steps to where Ben stopped and stared down the slope. Ted walked on, to an easier path down to the road, already thinking ahead. A CB radio is what I'll need. A car with a—or a truck. Truckers all have them. : . .

Ben watched him go, calling after him, "Watch for snakes from here on down," and then turned to look over the edge. The mountain was less steep, just past the sheer rock face, and scrubby bushes grew out of it. He could slide down on his belly, using bushes to plant his feet against and for hand grips. He was wearing Alex's ski jacket, which protected his skin from the brush and rocks. He would lower himself to the ledge that had not stopped Annie and Whitney, and look over to see what else he could do. Annie, hang on, I'll be right there. You'll be all right, we'll have another baby.

Hearing himself think that, he discovered what he believed: Annie isn't dead, she can't be, she's just too determined to live. But not even Annie could keep a baby through that. *Damn!*

Hanging from one skinny little bush, his foot slipping off another one, he became aware of his weight. In fact, he seemed to weigh hundreds of pounds. The weight pulled on his hands and wrists, where fatigue was making itself evident. And he could feel it pull and push at these frail bushes.

When Ben was about halfway down the thirty-foot drop to the ledge, the bush he was gripping with his right hand suddenly pulled out by the roots. For half a second he was supported by his other hand, and by the mountainside itself against his belly. Then the other bush gave way and he began to slide, slowly at first, then gathering speed, then—with a thump he landed on the ledge, on his side.

He was not seriously hurt, though he had landed on the pistol in his jacket pocket. That hurt like hell, and he thought he might have cracked a rib. He struggled to a sitting position and caught his breath painfully. Just a minute, Annie, I'm okay. There was a terrible ringing in his ears. Then, as that sensation cleared, he heard the worst sound he had known in his life—not for the first time, but for the hundredth, or so it seemed, and once too often to be tolerated. It was a rattlesnake, close to him.

Ben looked toward the sound, down the sloping grassy ledge, and there it was. A small one, coiled, its head raised, glaring at him. Oh, you bastard, just get out of my way. Get out of here.

The snake wasn't in his path, if he went straight over the edge where he was, but he didn't know where he wanted to go over the edge. He hadn't yet looked to see if he wanted to go down at all. If he did not, then the snake was directly in his way; if he did go over, he would be exposing his face and his hands to this killer as he lowered himself.

Well, all right, let's just find out . . . and he took the pistol from the jacket pocket, reached out with it—God! It's heavy—watched the sight waver and tremble, gripped his wrist and the heel of his hand with his other hand, steadied, wavered, steadied on—and had to stop to cock: Squeezing the trigger to pull the hammer back made the barrel dip and sway.

He lowered the gun to rest his arm for the second it took to pull the hammer back with his thumb, and the snake, which had seemed hypnotized by the barrel of the pistol, slid easily into motion toward him. He rushed the pistol back into the aiming position and fired—*Whamp!* The revolver kicked harder than he expected. This was a regular round, with a full load of powder. Ben felt the kick to his elbows, and saw the muzzle jump. He missed the snake, by how much he couldn't tell. But it flinched, then turned and crawled away into the underbrush.

Sshhit. He returned the pistol to his pocket and moved to the edge of the drop-off. Annie? Annie, I'm coming. Be there, goddamnit. Please.

The mountain king was resting under his log, barely conscious, when the first faint vibrations made themselves felt to him. Creatures on this mountainside. Above him. Moving violently, sliding, falling toward him.

His body was very cool, and as a result he was scarcely alert enough to be alarmed. Then came two great thumps in the earth very near him, and then one of the bodies slammed against his log, moving it inches across the needle-strewn earth. The creature rolled over the king's body and came to rest beside him.

It was stretched out on the earth as he was, and it was huge. Not as long as the mountain king, but much heavier. Not as large as the largest deer that lived in these mountains, but far bigger than any other creature he was used to seeing. It was alive—he sensed the warmth of its body, and the erratic exhalations of its breath. But it was absolutely still. Its scent on the tips of his tongue was sharp and strange.

The mountain king remained alongside it for a few seconds, gathering strength. Then he began to move away from it, gripping the slippery ground with the ridges across his belly. His senses were dull, and he had no information—in his memory, his instincts, his genes—to tell him if he were in danger from a creature that behaved so oddly, lying as still as death while still alive.

So he did not strike but moved away, in a state of dim uneasiness that had no clear focus and that gave his reflexes no message to act on. As he progressed, he slid into a pool of sunlight, and the temperature rose a few degrees—a very significant change, to the mountain king.

He moved laboriously up the slope for a distance of one of his lengths, two . . . and the tension began to leave him. He was out of reach of the big creature. The sun's warmth felt good to him, though it had not yet raised his internal temperature enough to restore his suppleness or the speed of his reflexes.

Then, suddenly, he sensed the other body, directly in front of him, also alive. First he sensed its warmth, then its scent, then he saw it move, just inches from his eyes.

CHAPTER

18

Baby? Annie said silently. Baby, are you with me? Baby, don't leave me, I'll take care of us after this, I promise. Annie was lying on her back, her feet higher than her head. She thought she'd been unconscious—for how long? Maybe only seconds. She could remember part of the fall, not all.

Damn, that hurts, she thought, meaning a dozen different things. She had a sharp pain in her side that hurt when she breathed, and a lot of raw, broad areas of pain that were probably scrapes. She moved one foot at a time; one ankle ached like hell, but the foot moved. She wiggled her toes, and the ankle stabbed her again, but the toes wiggled. I can't believe it, she thought; I'm not too bad.

Well, baby—and then she realized that she was warm and wet between her legs. Oh, baby, please, no. Oh, God, that's not fair, I'm all right, you didn't have to—. She steeled herself to reach and touch herself there. Her right hand was sore, torn and scraped, but it could feel the hot wetness of her jeans. She closed her eyes for a second, raised her hand and looked. Bloody. Oh, my God, baby, I'm so sorry . . . wait. Wait! The blood was from the cuts on her hand. She looked at her other hand—dirty and scraped, but not bleeding.

She touched herself again, and looked. The hand was wet, but not bloody. What, then? What? Oh, God, it's—her chest heaved with a burst of triumphant laughter, causing her side to jab her with pain—*ow*! Oh, that's wonderful, baby—baby, I've pissed my pants after all, isn't that wonderful? We'll be all right. We'll be all right 'til Ben comes. Come soon, Ben, please.

"Whitney?" she said, and turned and saw Whitney, lying below her, against a log. She was staring up at Annie, looking deadly calm. Looking, in fact, dead—but then she blinked.

Whitney Williams could not feel her body. She wondered if she could move, but she felt no urgency about doing it. The numbness was bearable, and she felt that motion might cause . . . something intolerable. Perhaps she'd shatter, or explode.

"Whitney?" Annie's voice, barely above a whisper. Whitney realized that she was looking at Annie, had been all the while. She saw Annie's shoulder and face; her body, stretched out in the opposite direction from Whitney's own, was hidden behind low bushes.

Then Whitney saw movement just in front of her own face. With difficulty she refocused her eyes to see what it was. It was blunt-tipped, grew wider for a couple of inches and then suddenly narrower: a head. It was black and leathery rough. Behind the wedge-shaped head it stretched out alongside her body farther than she could see, much thicker than her arm. Muscles rippled under the shiny, rough-grained black skin.

Moving. Toward Annie. No, don't do that. Don't hurt Annie. I could stop it—I could reach out and grab it, if I grabbed behind the head. But she could not make her hand move until the thing was out of reach. Then she reached, feebly, in what served as a sort of waved apology to Annie.

Annie thought: A snake—my God, that's a snake by Whitney. It seemed mammoth. It was longer than Whitney's body, at least a foot longer, and thick. All black. It can't be a rattlesnake, that size.

Annie saw Whitney squint her eyes at it, but Whitney's head didn't move, her expression didn't even really change. The snake was moving—Oh, God, no, snake, *Whitney, make it stop, you can*—it was moving toward Annie, up the slope, slowly and smoothly, death sinuously gliding. Whitney made a motion with her hand that may have meant, I'm sorry. Oh, *shit*, Annie said silently.

When it came near her face, she turned away and looked up at the sky, which bleared and sparkled as her eyes filled with tears.

In a moment she felt a nudge at her shoulder. She turned and looked and blinked. Four inches from her eyes, the black, shiny, leathery muscle moved, alongside her body, past her shoulder, toward her feet.

She could see waves of muscle flexions running along under the skin; flecks of a paler color on its back. She saw the skin wrinkle and become smooth again as the body curved and straightened. The sharp little belly ridges moved rhythmically along the forest floor like tank tracks, propelling the beast forward.

Annie could barely accept the idea that this might be a rattlesnake. Its body, she thought, is taller than my shoulder lying on the ground. And it just keeps coming, and coming—it's like one of those hundred-car freight trains that cross in front of your car.

Its skin was torn in places. At one place there was a ragged hole where flesh was ripped away to expose damp white ribs. Pale pink, watery blood had flowed from that wound and dried along the monster's side.

The scab cracked and bits of it flaked off as the skin moved under it.

Then Annie felt a weight on her left leg, below the knee—*It's crawling over me!*—and then a gentle nudge on the inside of her right knee as the belly ridges continued to ripple across her left leg. She strained to keep her legs still, not to flinch. She turned to look down the front of her body, but she could see nothing without raising her head, and she was afraid to move that much.

She turned back to watch the body sliding past her shoulder—she felt a terrible compulsion to see it end. As the weight moved to the top of her right thigh and then to her lower abdomen, the body in front of her eyes became narrower and then the rattles appeared, and passed—four, five inches of them.

The weight continued to make its way across her left leg, up her right, and onto her abdomen. She was determined to be absolutely still. Carefully, with infinite slowness, she turned her head to face the beast. It was still moving, heavy on her belly, cool and surprisingly hard on a strip of bare skin where her shirt had pulled up from her jeans; and now feathery-light between her breasts.

The head was not a head, but a weapon. It had a blunt snout, yellow eyes of absolutely no depth under hard, bony ridges that looked like fiercely frowning brows. It was small, the head. It was so close it filled her vision and she could see the scaly pattern of its skin in exquisite detail, but the head was tiny, considering the weight of the creature on her body. There was something awful about the grotesque disproportion.

Its skin was black, and its tongue was black. But the skin was the black of rotted leaves and the tongue the black of dried blood. Its tongue was shiny and forked and very long; it flicked just inches from her face before it disappeared into its slit of a mouth.

Still the motion continued across her legs and onto her torso, where its weight was becoming huge. The

head remained still; it was drawing the rest of its body
up to itself.

Don't you—interfere with me. You killer. It isn't
right, I'm going to have a baby. Please. Let me *alone*,
you—

The head began to sway in a tiny arc from side to side,
the tongue beginning to flick again. Annie glared at it
until she surprised herself by speaking aloud, in a soft,
tense murmur. "Ben'll kill you if you hurt me and my
baby," she told the beast. You dirty unspeakable
sonofabitch, *sonofabitch*! The head became perfectly
still when she spoke, then resumed its tiny motion when
she fell silent.

She heard a gunshot, then, up the mountain. Oh,
Ben, you can't hit him from there, what's the matter
with you?

And then she heard sounds from below her, near
Whitney—thrashing in the underbrush and the snuf-
fling, snorting moan of some animal. Oh, God, what?
What more? And the snake's head stopped moving
again, froze in a new attitude, stared down the slope,
flicking its tongue. After a moment it returned to its
scrutiny of Annie's face, swaying again in a slightly
longer arc.

Once again she spoke to the creature: "Ben won't
hurt you if you go away and leave me alone." She
couldn't take her eyes from it, though now she heard
sounds from up the slope. That would be Ben.

Why doesn't this horrible beast strike me? It's big
enough to kill me in seconds. Maybe it's hypnotizing
me? Do snakes really do that? It's so *heavy*. Oh, God,
please make this filthy brute go away and leave me alone
with my baby.

"Snake . . . listen, it's not fair, I'm going to have a
baby. You've no *reason*—" But her voice was beginning
to break.

Staring into the blank yellow eyes, the leathery lipless
mouth, she saw a perfect mask of indifference. Of cold-

bloodedness. The awful knowledge flowed through her just as the venom would: This is a rattlesnake, and a rattlesnake's business is to inject poison into living things with its horrible hollow fangs and kill them.

Indifferently. Cold-bloodedly.

The sounds from below her had ceased for a time, but now the bushes shook. Whatever it was was coming up toward her—coming for her. What will kill me, the rattlesnake, or—no picture formed in her mind of what the other creature could be.

The sounds in the brush above her were very close now. Ben? Oh, yes, Ben, come—but the monster on her belly began to produce his sound, penetrating and loud, half whisper, half rattle, filling her ears.

And then the head disappeared from her line of vision, pulling back—she closed her eyes and turned her face away. There was a gathering, and an increase in the weight on her abdomen, and then no motion but a faint, insistent vibration, as though the snake had an electrical current running through it. And the sound, the rattle filling her ears, filling her mind.

Oh, snake, please. . . . Ben, please. . . .

The mountain king, with his primitive brain that was scarcely a brain at all, did not have emotions, did not conceptualize, did not in any conscious way envision death. Yet he knew—his body knew—that he was nearer to dying than he'd ever been.

He was terribly battered, and he had bled a great deal. His nervous system was dulled; perhaps by the battering, but also because his temperature in the damp shade was so low. When his shelter was violently removed from him, his body had protested, but it had moved.

He had moved away from the huge living thing that had crashed down upon him, and the thing had not disturbed him, not required him to strike and kill it—for if the mountain king struck even a thing that size, it would die, and quickly. He knew that with his every cell.

He moved away from it in what must be called heedless confusion, though his brain could express no such humanly conceptualized emotions. His uneasiness had subsided just momentarily as he left that creature's presence, then leaped again to confusion and panic—desperation—when he came upon the second one.

He moved away from its head and found its lower part, found it warm and soft. Warmth and softness to rest his bruised and torn body, with its brutalized muscles and broken ribs. Struggling, he moved onto the faintly trembling, living bed.

Coming to rest in the warmth of the sun above him and the soft warmth under him, he found himself off the earth for the first time in his third of a century of life . . . and comfortable. He was distracted, confused by this odd restfulness. But in a second, he felt with the heat sensors in the pits in his skull the hot breath in front of him. Should he strike? But the reflex was blunted. The creature made no threatening motion. He tasted its scent with his tongue and ceased all other movement, not to provoke it.

As he rested, the sun's warmth and the creature's warmth suffused his body, beginning to restore his alertness and some of his strength. His pain became more vivid to him, but his suppleness was returning, too. Then something even more baffling occurred: The creature's mouth moved and he felt its voice, felt vibrations from its body, on which all of his own body now rested. There his senses focused, on that half-soothing, half-disturbing vibration that ran through him from the body of the other creature.

When it ceased, he regathered his attention and directed it to the creature's face. The tension was returning to him, now. There was something wrong—there was nothing right—about this situation. This huge thing could certainly kill him if he didn't kill it first. It had strong appendages to grab him with, a huge mouth to bite him. . . . But then the mouth moved and the irregular vibrations came from its body once again, and the mountain king was, once again, paralyzed by his divided attention.

When the voice stopped, he saw motion at a little distance from him, down the slope. Then that ceased, and he returned his gaze to the face in front of him.

The skin was furless, as smooth as his own, but soft. The bone structure under it was evident to him. The jaw, the cheekbone—his fangs would scrape against the hard bone and tear flesh, but would not penetrate as he wanted them to. The lips were soft and full, but he knew that flat, big teeth were just behind them. The eyeball was moist and soft. . . .

As the tension, the alertness, returned to his body, the mountain king drew himself up and began to make his own vibration, the familiar, comforting one that came from the lower part of his body, that meant nothing to him except that he was alive and strong, but that said to all other creatures: Here is the mountain king, holding pain and death for other living things, whatever their size, however sharp their hooves or their teeth or their claws. The mountain king has nothing for you but death.

CHAPTER

19

Alex Klein scrambled, crawled, climbed, slipped back, lay on his belly catching his breath and allowing his unwilling legs to rest; and returned to scrambling upward. The slope would be almost easy enough to walk on for a few yards, then would leap upward nearly vertical for a few feet. It was dotted with brush and trees.

At one point he had seen above him a relatively flat spot receding from his line of sight, then above that a short, steep bank about six feet high, then a ledge, and above that a bare, rocky cliff much too steep to climb. But as he ascended, bushes and trees interfered with his view upward, so he climbed blindly.

Finally cresting the first hump onto a flat spot, he grabbed a fallen log lying across his path. It shifted as he pulled himself up over it, turned and slid lazily, end-first, down the slope beside him. He grunted as he grabbed for something to stop himself sliding after the log, and shouted when what he grabbed was a leg—a slender woman's leg wearing blue jeans. Whitney's leg.

"What?" he meant to say, but his slack and painful

jaw produced a shapeless sound. Alex's inadvertent tug pulled Whitney over the edge. She slipped sideways along the sloped earth, sliding downward slowly, gently, a couple of yards, coming to rest on a flat, shady spot, her face obscured by deep grass. Alex had caught a glimpse of her face as it slid away from him.

Whitney hadn't spoken, but she had looked at him with an oddly apologetic expression. She looked sad, opened her mouth to speak but didn't, raised her eyebrows and crinkled them over the bridge of her nose—I couldn't help it, she had seemed to say.

What? he thought. For a moment he didn't move toward her, as he struggled to get a solid purchase on the earth, to avoid sliding helplessly downward. Then he heard a soft voice murmuring above him. A woman—Annie or Karen? He looked upward toward the sound and saw Annie's long, reddish-blond hair spread on the earth. He saw her head and shoulders; the rest of her was obscured behind bushes.

He was about to move back down toward Whitney when he heard the rattle, coming from near Annie. He froze for a moment, then very slowly, making as little motion in the bushes as he could manage, he crawled up farther so he could see along the length of Annie's body.

Coiled on Annie was a rattlesnake of appalling size. Its head was raised up off the heap of its body, swaying gently.

And a few feet beyond the black head was the muzzle of Alex's pistol, in Ben Axelrod's hand, pointing at the rattlesnake's head and at Alex Klein's face. Ben looked coldly down the barrel and squeezed the trigger.

Ben looked over the edge of the grassy shelf and saw that the sheer drop was only about six feet. After that, the earth fell away in an incline not so steep as the drop he had just climbed down, and then there was a broad, mounded flat area, and past that another drop-off. The whole space was dotted with trees; some of it was grassy, and in some places it was overgrown with thick brush. He could see Whitney, lying at the edge of the last drop-off, perhaps fifty feet from him. Nearer, through underbrush, he saw glimpses of Annie.

He moved carefully down the slope. Don't get careless, now, a few seconds isn't going to make any difference, just watch your step. In fact he wasn't so much stepping as sliding on his backside, slowing and controlling himself with his heels and his hands. He lost sight of both women as he moved downward.

As he edged around the last big bush obscuring his view of Annie, he saw—but he hardly believed what he saw. It took him a moment to sort out the great, dark heap on Annie's abdomen. When its head swayed—less than a foot from Annie's face—it suddenly became clear what he was seeing.

Ben never wondered what he might do, only set about doing it. He was pulling the pistol from his pocket as he estimated the distance to the snake—too far, much too far to be sure of hitting it. Twelve, fifteen feet, to hit an object—he was sure he had to hit the head, or near it, to kill it before it could strike—an object maybe two inches by three. And in motion—slowly, regularly swaying.

He did not wonder whether he could kill it before it struck. There was simply no reason to consider that he might not, even though he knew his chances were scarcely even. He did wonder, as he sidled along the slope to get nearer, what was preventing the rattlesnake from striking—though Annie's stillness was surely helping. Oh, Jesus, has he killed her already, is she dead? What's it doing just sitting there? Playing, like a cat? You're gonna die, you sadistic sonofabitch.

Down to about six feet now, and the snake still hadn't detected his presence or changed its position. He could hear Annie's voice—for God's sake, she's talking! Well, she's alive, then, goddamnit, right. He stopped and planted his feet so that his knees came up and made a rest for his elbows. As he did, he dislodged a little rock, which rolled down the slope a few inches toward Annie's foot. Oh, Christ, Annie, don't flinch!

The rock stopped short of Annie, but the snake apparently detected the motion, because it suddenly began to rattle—loud! Jesus, what a *sound*—and drew itself up, its head back away from Annie's face, as though to strike. Ben pulled the pistol up, with just one hand, squeezing the trigger—and froze, the hammer halfway back, as the snake held its new position.

Oh, good God, if I'd have fired there's no chance I'd have hit him, and that would have set him off. I'm not gonna get a second chance. As this thought formed, Ben was pulling the hammer back with his thumb, reaching out with the pistol, resting both arms on his knees, gripping his right hand in his left, and taking aim.

Through the U of the rear sight, he saw the post of the front sight. It was painted pink for sharper visibility. He centered U and post on the rattlesnake's black head, which just filled the U at this distance. The head then swayed out of his line of fire, only to sway back in for a split second, then out again.

He began to squeeze the trigger—it needed only a tiny pull in the cocked position—to time the firing with the swaying of the head into the U, and saw the front sight dip infinitesimally; he was squeezing the grip too hard. Indeed, he could feel the diamond pattern of the brown Bakelite grip being impressed into his palm. He made no adjustment, but ordered his hands to relax. The post moved, barely perceptibly, back into position.

He only vaguely saw Alex Klein's oddly misshapen face when it materialized in his line of fire. Alex? he thought dimly—Alex is alive?—just as the rattlesnake's black head floated back into his intensely focused, narrowly closed-down line of sight. He saw the blue-black U, the pink post, the wedge-shaped head, and he fired.

Later, when he thought about it, he knew that he would have fired even if his view of Alex had been sharp and had lasted longer. He'd have fired at that snake, taken the one chance he had to save Annie, and maybe his baby, even if he'd known for certain that it meant blowing Alex Klein's face apart.

He fired, and felt the kick, and saw the muzzle jump away. His vision was obscured by a puff of powder smoke for a moment, but he saw the snake's head dart forward and he saw Alex duck.

The mountain king's instinct was beginning to reassert itself. His natural reaction to so much uncertainty was to strike, to inject his deadly secretion into a living body. His instinct told him now, at last to ignore the oddly comforting quality of the shifting softness beneath him and the mesmerizing, rhythmic vibration that the body produced sporadically; these things were not for him, would destroy him.

The mountain king was reclaiming his own nature. He tensed the muscles of his upper body eagerly as he stared at the creature's bulging eye.

The mountain king did not die when the .38-caliber slug tore through the base of his skull and the top of his long spinal column, but his awareness ceased and all control over his body was lost. He died a few seconds later, when all his marvelous nervous system and musculature had exhausted their last, reflexive attempts to remove him from this terrible place.

CHAPTER

20

Alex Klein might have felt the bullet tear harmlessly through a disorderly tuft of hair at the back of his head, but his head was flooded with pain from his jaw as he slammed his face to the earth. He nearly passed out from it—or maybe did, he thought as he raised his head slowly while his vision cleared.

He saw the snake writhing on the ground beside Annie, the back of its head gone. It turned over, showing its ridged belly, very slightly paler in color than its back; then over again, spiraling along its incredible length. Then it stopped turning—first at its head, and then the stillness moved along its body until the great snake stretched, full length, belly up.

Alex's mind was rapidly filling with—terror. The realization was forming that Ben had looked him in the face and pulled the trigger without changing expression. Ben Axelrod killed me, by God, Alex thought wonderingly—he pulled the trigger without batting an eye. He didn't even look to see if I was all right afterward, until he'd moved to Annie and talked to her.

They were holding each other now, Ben laughing, Annie crying. "The baby's all right," Annie had said first, "—at least I think so," and had pushed herself up to a sitting position. "Oh, Ben," she said as she buried her face in his neck, "Ben, he was—it was—" but she was sobbing uncontrollably.

Ben took her in his arms and then looked past her at Alex. He shook his head slowly, as though to apologize.

Alex glared at him. You sonofabitch, you killed me. Jesus! I wondered if he was a killer? *Jesus!* And I didn't even *mean . . . killer!* The sonofabitch shot an actual bullet at my *head*.

Doesn't look like a killer now, does he, holding his wife, crying in her hair, laughing? Sonofabitch bastard—

But the rage just wouldn't take hold. Alex's feeling, over all other feelings, was fear. *Ben Axelrod killed me.* And he would again if he thought he had to. He could and would.

Suddenly Alex Klein felt old, as if something in him—something that he wasn't sure he could live without—had died.

He remembered Whitney then, and turned to move down toward her.

Randall Madison was dead. He hadn't stirred since a convulsive shudder swept through his body some time ago—Karen wasn't clear-minded enough to know just how long. Twenty minutes? Five?

Tim lay on the bed with Randall, hugging him, trying to give him warmth and comfort. Karen supposed that Tim did not know—had not allowed himself to believe—that Randall was dead.

Though her leg still hurt and her mouth was dry and she felt feverish, Karen was certain that she was not in danger of death. She felt restless and energetic one minute, tired and listless the next. Now she shifted, pulling herself up to a sitting position.

As she did, the bedsprings squeaked—and the rattlesnake on the floor began to make its threatening sound. *Oh!* She froze as her heart leaped. *I'd forgotten that awful thing was there.* She took a deep breath and closed her eyes and felt the bedsprings react to another motion on the bed.

Tim was sitting up. His eyes were dry, his expression blank. His hand trembled slightly as he reached to pat Randall's face.

Then he put his feet to the floor. Karen said, "Tim—" He walked stiffly to the foot of the bed, leaned over and took hold of the frame, and yanked it violently. It rolled on its casters, two, three feet from the wall. Tim, still without expression, as though he were going to pick up a pencil that had rolled out of sight under the bed, walked around and reached down toward the rattling sound.

Karen followed him with widening eyes. "Tim, you mustn't—" The snake struck him in the forearm. He gasped and flinched back momentarily, then reached and grabbed the snake behind the head.

He lifted it and stared into its tiny face for a moment. The creature hung down from Tim's fist, writhing and twisting, its knobby tail brushing the floor. Tim's face crumpled then, and he began to talk, softly at first, his voice quickly rising to a scream. "You vicious, obscene little poisonous mother*fucker*! You'll *pay*—"

He flung the snake then, and it sailed through the air across the room, slamming flat against the opposite wall. It slapped down on the floor, drew into a coil and resumed its rattle. "You filthy little killer," Tim said in a low voice, and walked to it. Tim's right arm, which had been struck, seemed a little stiff now, but no hesitation had entered his movements.

Karen heard another sound, a motor outdoors. For a second she thought the man who came to mow the lawn was out there, riding cheerfully around on his machine. But the sound grew and took on a different character: a roar, a whistle under it and a thwacking noise.

Tim reached down and grabbed the snake again—it

didn't even attempt to strike him this time—picked it up and slammed it to the floor. It made as if to crawl away, but the creature seemed to be broken. It flopped over on its back, then flopped again—then Tim grabbed it once more and slammed it down.

The snake was still. Tim picked it up and held it, in his left hand this time, leaving his right arm hanging limp, and screamed something unintelligible under the sound of the helicopter outside.

When Karen heard the front door slam open, she finally understood that the rescue party had arrived. Oh, Ted, thank God—Ted?

The first man through the bedroom door carried a wooden pole with a wire loop on the end. He froze just inside the door, staring at Tim. Tim stood, holding the rattlesnake down away from his face, weeping; his face was slack, expressionless and chalk-white.

The second man carried a white box with a red cross on it, a sort of medical attaché case. He looked at the first man, then at Tim, then moved to Tim and took him gently by the left arm. Tim dropped the dead snake and allowed himself to be led to the bed.

While the medical man opened his case and began to extract hypodermics and bandages, the man with the snake-catching stick turned to Karen and said, "Karen? Your husband said on the radio to tell you Charley's fine and he's fine. Wants me to radio and tell him you're OK."

Karen was weeping with relief and with sudden grief for Randall and sorrow for Tim. She couldn't speak, but she nodded. Ted saved me after all, she thought. He got a radio! How in the world did he do that?

CHAPTER

21

Annie Axelrod shifted gingerly in her favorite chair, turning her knees this way and that, settling her feet on an ottoman. It was no use; she was not to be comfortable. Her ribs were taped; one of them had been cracked. That same side of her body, from just under her rib cage all the way to her hip, was loosely bandaged, to protect a nasty-looking mass of scabs. Her sprained ankle was tightly wrapped.

The scrapes didn't hurt much anymore, except when she stretched, but they itched maddeningly. Her ankle was only a little tender, and the rib hurt only when she moved just so. Annie's real discomfort was in her mind, which had, it seemed, taken its own battering.

It was early Monday evening, just a week after the . . . ordeal, she called it when she had to have a word for it. She had returned to work this day. Probably too soon, but she'd wanted desperately to get back to normal, to become involved with the everyday business of life. She wished to get over the consuming feeling that her entire

existence was defined, now and forever, by the word
survivor. She wanted to get back to her life.

Every night this past week she had dreamed. Creepy
dreams, never about snakes, but about desperate
struggles to escape from narrow places, each escape
more difficult than the last. And in each dream someone
important to her had died. Never Annie, but
others—everyone who'd been on the mountain, and
others, including her younger sister and her mother.

The office routine had scarcely penetrated the fog of
her malaise. Quite a nice fuss had been made over her
for the first hour or so. She was something of a
celebrity; her station's news program had mentioned her
in its coverage of the incident—though its lead had been
Randall and Whitney, of course. The *New York Post*
had featured the story on their front page, which had
made Annie feel like just another of their tacky cir-
culation-boosting stunts: HORRIBLE DEATH OF THE
LOAN ARRANGER—"Randall Madison, the actor
famous as Mr. Reid, the bemused loan officer in . . ."
And "Pretty Whitney Williams, her role in a major new
film just announced, lived through a nightmarish real-
life . . ." with a publicity still of Whitney in a clingy
silken blouse. Ugh. The sleazy bastards. Whitney hadn't
seemed to mind, though.

Albie, Annie's good old cat, another survivor,
hopped into the chair with her. He'd become more
friendly since last weekend, because he missed Dinny
and the kitten, maybe. Or maybe Albie just felt
as awful—as anxious and depressed and isolated—as
Annie did.

Because of the vividness of the dreams, with someone
forever dying in them, Annie sometimes forgot that
Randall actually had died. Remembering now, she was
stabbed by grief—again, and as painful as the first time.
She was *never* going to come out of this. Randall, whom
she'd loved, was lost to her; and so was Tim. Tim, it
seemed, would be her friend no more. He blamed
everyone who'd been on the mountain for Randall's

death. He was inconsolable, and unforgiving. Randall and Tim had been the brothers Annie had never had, and now she'd lost them. Well, maybe in time Tim would. . . . He must be in terrible pain. I really must find a way to approach him. Lift him out of his awful, furious grief. Later. In a few days, maybe.

For now, she couldn't lift herself out of her own funk. She didn't even know what troubled her, why she was so fitfulminded, unsettled, by turns terrified and hopeless. Why her hands shook sometimes and she constantly wanted a cigarette—she hadn't smoked for more than four years. Too much, she thought, it had all been too much. She had been in the presence of her death, and she couldn't scream, couldn't run. She shuddered. Whatever it was, she seemed to be alone with it. The others were not reacting in the same way at all.

Ben seemed to have put it all behind him pretty well by now. Of course, Ben had other things to think about, new things. Whitney was off to California, full of high hopes and ambition. Karen—well, Karen's reaction to the whole business had been very strange.

Annie had talked to Karen twice in the last week, and had come to realize that the big jolt for her had not been the bite of the killer snake, or lying beside Randall as he died. All of the horror was just a sort of footnote. What had affected Karen was learning about Ted having had an affair. Of all things. And almost two years ago, for heaven's sake.

The effect on Karen seemed to be a healthy one, though—it might have grown her up a little. Annie would be glad of that, if she had it in her to be glad about anything. She liked Karen a lot, enjoyed her, but Karen had always been a little . . . well, callow. She would be more interesting with a more complex sense of the world.

Annie hadn't talked to Ted, but Ben said he seemed amazingly unaffected by the adventure on the mountain. Ted was cheery and energetic, Ben reported, as though he was enjoying life just fine. Well, okay. Good for both of them. For now, though, their cheer just seemed to isolate Annie the more.

She shifted in the chair again and Albie, as he had done once before, got up, shook his head in apparent exasperation, and hopped to the floor. Well, I beg your pardon, you snooty little shit. But he stopped a few strides from her and looked back over his shoulder. She pursed her lips and coaxed him back. He plodded to her, as though to give her just one more chance. Right, hop up and settle in there. You don't want to be alone, either. Albie stretched up and butted her chin hard with his nose and cheek.

Whitney had telephoned Annie to say good-bye. She was up and about in an awful hurry—on crutches, an arm and a leg in casts. Whitney had gotten a principal role—not the part she'd tested for, but a better one—in a film that wouldn't start shooting for at least a month. And the director liked her enough to postpone it even further, depending on her progress. Annie had the feeling that Whitney would be a fast healer.

The phone conversation had been hurried and rather strained. "Hi," she'd said, "it's Whitney Williams." How many Whitneys does she imagine I know?

Whitney was going to California for good. Even if she doesn't make this movie there'll be others. Career there. The place for an actor now. Time I made the move. . . . Alex? About Alex she had said, among other things, "It's about time *I* left one." A chill had run through Annie at the time, but as she heard the words again now in her mind, she heard the brittle, short laugh that had come with them, and it sounded hollow. Like bravado.

Well, good luck in the Golden West, Whitney Louise. Annie was a little surprised to realize that, though she scarcely knew Whitney, she expected to miss her.

She resisted an impulse to shift again, not wanting to disturb the cat. Then, thoughtlessly, she reached to the cable-TV box beside her, to turn on the news until Ben got home. But in doing that she stretched her side, stinging, probably tearing a bandage loose and starting a little blood seeping. Oh-h-h, *damn!* She felt tears start, but she set her jaw and blinked them back. She didn't want to be red-eyed and snot-nosed when Ben got home, as well as disgustingly scabby. Tears leaked out anyway, though, and she sniffled once.

Ben had been a regular prince about helping her with her bandages and not being disgusted—or not showing it, she thought. But Annie was feeling so out of sorts, so childish-grumpy—so *lonely*—that it made her all the more miserable to be deprived of warm, all-over physical closeness with Ben. She'd like to make love with him, that's what she'd really like. That'd be nice just for its own sake, but it would help her feel more normal, too.

We could, really. . . . He'd have to be careful with his hands, but with the lights out he wouldn't see me . . . no. He wouldn't. He *is* a prince, but I'm just too nasty-looking. Only on my side, though, almost around on my back. . . . No. She sighed heavily.

Her mind wandered to Alex Klein. She could not find in herself a whole lot of feeling for Alex, but losing Whitney so abruptly did seem a little hard on him. Whitney had said she had asked him to move out there with her. But could she really have expected Alex to do that? Of course, Alex had a consolation prize—though he didn't seem to know it yet. Whitney had told Annie that Alex was surprisingly resigned to working for Ben. He had become convinced that Ben would get the executive vice-presidency they both wanted. Whitney didn't know why he thought that, but he was so matter-of-fact about it she had assumed at first it had already happened. Annie knew better: Alex was going to get that job, because Ben was going to leave Arthur Bradley Associates to set up shop for himself.

A breeze of anxiety wafted through Annie when she thought of that. She had approved of the idea immediately, for reasons that were no longer quite clear to her, if they ever had been. Last Tuesday evening, driving to the city after Annie was discharged from Schoharie Valley General Hospital, Ben had broached the subject—in rather gingerly fashion, as Annie recalled it now. But they had agreed surprisingly easily that Ben should make the move. That he'd do fine on his own, that he'd have no trouble doing whatever had to be done to make it work.

Now, Annie had her doubts. Actually, she still believed that Ben would do fine, but she couldn't think *why* she believed it; and that made her uneasy. She tried to think it through, to discover what made her so confident, when only a few days ago she hadn't been. But she couldn't keep her thoughts focused. She sighed and allowed her mind to sink downward, out of this scattery fitfulness, into depression.

Shit, she thought. Shit on this, I'm going to . . . take a shower. Right. Get out of these disgusting bandages. She got up, and realized as she did that something had changed, some pain had eased. What? Her rib! Her cracked rib hadn't stabbed her when she arose. What a lovely feeling of freedom! She hadn't been able to do that without pain in all this time.

It was such a pleasure that she sat back down to do it again, to test it, to see if that little torment, at least, really had left her. Easy . . . up . . . all *right*! There had been a twinge that time, but just a tiny one, almost pleasurable.

She removed her clothes and walked to the bathroom, unwrapping bandages as she went. The tape around her ribs would get wet, but she'd keep it warm as she dried, and it would come off in a day or so anyway, maybe. Nice soft shower, and then I'll wrap up in that fat terrycloth robe that's usually too warm to wear. I'll look nice when Ben comes home, and who knows? She took the Ace bandage off her ankle. The ankle was still a weird color, but not so swollen anymore.

As she stepped into the shower, she looked down at

herself. Not bad, really. Little scrapes here and there, down one leg, some all but healed; one on her right elbow still had a little scab on it. The big area under her ribs was not so nice, but not bloody after all. The tape around her ribs was dingy gray and dismal-looking. But most of her was smooth and pink as ever, and shining wet now. Her belly—*oh*! Oh, my Lord, I—*Hey, baby, how are you?*

Annie realized suddenly that she had not once talked to her baby in the past week; not since the moment the monster had crawled onto her body. She touched her belly now and smiled. *Gee, baby, how're you doing, are you okay in there?*

How awful that I forgot you. How did that happen? No wonder I've felt so alone. Listen, I'm—I've had some trouble, but we're okay now. We're gonna heal up just fine. All right? We'll be fine. Ben'll take care of us, won't he? Sure he will, Ben can do anything he wants. Annie stepped back under the soothing, soft spray.

When she left the bathroom, wrapped in the luxurious white robe, she felt infinitely better. The damn wet tape was becoming clammy as it cooled, but except for that she felt warm, and much softer and more supple. She limped down the long hallway toward the kitchen. Nice glass of wine—what do you say, baby? Soften me up some more.

As she passed the front entranceway, she heard a key in the lock. She stopped and waited. When the door swung in, Ben looked up in surprise and grinned. "Hey, lady!" He had a package in each arm—something flat in a Brentano's bag, and a bottle from the liquor store. He stepped to Annie and, arms at his sides, moved against her and touched her cheek with his, then her nose with his, then kissed her softly on the mouth. "You look nice," he said softly, still nose to nose.

He smelled a little beery—she knew he'd stopped after work with a prospective client—and a little like cigar, a smell Annie liked. She put her hands on his shoulders. "Mm-hmm," she said. "Neat and clean, anyway."

"Oh, at least that, yeah." He grinned and stepped back.

"How'd it go?" Annie said.

"Oh. Oh, fine, same as the last two—exactly. He'll give me work if I want it, but he also wants to hire me. Hell, I'm a star!"

She laughed and they stood silent for a moment. "What've you got in the packages? Presents?"

"Oh. Well, uh—I got some champagne," he said, and offered the bottle.

Annie took it. It felt cold. Why does he seem so awkward? "That's wonderful," she said. "And what's that?" She nodded at the book-shop bag.

"Oh, well." He fell silent for a second. Annie thought he might be blushing. What in the world? He removed the book from the bag: *The Joy of Sex.* "It's—you see, I thought—"

He *is* blushing! Annie smiled wonderingly. "You're —well, here, ladies and gentlemen, is the suave and urbane, old married crock pushing forty, blushing like a schoolboy."

"Look," he grumbled, "don't be a smartass. It's got *positions* in it, you know, and I thought we could—because of your—aches and pains, I thought we might find some . . . you know, there's probably some way—well, shit, if it didn't throw my back out—"

Annie stepped toward him, careless of her tender ankle, and almost fell at him. Ben dropped the book and grabbed her, alarmed. "Whoa! Are you—?"

"I'm fine, I'm just fine," she said, and held him close to her. Her rib scarcely complained at all. She rubbed her cheek gently against his beard. "You're something, you are," she said softly. "I've needed terribly to be close to you—how did you know that?"

Actually, Ben hadn't known it, at least not consciously; in fact he'd thought it was the farthest thing from her mind. The silly sex manual was meant to be a persuader. He felt very foolish. But he shrugged a tiny shrug against her chin and said, "Well, I'm just awful smart, is all." What the hell, he thought; you're supposed to get lucky once in a while, too.

Annie laughed and stepped back. "Open the champagne," she said, and handed him the bottle. She bent carefully and picked up the book. She smiled and turned to walk down the hall toward their bedroom. As she walked, she opened the book and leafed through it. "Oh! . . . Oh, hey"—she turned to call into the kitchen, but Ben was still standing in the entranceway, watching her walk away from him, smiling. She said, "There's—there are some nice things in here."

Ben grinned and nodded. Annie shook her head slowly and smiled. "Well, hurry up then," she said.